The Emergence
A Mystical SELF Saga

Book one

Written by Randy Grasser & Annet van Duinen

LEGAL DISCLAIMER & LIMITATION OF LIABILITY
First Edition March 2025
ISBN (paperback) 979-8-9928422-0-3
ISBN (ebook) 979-8-9928422-1-0

LEGAL DISCLAIMER & LIMITATION OF LIABILITY

General Disclaimer
The *Mystical SELF book* series, including *The Emergence* and all subsequent works, is a work of fiction created for entertainment and personal reflection. Any resemblance to real persons, events, or places is purely coincidental. The themes, characters, and concepts within the series are designed to inspire self-discovery and personal growth but should not be considered a substitute for professional psychological, medical, or therapeutic advice.

Reader Responsibility & Interpretation
The *Mystical SELF* series explores themes of personal growth, self-awareness, and emotional challenges. Readers are encouraged to engage with the material in a way that is meaningful to them, but they remain solely responsible for how they interpret and apply the book's concepts to their own lives. Neither the authors nor their representatives assume responsibility for personal decisions, actions, or interpretations made as a result of engaging with this content.

Limitation of Liability
To the fullest extent permitted by law, the authors, publishers, and any affiliated representatives of *Mystical SELF* disclaim all liability for any direct, indirect, incidental, consequential, or special damages arising from the use, interpretation, or application of the book series, its content, or related discussions. This includes, but is not limited to, personal decisions, psychological effects, or any perceived emotional impact resulting from reading or engaging with the material.

If you would like to inquire about the authors' availability to speak at your event contact info@thelivingadventurers.com Examples of topics they can speak on are:

- The Power of Being Highly Sensitive: Understanding and harnessing emotional depth in a chaotic world.
- Thriving as a High Sensation Seeker: How adventure, challenge, and self-discovery fuel a meaningful life.
- Emotional Intelligence & Mental Resilience: Understanding how thoughts, emotions, and beliefs shape reality.

www.thelivingadventurers.com

Ripples of Change

To the young souls navigating a world not of their making, this book is for you. May you find the strength to embrace change, the courage to seek your truth, and the wisdom to shape the world into something greater than what was passed down. Your journey is just beginning, and the power to transform the future is already within you.

To Elaine Aron, Ph.D. and William Allen, whose groundbreaking work on Highly Sensitive People set in motion a ripple effect that transformed countless lives, including our own. If we had never discovered the HSP trait through your books, and we had never heard William Allen speak about it on a podcast, our paths would never have crossed. That first conversation we had for the Sensitive and Strong podcast may have been just an interview, but it became the spark that set us on an extraordinary path, one of connection, collaboration, and creation.

With our deepest and most heartfelt gratitude, your work not only transformed our understanding of ourselves but also led us to one another, a deep connection that has become the foundation of our love, growth, and the courage to fully step into who we are. You set in motion a cascade of events that brought us together, allowing us to see and embrace each other completely, to challenge and uplift one another, and to walk this path side by side as partners in both love and self-discovery. For the wisdom you've shared, the connections you've unknowingly fostered, and the profound impact you've had on our lives, thank you.

Never underestimate the power you have to create ripples of positive change. You never know where they might lead.

"Life is not just the passing of time, it is the collection of experiences. Their frequency and intensity define who we are, and what we are capable of... Live an adventurous life!" - Randy Grasser

"Life isn't about waiting for the storm to pass. It's about learning how to dance in the rain." – Annet van Duinen

Prologue
A Realm in Disarray

Ethan Rivers perched on the edge of his rooftop, his legs dangling over the side as a soft breeze ruffled his dark hair. The cool night air wrapped around him like a fragile shield, holding back the weight of the day. Above him the sky stretched endlessly, its vast expanse speckled with stars that twinkled like distant promises. Ethan's gaze traced their patterns, his mind flexing with a longing he didn't understand. Was there life out there, somewhere beyond the shimmering constellations? Was there a place where things made sense, where he could belong?

The distant sound of a car passing down his suburban street brought him back to reality, but only for a moment. His thoughts quickly drifted to the tangled mess of his life. At school he felt invisible, awkward, and misunderstood. His classmates barely noticed him, except when they mocked his intense reactions to everything around him. At home things weren't any better. His family seemed to view his sensitivity as a weakness, a problem to be fixed or ridiculed.

"Hey, crybaby!" The sharp voice of his older brother cut through the stillness, pulling Ethan out of his thoughts. "Where you at? I got a knuckle sandwich waiting for you!"

Ethan tensed, his jaw tightening as his brother's taunts echoed in the night. He knew better than to answer, but the words still found their mark, sinking into the ache he carried. Being sensitive often felt more like a curse than a gift, a vulnerability he couldn't escape, no matter how high he climbed to get away.

Across town, Sarah Halloway sat on the back porch of her house, her knees pulled up to her chest and her arms wrapped tightly around them. The cool wooden planks pressed against her legs, grounding her as she stared up at the same infinite night sky. Her emerald-green eyes searched the heavens, wondering if life existed out there among the stars. She wanted to believe it did. It was easier than believing she was meant to spend her days feeling like an outsider in her world.

Sarah's mind wandered to the things her therapist had said during their last session, about embracing her uniqueness, although her therapist knew nothing about Sarah's highly sensitive nature. The words had sounded good in theory, but in practice? In the real world, where people misunderstood her intensity and her need for connection, they seemed like empty statements. She had tried to blend in, to hide the parts of herself that felt too much, but it made the emptiness worse.

Inside the house, her father's silhouette appeared at the window, his eyes filled with concern as he watched her. He wanted to help but didn't know how. Sarah had always been a puzzle to him, brilliant, creative, and fiercely independent, but also distant and guarded. He didn't know the depth of her struggle or the aching weight of her self-doubt.

Both Ethan and Sarah sat in silence, separated by miles of suburban sprawl yet connected by a shared yearning. Neither of them noticed the faint streak of light cutting through the sky at first. But then it happened, sudden, brilliant, and impossible to miss.

A shooting star blazed across the heavens, leaving a shimmering trail in its wake. Ethan straightened, his heart quickening as the streak caught his eye. He closed his eyes, feeling the momentary spark of hope that always came with making a wish. I wish I were Shadow Sage, he thought, imagining the fearless, cunning warrior he became in the virtual world of Mystical Quest, a multi-player video game where he felt he could truly be himself.

Sarah saw it too, her breath catching as the star streaked above her. Her mind raced with the possibilities; with a longing she couldn't quite put into words. As her eyes fluttered shut, her wish rose like a quiet prayer. I wish I were Luna Whisper, she thought, picturing the clever, powerful mage who always knew how to navigate the challenges of *Mystical Quest*.

In the stillness of the night, two wishes whispered into the vast expanse of the universe, carried on the faint hope that maybe, just maybe, the stars would listen.

From the endless depths of the Ethereal Nexus, where rivers of light flowed through infinite space like celestial veins, the Orb of Reflection emerged. This radiant golden sphere, its surface alive with swirling bands of mirrored light, glided forward with purpose. Known as Aerthis, the Orb shimmered with an otherworldly brilliance, exuding the wisdom of the Nexus itself. It was more than a glowing artifact, it was a living, sentient being, created to bring balance when realms teetered on the edge of collapse. Now, a crumbling was beginning to emerge.

The Nexus had felt the warning first, faint and trembling, like the rustle of leaves before a storm. The ripple grew stronger, sharper, shaking the very fabric of the young and fragile Realm. As the Orb descended, the Nexus's ancient energy hummed within its core, urging it forward. This was no ordinary disturbance. Something vital was breaking.

When the Orb pierced the veil and entered the Realm, a vision of despair unfurled before it. Below, the once-lush Plains of Rejuvenation stretched out like a shadow of its former glory. Golden meadows that had once rippled with healing light now lay scorched and gray, its beauty and serenity stolen. The air above was heavy and dull, suffused with an unnatural stillness that pressed down on the land like a suffocating weight. The Plains, once teeming with vibrant flora and serene streams, had become the Barren Lands, a scar across the entire Realm.

As the Orb moved closer, its glowing surface reflected the shattered remains of the once elegant Core City, rising at the center of the Realm. What had once been a radiant beacon of harmony and strength now stood in ruin. Cracked spires jutted into the sky like broken fingers, and the city's once-vivid golden light flickered weakly, as if struggling to stay alive. Its pathways, once alive with energy, were silent now, strewn with the remnants of a forgotten peace.

And at the center of it all was the source of the ruin: the 13 Dragons, now looming shadows of their former selves. These towering creatures, once revered as the Eternal Guardians of Origin (E.G.O.), had been protectors of the Realm's growth and evolution. Each dragon embodied a piece of the Realm's psyche, their harmonious forms once brimming with resilience, courage, and a desire for adventure. But now, their once-majestic scales had darkened, corrupted by chaos. Their glowing eyes, once filled with clarity, burned with volatile, destructive energy. No longer guardians, they had fallen prey to Dysquinox, their now twisted natures spilling destruction like poison across the land.

The Orb hovered, its mirrored surface trembling as it observed the devastation. The Dysquinox Dragons moved restlessly within the Core City, their immense forms radiating imbalance. Their once-unifying presence now fragmented and frayed the very fabric of the Realm, breaking its connection to the Five Mystical Enigmas, the advisors meant to aid the Realms custodian. Without their harmony, the Realm's balance of thought, emotion, and action had unraveled into chaos.

The Orb hovered, its mirrored surface trembling as it observed the devastation. The Dysquinox Dragons moved restlessly within the Core City, their immense forms radiating imbalance. Their once-unifying presence now fragmented and frayed the very fabric of the Realm, breaking its connection to the Five Mystical Enigmas, the advisors meant to aid the Realms custodian. Without their harmony, the Realm's balance of thought, emotion, and action had unraveled into chaos.

Yet amid the wreckage, there was a glimmer of hope. The Orb's gaze turned to the Mystical Forest, untouched by the spreading corruption, for now. Its towering trees shimmered with an inner light, their crystalline leaves whispering with life. Hidden deep within this forest was a sanctuary known only to the Nexus and its emissary: the Chamber of Secrets, a place shielded by layers of ancient protection. . This would be the refuge for the Sacred Book of Wisdom, the beating heart of the Realm's existence.

The Orb goal is to ensure the book's salvation by finding it and ensuring the forest will be its sanctuary until the Realm's rightful Custodian could rise.

The Orb moved through the desolation with silent determination. Entering the city undetected, it glided into the shattered Celestial Atrium, its mirrored light reflecting the broken beauty of the chamber. Crumbling mosaics of balance and harmony adorned the walls, now fractured and dulled. At the room's center, the Sacred Book rested atop a cracked pedestal, its cover glowing as if struggling to stay alive.

The Orb wrapped itself around the book, its golden rays embracing it protectively.

With the book in its possession, the Orb fled the city, its light dimming to conceal itself from the watchful gaze of the Dysquinox Dragons. It moved swiftly across the Barren Lands to the Mystical Forest, the whispers of the trees welcoming it as it entered the Chamber of Secrets. Inside, the chamber walls pulsed, their energy mingling with the Nexus's as the Orb placed the book gently on the central pedestal. The book's glow steadied, protected now by the Orb's vigilance.

But the Orb's task was far from over. Beyond the chamber's walls, the Realm teetered on the brink of collapse, its balance hanging by a thread. The Orb turned its gaze outward, searching for signs of hope. Its mirrored surface caught faint sparks in the chaos, two faint but resilient threads of potential.

One was a girl, her sharp mind encased in emptiness, her heart guarded by walls built from years of self-doubt. The other was a boy, believing his sensitivity was his weakness that weighed him down, yet his spirit held a strength waiting to emerge. They were fragile, yes, but the Orb could see the seeds of courage within them. They were the Realms only hope.

With a pulse of radiant energy, the Orb sent out its call. A ripple spread across the chaotic ether of the external world in hopes of reaching the two sparks. If successful, they would be drawn toward the chamber. Time was of the essence, and the future of the Realm now rested in the abilities of these two unwitting souls. If proven worthy, they would have to face the trials, uncovering the hidden truths within themselves, and, if they were strong enough, mend what had been broken.

The Orb dimmed, its light settling into a steady glow as it waited. Somewhere in the distance, a Dysquinox Dragon stirred, its eyes burning as it sensed the faint stirrings of resistance.

Chapter 1

Ordinary Lives
Hidden Struggles

Ethan Rivers climbed the front steps of his suburban home, his posture weighted down by the exhaustion of yet another draining day at school. The late afternoon sun draped the neighborhood in hues of fading gold, but Ethan barely noticed; his mind had already shifted to the only place where he felt like he belonged: the virtual realm of *Mystical Quest*.

As Ethan opened the front door, a knot of apprehension tightened in his chest. Was his older brother home? He stepped inside quietly, his movements careful and deliberate, hoping to slip by unnoticed. From the kitchen, he could hear the familiar chatter of his mom and little sister, but he didn't dare risk drawing attention. If his brother was nearby, even a brief encounter could spiral into something he wasn't ready to face.

Ethan made his way to his room as quickly as possible. Once inside, he shut the door with a soft but purposeful click, turning the lock for good measure. His backpack landed on the floor with a muted thud as he collapsed into his chair. Reaching for his gaming computer, Ethan powered it on, the low hum of the machine bringing an instant sense of relief. Letting out a sigh, he felt the tension begin to melt away. Here, in his sanctuary, he was safe.

The gentle hum of his computer greeted him like an old friend. To Ethan, it wasn't just a machine; it was the portal to a world where his sensitivity wasn't a burden, it was his greatest strength. For as long as he could remember, Ethan had felt out of step with the rhythm of the world. At school, his heightened awareness to the emotions of others left him perpetually drained. The harsh banter of classmates, the unspoken expectations of teachers, it all pressed down on him until his thoughts spun into a storm. Group projects were torture, social events a waking nightmare. Even when teachers praised his intelligence, he felt invisible, as though his potential was a rumor whispered behind his back.

In the game, everything changed. The quiet, cautious boy became Shadow Sage, a daring, intuitive warrior whose legendary reputation preceded him. As Shadow Sage, Ethan's sensitivity sharpened into an advantage, a gift that let him anticipate danger, unravel puzzles, and outwit opponents. The world of *Mystical Quest* was chaotic, but in it, Ethan felt more in control than he ever had in real life.

Tonight, Shadow Sage would attempt a level he'd tried to beat for weeks. Ethan's heart beat faster as his avatar climbed through the dense, vine-strangled jungle of the game's map. His mind buzzed with strategies and intuition, each choice flowing seamlessly into the next.

It was as though the game was wired into his very thoughts.

A sudden knock on Ethan's door jolted him out of his concentration. He ignored it at first, hoping whoever was on the other side would go away. But the knock came again, louder this time, followed by his father's stern voice: "Ethan! Dinner!"

Ethan sighed heavily, reluctantly pausing the game. The glow of the screen faded, and with it, the fragile sense of safety he'd felt moments earlier. Bracing himself for another grueling evening, he stood and made his way toward the stairs. As he walked, the pungent odor of cooked cabbage hit him like a slap. His stomach churned, and an unshakable feeling of rejection settled over him. The smell wasn't just unpleasant, it was a reminder of how little his voice seemed to matter in this house.

He'd told his parents countless times that he hated cabbage, how its slimy texture made him gag, but it never seemed to matter. It was always there, steaming on the table like an unspoken challenge. He entered the dining room, the tension in his stomach tightening as his eyes flicked to his older brother, Jason, already seated and smirking. Ethan's stomach sank further. Jason lived for moments like this, where Ethan's discomfort became his entertainment.

Dinner began, and there it was, the bowl of cabbage, glistening under the overhead light, the smell even worse up close. Ethan tried to steel himself as his mother passed it to him, her expression indifferent, as though his protests over the years had been a passing breeze. His little sisters' eyes cast an empathetic grimace. Ethan gently gives her a knowing smile back. He hesitated before taking a spoonful, every fiber of his being screaming against it. But he knew better than to refuse. His father's glare was enough to silence him.

"Don't make a scene," his dad had said countless times before, and Ethan knew what that meant.

He forced himself to take a bite, the texture was as revolting as always. Each slimy mouthful felt like swallowing betrayal.

Jason chuckled from across the table, his cruel amusement unmistakable. "What's the matter, Ethan?" he sneered. "You don't like Mom's cooking? You're so ungrateful."

Ethan's face burned as he chewed, his throat tightening against the urge to gag. His parents didn't intervene. They never did. It was as if his discomfort didn't exist, or worse, as if it was deserved. With every bite, Ethan felt smaller, more invisible, more unwelcome. The laughter, the silence, the slimy cabbage, they all piled on top of him, suffocating any shred of worth he tried to hold on to. He felt like a stranger, an outsider forced to endure a ritual he despised. He didn't belong here. He wasn't sure he belonged anywhere. Ethan shifted uncomfortably in his seat as his father's sharp gaze fixed on him, his voice slicing through the uneasy silence of the dinner table.

"Anything happen at school today I should know about?" The question wasn't casual, it was loaded, the tone carrying an unspoken accusation, as if Ethan were constantly teetering on the edge of trouble. The familiar knot in Ethan's stomach tightened. This nightly inquisition deepened his sense of isolation, a constant reminder of how out of place he felt. *If I could just stay invisible*, Ethan thought, *I'd be safe.* But safety was never guaranteed, no matter how much effort he put into fading into the background. His father's voice rang in his ears, but Ethan's mind drifted to a memory he had tried to bury, a moment that had shaped the way he saw himself and the world around him. A moment his father seems to never forget or understand.

It was third grade, nine years ago, on a cold, rainy day. The teacher was late, leaving the entire class stranded outside, shivering and soaked.

Ethan had felt the misery of his classmates like it was his, the challenge of being highly sensitive, the weight of their unhappiness pressing on him. He couldn't bear it. Spotting an open window, he climbed through, ignoring the scrape of the sill against his hands and knees, and unlocked the door from the inside. He had felt a flicker of pride, believing he had done the right thing, sparing everyone the discomfort of standing in the freezing rain.

But that small act of kindness had cost him dearly. The teacher, arriving minutes later, didn't see a boy trying to help. She saw a rule broken, and Ethan was sent to the principal's office. He still remembered the strap, a thick leather belt wielded as punishment. The sting on his hands was nothing compared to the humiliation, the way it made him feel like he was less than everyone else, like he had done something unforgivable.

But the worst part came later. When he got home that evening, his older brother wasted no time in announcing Ethan's "misdeed" to their father. Ethan could still hear the fury in his father's voice, the disgust on his face. "You brought shame to this family," his father had said, unbuckling his belt. The punishment that followed was harsh, leaving Ethan more bruised on the inside than out. It wasn't just the pain; it was the message: *You don't belong here. You're a failure.*

Now, sitting at the dinner table years later, that memory lingered like a dark shadow. Ethan clenched his jaw, his appetite gone, his hands curled into fists under the table. He kept his eyes down, avoiding his father's penetrating stare and his brother's smug glances.

"I asked you a question," his father pressed, his voice sharper now.

Ethan swallowed hard, willing his voice not to shake. "No, nothing happened."

His father's eyes narrowed, as if he didn't believe him. The air felt heavy, the unspoken tension pressing down on Ethan until he could hardly breathe. Inside, Ethan screamed at himself to hold it together, to endure the interrogation, the judgment, the memories that told him he didn't belong. But the weight of it all, his father's words, his brother's smirk, the endless feeling of always being wrong no matter what he did, was suffocating.

Ethan longed to retreat, to escape into the digital sanctuary of *Mystical Quest*, where he could transform into Shadow Sage, a figure of courage and strength, a hero instead of the burden he felt like in real life. Somewhere inside, he wished for a place where he could simply be, where he wouldn't have to fight so hard to prove that he mattered. A place where he could just be himself.

He kept his answers vague, carefully choosing his words, hoping to avoid drawing his father's attention any further.

But predictably, his older brother Jason wasn't about to let him off so easily. "Yeah, Ethan," Jason said with a smug grin, leaning back in his chair as if he owned the room. "You're quiet. What are you hiding this time? Did you break any more rules?"

The words hit Ethan like a slap, and uncontrollable anger surged through him. His face flushed red as he snapped. "Why do you have to always be so mean?" His voice trembled, frustration bubbling to the surface despite his effort to keep it down.

Jason's grin widened, a predator savoring the weakness in his prey. "Mean?" he mocked, his tone dripping with false innocence. "I'll show you mean, you little crybaby." Jason hoping to see Ethan breakdown as his emotions overwhelmed him, like so many times before. Ethan clenched his fists under the table even more, his nails now digging into his palms. Jason's torment wasn't new. It was endless.

For as long as Ethan could remember, his brother had been relentless, poking, prodding, and humiliating him at every turn. Ethan had never understood why Jason hated him so much, but he had learned to deal with it in the only way he could: survival.

Ethan's parents never saw the impact Jason's torment created, for he was the perfect child in their eyes. People tend to see the reactions of others, not the instigators causing the torment. Over the years, Ethan developed a hyper-vigilance so intense it became second nature. Every sound, every glance, every subtle shift in the air put him on high alert. He had trained himself to read both his brother's and father's body language with uncanny precision, detecting the smallest flicker of malice before it turned into action.

This constant state of watchfulness had followed Ethan into adolescence, growing sharper with each passing year. While it helped him avoid Jason's worst attacks, it came at a cost. Ethan could never relax, never let his guard down. His home, the one place that was supposed to feel safe, had become a battleground where he always had to be one step ahead.

The hyper-vigilance bled into every part of Ethan's life. He couldn't enjoy simple moments or let his mind wander without the nagging awareness that Jason might strike, or worse, trigger his father. Even in the rare moments of peace, the tension never fully left him. He was always playing the watchful eye, constantly scanning for danger, constantly protecting himself.

But that vigilance came at a price. It drained him, left him feeling hollow. Ethan could never be himself, not here, not in this house. The weight of always being on guard pressed on him until all he could think about was escaping, into his room, into *Mystical Quest*, into a world where he was strong, where he could fight back, where he mattered.

"That's enough!" Ethan's mom interjected, her tone sharp but weary. "Let's just have a nice family dinner for once, okay? No more of this back-and-forth." The tension lingered, the air heavy with unspoken words.

Ethan stabbed at his food, doing his best to appear unaffected, though his heart was racing. After a few awkward minutes of silence, he set his fork down. "Can I be excused? I have a lot of homework to do," he asked, his voice subdued.

His father frowned, clearly unimpressed. "Not until you clear the table." Something Ethan seemed to be tasked with every night, while Jason went out to shoot hoops in the driveway.

Ethan swallowed the retort that sprang to his lips and nodded. "Fine."

As soon as dinner was over, Ethan carried plates to the kitchen, rinsing them before placing them in the dishwasher. The moment the last dish was put away, he made a beeline for his room. Once inside, he locked the door behind him, leaning against it as he let out a heavy sigh. "I feel so unwanted in this house," he muttered to himself, the words filled with a bitter sadness.

Ethan walked over and sat down in his chair, reaching for the mouse, he prepared his escape as he woke his computer up to the *Mystical Quest*, the one place where he could forget the chaos of his life and the weight of his insecurities.

Just as his hand hovered over the keyboard, a strange sound made him pause, a faint buzzing, low and uneven, emerged from his computer.

He froze, his heart skipping a beat. The sound grew louder, like the hum of static building in intensity. His eyes locked onto the screen as it began to flicker erratically, the bright glow of the game collapsing into jagged lines of distortion.

"No, no, no, no!" Ethan muttered, panic rising. The flickering escalated, the screen flashing a pale blue before cutting out. Ethan's stomach sank, his mind racing with worst-case scenarios. *Don't crash? Please, don't crash. Not now.*

For what felt like an eternity, the screen remained blank. Ethan sat there, hands hovering uselessly over the keyboard, his pulse pounding in his ears. Then, without warning, the screen flickered back to life. Ethan blinked, his breath hitching. The *Mystical Quest* logo briefly appeared, but instead of loading the familiar map he had memorized down to the last detail, something different filled the screen. His game avatar, Shadow Sage, stood at the edge of an unfamiliar jungle. Thick, tangled vines hung from towering trees, and a narrow path carved its way through the dense foliage. The environment pulsed with an eerie glow, as if alive.

"What the ...?" Ethan muttered, leaning closer to the screen. His fingers hovered over the keyboard, his eyes scanning every detail of the scene. "Where is this?"

The unfamiliarity of the place sent a jolt through him, equal parts exhilaration and unease. The graphics were stunning, more immersive than anything he'd seen in the game before. His pulse quickened as his thoughts raced. *Is this an update? I've never seen anything like this before.*

Suddenly, a sharp ping broke the silence, making him jump. A message box appeared on the screen, the sender listed as: Unknown.

The message was simple: "Seek the Chamber of Secrets."

Ethan's hands trembled as he placed his headphones on his head and adjusted the mic. Ethan spoke, as he had many times to other players in the game: "Who are you?"

He waited, his eyes darting between the message box and the jungle on the screen and any sound that might provide answers.

Seconds stretched into agonizing minutes. There was no response.

The jungle remained still, its shadows shifting as though inviting him forward. Ethan's curiosity and apprehension warred within him. His mind raced with questions. *Who sent that message? What's the Chamber of Secrets?*

Taking a breath, Ethan's fingers tightened on the mouse. His curiosity outweighed his fear, and with a nervous exhale, he guided Shadow Sage down the narrow path, deeper into the unknown.

Across town, Sarah Halloway leaned back in the worn desk chair of her attic apartment. The space, cluttered with notebooks, pencils, and half-finished sketches, wasn't just a room, it was her sanctuary, the one place in the world where she felt safe. She had fought hard for this haven, convincing her father to let her move up here despite his reluctance. He, ironically, worried she was isolating herself too much, but Sarah knew better. The attic wasn't isolation, it was survival.

Her day had been as frustrating as she'd expected. Therapy was a complete waste of time with its carousel of clichés, recycled metaphors, and questions that led nowhere.

Sarah could predict every word her therapist would say before he even opened his mouth. *Talk about a lack of authenticity,* she thought bitterly. He didn't know her. No one did.

She went because her father insisted. "You need to talk to someone," he had said, his tone flat and detached. *Why couldn't that someone be him?* she thought for the millionth time. She wanted him to see her, to hear her, to really understand her. But deep down, Sarah knew that would never happen.

Her father was kind in his own way, but he had always been emotionally distant, like a shadow of the man he might have been. Sarah couldn't remember a time when he wasn't like this, though she knew why. Her mother had passed away suddenly when Sarah was two years old. She had no memories of her, just blurry photographs and the constant reminders told by father. The grief of losing his wife had shattered him, leaving behind a man who seemed hollow, incapable of connecting with anyone, even his own daughter.

As a child, Sarah had desperately craved her father's love, clinging to the rare moments of warmth and approval like fragile lifelines. But his grief had built an impenetrable wall between them, a wall she could never climb, no matter how hard she tried. He was there, physically present, but his spirit seemed trapped elsewhere, wrapped so tightly in sorrow that nothing and no one could break through.

She had learned early on that his grief wasn't something she could fix. As much as she longed for his attention, for him to see her, she always came up empty. Instead, his silence and detachment became the constant backdrop of her life.

So, Sarah learned to exist on her own. She stopped expecting anyone to show up for her, stopped hoping for someone to see her. The ache of being unseen, unheard, and unacknowledged carved out a void inside her, a hollow space she had to fill herself. She poured her heart into her art, sketching intricate worlds and characters that reflected the emotions she couldn't voice aloud. And she found refuge in the digital realm of *Mystical Quest*, where she could become someone else.

Sarah knew she was different from other kids. Her mind worked at a speed others couldn't seem to match, processing every subtle detail, every unspoken word.

She noticed things others overlooked, connected dots that no one else even saw. But instead of feeling empowered, her sharp mind often left her isolated. Teachers praised her intellect but misread her withdrawal as aloofness or disinterest. Her peers dismissed her as weird, her incisive observations cutting too close to truths they weren't ready to confront.

It hurt, being so sensitive to the world around her, feeling like an outsider no matter where she went. But here, in her attic sanctuary, she was free from judgment. This room, cluttered with notebooks, art supplies, and books, was her fortress.

As she turned on her computer, the glow of the *Mystical Quest* login screen filled the space, she became someone else. In the game, she was Luna Whisper, an Amazonian Warrior mage renowned for her brilliance, her ability to solve the most complex puzzles, uncover the most hidden secrets. Luna wasn't burdened by doubt or trapped by emptiness. Luna had clarity, purpose, and respect, things Sarah craved but could never find in the real world.

Sarah leaned forward, the hum of her computer grounding her in a way nothing else could. Around her, scattered sketches lay in disarray, fragments of worlds she had created, pieces of herself she couldn't share with anyone. They usually brought her some sense of solace, but not tonight.

Tonight, the weight pressing on her mind was too much. She needed more than paper and pencils. She needed escape. She needed *Mystical Quest*.

Her fingers hovered over the keyboard, a sigh slipping from her lips as the glow of the screen illuminated her face. In the real world, she was invisible, a puzzle no one seemed to want to solve. But here? Here, she mattered. Here, she was Luna Whisper, sharp, powerful, respected.

The title screen flickered to life, inviting her into the one place where she felt alive. "At least here, I can be someone," she whispered to herself. With a decisive press of a key, the login screen faded, and her heart lifted. As the game began to load, the screen flickered violently. Jagged lines replaced the familiar *Mystical Quest* launch screen, crackling with erratic energy. Then, as abruptly as it started, the screen went dim, the faint glow of blue filling the room.

"Great," Sarah muttered, throwing herself back into her chair, frustration bubbling to the surface. "Just what I need right now."

Every now and then her computer glitched, and she knew how to deal with that, but this was different, something else was going on that she couldn't quite get... She was about to hit the keyboard to take action when the screen went back to what looked normal. "Hmmm, strange..."

She leaned forward instinctively, her breath hitching in her throat. This time, *Mystical Quest* loaded, but not the way it usually did.

As the graphics sharpened, Sarah's avatar, Luna Whisper, appeared on the screen. But instead of the familiar settings she had memorized over the years, Luna was standing on an unfamiliar jungle trail. Thick vines twisted around towering trees, the foliage casting dappled shadows across the ground. The air seemed to shimmer, as if the jungle itself were alive, the detail so vivid that Sarah could almost feel the humid air against her skin.

"Whoa," she murmured, her fingers tightening around the edges of the keyboard. "That's... so real. But where is this?"

She frowned, her eyes scanning the screen. Sarah had played *Mystical Quest* for years. She knew every level, every map, every corner of the game.

She even knew most of the long-time players by their avatars. But this place? She didn't recognize it at all.

Her confusion deepened as a soft chime broke the silence. A message box appeared at the top of the screen, the sender listed as: Unknown.

The message was short, cryptic: "Seek the Chamber of Secrets."

Sarah's heart raced as she reached for her headset and slipped it on, her fingers fumbling. Pressing the mic button, she spoke, her voice steady but tinged with curiosity. "What's the Chamber of Secrets?" she asked, her words hanging in the air like a challenge.

She waited, listening intently for a response, but none came. The message box remained still, no typing indicator, no follow-up replies. Whoever, or whatever, had sent it had vanished as quickly as they'd appeared.

A chill ran down Sarah's spine as she stared at the screen, the unfamiliar jungle trail stretching out before Luna Whisper like a path beckoning her forward. The mystery sent a thrill through her veins, mingling with unease. She didn't know who or what was guiding her, but she couldn't shake the feeling that this was something she needed to explore.

Taking a breath, she tightened her grip on the mouse. "Guess I'll find out myself," she muttered, moving Luna Whisper forward into the unknown.

Tonight, under Sarah's watchful eye, Luna Whisper planned to tackle this new and elusive challenge. Sarah's fingers hovered over the keyboard as her avatar navigated through the dense jungle growth, thicker than any of the other game jungles she had worked her way through.

As the dense jungle began to thin, a mysterious clearing began to emerge.

Luna Whisper, her sharp eyes scanning every detail, stepped lightly into the moonlit space.

To her left, Shadow Sage emerged from the jungle with calculated hyper-vigilance, his blade drawn as if ready to battle at a moment's notice.

They both froze, spotting each other immediately. Their gazes locked, each sizing the other up like rival predators. Before them, what appears to be a massive stone door drew their attention briefly, its glowing golden inscription casting an eerie light across the clearing.

"Well, well," Luna said, her voice edged with sarcasm. "What are the odds? You always seem to show up where you're least wanted, Shadow."

Shadow Sage's lips curled into a smirk. "Funny, I was just thinking the same about you. What are you doing here, Luna? Decoding riddles and dragging your feet as usual?"

Luna raised an eyebrow, crossing her arms. "Unlike you, I actually use my brain. And by the way, brute force isn't going to open that door." She nodded toward the ancient entrance, her tone dripping with superiority.

"Thanks for the tip," Shadow shot back, his smirk unfaltering. "But if you think you're claiming whatever's on the other side, you're delusional."

"Me?" Luna scoffed, stepping closer to the door. "At least I'm not the one trying to cut my way through a challenge. Maybe leave this one to someone who knows what they're doing."

Shadow Sage moved in tandem, closing the gap between them, his voice dropping to a competitive growl. "You talk a big game, Luna, but let's not pretend you've got this figured out either. Admit it, you're as puzzled as I am about this."

Their heated exchange was interrupted as the golden inscription on the door pulsed brightly.

Both of them turned toward it, the light commanding their attention. Below the inscription, a shimmering pool of water materialized at the base of the door, its surface unnervingly still. But as they stepped closer, the water began to ripple.

"What is that?" Shadow Sage muttered, his usual bravado cracking as a twinge of unease slipped into his voice. His sharp eyes flickered toward the shimmering pool of water at the base of the door, every muscle in his body now tense.

"Don't be so jumpy, Shadow," Luna Whisper quipped, her voice laced with playful arrogance, though there was a hint of hesitation beneath it. "It's just a puddle of water. Best stand behind me if you're that scared."

The eerie glow from the door intensified, washing over the clearing like a pulse of energy.

Shadow Sage instinctively stepped back, his hand tightening around the hilt of his sword. "I don't like this," he said cautiously. "It feels like some kind of trap."

"Typical," Luna said with a sigh, shaking her head. "Always assuming the worst. It's just water. Tell you what, why don't *you* splash around in it while I figure out what that message above the door means?"

She gestured upward, her sharp gaze locking on the inscription etched into the stone:

'ONLY THE AUTHENTIC SHALL ENTER.'

"It's got to be a riddle," Luna said, her tone thoughtful now, the sharp edge of her teasing giving way to curiosity.

"Maybe," Shadow Sage replied, inching closer to the door despite his wariness. He couldn't resist the pull of the challenge, the need to uncover the mystery. As he approached, his focus narrowed to the faint hum emanating from the stone.

Without thinking, he reached out, his fingers brushing the door's surface. As he did, his foot stepped into the pool of water, and the world seemed to explode. A flash of light tore through Ethan's senses like a bolt of lightning. The impact threw him backward off his chair, and his headset went flying as he hit the floor with a loud thud. For a moment, he lay there, stunned, his mind reeling. He scrambled upright, grabbing his headset and shoving it back on.

"Holy crap, you won't believe what just happened," he blurted, his voice shaky as adrenaline coursed through him.

"What? Did your game freeze?" Luna Whisper's voice came through the headset, laced with confusion. "You stopped moving completely, like you were frozen."

Ethan hesitated, rubbing the back of his neck as he glanced at his computer screen. "I don't know," he said, his voice quieter now. "I think my chair broke or something. I reached for the door, and…" He trailed off, embarrassment creeping into his tone. "Never mind."

"You reached for the door and what?" Sarah's voice was sharper now, tinged with concern.

Ethan hesitated again, his pride warring with the strange vulnerability that had washed over him. "It's crazy," he admitted. "I think I'm just… off today."

His words were stiff, almost apologetic, but they carried a weight that Sarah hadn't heard before. Through her headset, Sarah immediately picked up on the shift in his tone. This wasn't like him, not like Shadow Sage, the unshakable warrior she was used to seeing. This was something else.

"I get it," Sarah said, her voice unusually gentle. "Life can suck sometimes."

"You're not kidding," Ethan replied with a bitter laugh, the crack in his armor widening.

"So, what happened?" Sarah pressed gently, her voice curious. "I saw you reach for the door, your foot hit the water, and then... you froze."

Ethan hesitated, swallowing hard. "Promise you won't laugh?" he asked, his voice quiet, almost vulnerable.

"Promise," Sarah replied firmly, her tone carrying a rare sincerity that cut through the usual banter between them.

Ethan exhaled, trying to find the words. "It felt... real," he said at last. "Like I wasn't just playing the game. I was in it, standing there, like I could feel the air and the energy from the door. It's stupid, I know."

Sarah didn't laugh. Instead, her voice softened, carrying an unexpected warmth. "It's not stupid," she said, her words deliberate and genuine. After a moment, she added. "Honestly... I get it. Sometimes I wish I could actually be in the game too, just to escape this life for a while. It's easier there."

Ethan blinked, her response catching him off guard. For the first time in a long while, he felt the faint stirrings of something unfamiliar yet comforting, was that connection? It was like being seen, not as Shadow Sage, but as himself. He let out a breath he hadn't realized he'd been holding. "Thanks," he murmured, his voice quiet but laced with gratitude.

Sarah smiled, even though she knew he couldn't see it. She could feel the shift between them, the rivalry that usually defined their interactions giving way to something more, something human. "So," she said, her tone turning thoughtful as she gently steered the conversation back. "What do we do now?"

Ethan straightened in his chair, the weight of what he just experienced easing. "We figure it out," he said, his voice regaining some of its usual steadiness. "Together, I guess."

"Together," Sarah echoed. Her grip tightened on the mouse as a small, determined smile played on her lips.

For the first time, Luna Whisper and Shadow Sage weren't rivals; they were allies, standing on the brink of something far bigger than either of them could comprehend.

Shadow Sage glanced back at the glowing pool of water. "Luna," he said cautiously, his voice tinged with curiosity and challenge. "There's something strange about that pool. Why don't you touch it and see what happens?"

Luna Whisper huffed, the familiar competitive edge creeping back into her tone. "For God's sake, Shadow. It's just a puddle of water," she muttered, stepping closer. She reached out, her movements bold and unflinching, as if to prove him wrong.

The moment her foot touched the water, the world seemed to tilt. A sudden flash of light rippled through the pool, and Sarah's breath caught in her throat. It wasn't just a reflection of Luna she saw, it was herself, standing there in front of the door, not as her avatar, but as Sarah Halloway.

Her heart pounded as she turned to Shadow Sage finding him standing next to her, his presence startlingly real. The line between the game and reality blurred in a way that made her stomach flip.

Startled, Sarah yanked Luna's foot out of the water, jerking back in her chair. She sat frozen for a moment, her chest heaving, her mind racing to process what she had just experienced.

"Shadow," she said, her voice trembling with nervous energy. "I... I was there. In the game. Standing right next to you, or, I mean, your avatar. But it wasn't just a game. It felt so real."

Ethan's grip on his mouse tightened as he processed her words. His voice, normally steady and teasing, wavered. "You mean... like you were actually there right! In the jungle! With me! I know!"

"Yes," Sarah shouted, her tone filled with awe and a flicker of fear. "I don't know how, but I was there!"

The two sat in stunned silence, the realization settling over them like a heavy fog. Whatever they had stumbled into wasn't a glitch or a hidden level, it was something far deeper, something neither of them could understand yet. For the first time, they weren't just players navigating a virtual world; they were part of something real, and it was both exhilarating and terrifying.

'Only the authentic shall enter?' Luna Whisper murmured aloud, her voice trembling with equal parts curiosity and apprehension as she took another step back from the glowing pool. She turned to Shadow Sage, her expression unusually serious. "Shadow," she said, her tone charged with urgency. "I think… I think we're meant to step into that pool together…"

"What? Are you crazy?" Shadow shouted, his voice sharp with disbelief.

"Listen," Luna said, her eyes locking onto his. "You stepped in and saw yourself, right? Your real self?"

Shadow hesitated, the memory of the flash still fresh in his mind. "Yeah… I think so…"

"Well, I did too," Luna continued, her voice firm but tinged with awe. "I saw myself, Shadow. Not Luna Whisper, but me, my true self. Standing right here."

"And?" Shadow replied, his skepticism still intact, though it was clear he was beginning to waver.

"Think about it," Luna pressed, her hands gesturing emphatically. "The inscription says:

'Only the authentic shall enter.'

Don't you see? Our avatars, they're not real. They're just characters we wear to hide behind in the game. But if this pool is showing us who we *really* are, maybe that's the key. Maybe we're supposed to step in and show our true selves, not as Shadow Sage or Luna Whisper."

Shadow shook his head, his hand running through his hair as if trying to pull himself back to reality. "Luna, I hate to break it to you, but this is a video game. It's *not* real life," he said, his voice laced with frustration, though the uncertainty in his tone betrayed him.

"Oh, really?" Luna shot back, her sharp tone cutting through his defenses. "Then how do you explain what happened, to you *and* to me? Wise guy?"

Shadow opened his mouth to respond but faltered. He couldn't deny what he had felt when he stepped into the pool. It had been real, too real. He sighed, his voice softer now. "I don't know," he admitted. "But come on... you can't actually *be* in the game as real people. Can you?"

For the first time, Shadow's voice wasn't just questioning; it was vulnerable, tinged with an uncertainty that Ethan rarely allowed himself to show.

Luna's expression softened as she picked up on the shift in his tone. "I don't know either, maybe this new update uses our camera somehow?" she questioned, the weight of the moment pressing down on her.

"Maybe it's a new AI thing, whatever this is, it's not the same game anymore, it's different. You know that as much as I do."

Shadow looked at her, the usual tension between them melting into something deeper, something real. "So, what do we do?" he asked, his voice steady but his eyes filled with uncertainty.

"We step in," Luna replied, her voice resolute despite the tremble in her hands. "Together."

The two stood in silence for a moment, the glowing pool of water casting shifting reflections on their avatars' faces. It felt like a threshold, like the next step would change everything.

Chapter 2

The Call to Adventure

Both Luna Whisper and Shadow Sage stood at the edge of the glowing pool, the light dancing on their faces as if daring them to step forward. The tension between them hung heavy in the air, laced with the uncertainty of what would happen next.

Luna reached out her hand, her fingers trembling despite her bold expression. "Together," she said, her voice steady but carrying an urgency.

Shadow hesitated, glancing down at her outstretched hand. His hovered for a moment, doubt flickering in his eyes. He looked up and met Luna's gaze. In her eyes, he saw something he hadn't expected, determination tempered by a vulnerability that mirrored his. Slowly, he took her hand, their grip firm, grounding them both in the moment.

"On the count of three," he said, his voice low but resolute.

Luna nodded, her grip tightening. "One," she began.

"Two," Shadow continued, their voices overlapping.

"Three."

In unison, they stepped into the pool with both feet. The world erupted in a cascade of light, the pool dissolving into a swirling tunnel of colors that enveloped them. Ethan and Sarah felt themselves spinning, being pulled forward with an unrelenting force. It wasn't just falling, it was as if they were being drawn into something far beyond their understanding.

Around them, the walls of the light-filled tunnel shimmered with vivid, shifting images. Scenes from their lives played out in fragmented flashes, each one striking with raw emotion. Sarah saw herself sitting stiffly in her therapist's office, the weight of judgment heavy on her shoulders. The scene shifted, Sarah being teased at school, the taunts echoing in her ears as she clenched her fists, trying not to cry.

Ethan's images unfurled next: his brother yelling at him, the cruel words slicing through him like knives. Then his brother's fist came down, and Ethan flinched as his father stood by, laughing, a cold, mocking sound that made his stomach churn even now.

The images swirled faster, changing again. This time, they weren't echoes of pain but something different. Sarah stood boldly, her presence commanding as she donned the elegant armor of Luna Whisper. Beside her stood Ethan, strong and unyielding in the armor of Shadow Sage. Together, they seemed ready to face the unknown with a strength neither had yet claimed in their real lives.

Abruptly, the tunnel shifted again. A flash of brilliant light revealed an enormous reptilian beast, its scales glinting like molten metal, its wings spanning the horizon, and its eyes glowing with an ominous intensity. The creature loomed before them, radiating both power and malice. Before they could process what they were seeing, the tunnel collapsed into darkness, and the sensation of falling stopped abruptly.

With a heavy thud, Ethan and Sarah landed on a cold, sand-covered floor. The impact jarred them, the breath knocked from their lungs as they lay still for a moment, disoriented. They turned their heads toward each other, locking eyes, no longer as Shadow Sage and Luna Whisper, but as themselves.

They were face-to-face, their avatars stripped away, leaving Ethan and Sarah as their true selves. The jungle, the door and the pool were gone, replaced by an ancient chamber that seemed alive.

Ethan and Sarah stared at each other, both frozen in shock. Their breaths came in shallow bursts, their minds struggling to process what they were seeing. They had seen each other before, passing glances in the crowded hallways at school, casual glimpses during classes, but they had never spoken. Never thought they would.

"You…" Ethan began, his voice uncertain. "You are Luna Whisper?"

"And you are… Shadow Sage?" Sarah whispered back, her voice just as tentative, her wide eyes scanning his face.

They stared at each other for a long, silent moment, each wrestling with a mix of disbelief and recognition. Neither had imagined the other was more than a face in the crowd at school. Both had assumed the other would be dismissive, maybe even cruel, like so many in their lives. And yet here they were, not as their avatars, but as themselves, face to face in a place that defied explanation.

"I've seen you before," Sarah said, her words hesitant, as if she weren't sure she should speak them aloud.

Ethan nodded. "Yeah… at school. But we've never… you know, talked."

"Never had a reason to, I guess," Sarah replied, her voice carrying a trace of guardedness, though her eyes betrayed curiosity.

Ethan let out a shaky laugh, running a hand through his hair. "Well, this is definitely a first."

"Yeah," Sarah agreed, her lips curving into a faint, uncertain smile.

For a moment, they stood there, two strangers brought together by something far beyond their comprehension. Then, as if drawn by the same invisible force, they both turned to take in their surroundings. The chamber stretched out around them, ancient, its stone walls covered in twisting vines that shimmered with an ethereal glow. The light seemed alive, shifting between shadow and brilliance, creating an atmosphere both unsettling and awe-inspiring. The air hummed, charged with energy that made their skin tingle.

"What is this place?" Sarah whispered, her voice filled with awe and trepidation as she rose to her feet.

Ethan stood beside her, his gaze fixed on the centerpiece of the chamber: a pedestal in the room's center, upon which rested an ancient book. Its cover glimmered, intricate patterns etched into its surface shifting like ripples on water. Ethan's stomach tightened as he stared at it, the sheer weight of its presence seemed overwhelming.

"I don't know," he replied. "But… something about this place feels …familiar."

Sarah stepped closer to the book, her movements slow and deliberate.

The energy radiating from it seemed to pull her in, her breath growing shallow as she felt a presence. "Do you feel that?" she asked, her voice trembling. "It's like I have been here before."

Ethan nodded, his hand twitching as if drawn to the book before he hesitated and pulled back. "That feels like it's more than just a book," he said, pointing at the ancient book on the pedestal.

Side by side, they studied the glowing patterns on its cover. The lines pulsed, as though responding to their proximity. The hum in the chamber grew louder, not a sound, but a vibration, something they felt deep within their bones, as if the room itself was alive and aware of their presence.

"Shall we open it?" Sarah said, glancing at Ethan. There was an urgency in her voice but also fear.

"Why not." Ethan stated.

Sarah's hand trembled as she reached toward the book, hovering above its surface. She hesitated, her mind racing with possibilities. She spoke. "Maybe we should do this together?"

Her words hung in the air, heavy with meaning. For a long moment, neither of them moved, the weight of the moment pressing down on them.

Ethan stepped forward, his hand moving to meet hers. Together, they placed their hands on the book, their fingers brushing against its surface.

The reaction was instant. Warmth surged through their hands, spreading up their arms and into their chests. The light from the book exploded outward, filling the chamber with a brilliant, golden glow. The patterns on its surface danced and shifted, forming shapes and symbols they couldn't comprehend, yet somehow felt connected to.

Ethan and Sarah felt the energy of the chamber engulfing them, as though it were pulling them into something far greater than themselves. The air around them seemed to hum with purpose, and for the first time, they weren't just standing in a strange, magical place. They were a part of it.

Instinctively they stepped back as the book before them began to move, its ancient pages flipping open on their own as though guided by an unseen force. A faint golden glow seeped from its center, growing brighter with each turn of the page. From the heart of the book, a radiant orb floated upward, its golden surface shimmering with a mirror-like quality that seemed alive.

Both Sarah and Ethan froze, their eyes locked on the orb as its surface began to shift, revealing reflections, not of who they were now, but of who they had once been. Ethan saw himself as a quiet, isolated boy, his brother's cruel words cutting into him, his father's indifference reinforcing the belief that he didn't belong. Sarah saw herself sitting alone in the school cafeteria, her sharp observations and withdrawn demeanor making her a target for teasing and whispers.

The images rippled across the orb's surface like water, shifting intensely. Now, they saw themselves transformed: confident, vibrant, and unshaken by the weight of the world. Ethan stood tall, radiating strength, while Sarah exuded an unyielding brilliance, her eyes filled with clarity and determination.

The hum of energy that had been building in the chamber grew louder, vibrating in the air like a living heartbeat. The orb stopped in midair, hovering above the book, its glow illuminating the entire room. Sarah and Ethan exchanged a glance, unsure whether to move closer or retreat further.

"Maybe... maybe we're supposed to touch it too," Ethan whispered, his voice trembling as his gaze flicked back to the floating orb.

Before Sarah could respond, the orb spoke.

"My name," it said, its voice deep and resonant, like a melody echoing through the chamber. "Is Aerthis, and I am the Guardian of the Book of Wisdom."

Ethan jumped at the sound, his nerves jolted. "Whoa!" he exclaimed, his face a mix of awe and disbelief. "That's... wicked!"

Sarah, her eyes never leaving the orb, found her voice, though it came out as a soft whisper.

"Hello, Aerthis... can you please tell us where we are?"

The Orb's surface rippled like liquid silver as it hovered closer to them, its enigmatic glow bathing them in a warmth that felt both soothing and intense. "You," Aerthis said in a voice that seemed to sing. "Are the Seekers, chosen to restore harmony to this realm."

Ethan and Sarah exchanged another glance, their confusion clearly visible. The rivalry and distance that had defined their encounters in *Mystical Quest* evaporated, replaced by a shared sense of something far greater than either of them could comprehend.

"What do you mean, we're Seekers? What realm?" Ethan asked, his words spilling out in a rapid stream.

"Are we still in the game? Is this some kind of advanced AI thing?"

Aerthis seemed to pulse with amusement as it responded. "Yes, you have many questions," the orb replied, its tone patient and calm. "And in time, they will be answered. But first, you must be willing to accept the quest. Only then can I guide you forward."

"What quest?" Sarah asked, her brows furrowing. "What are you talking about? What does it mean to accept?"

Aerthis hovered closer, its glow intensifying as its voice softened. "The realm is in jeopardy," it said, the weight of its words filling the chamber. "It has lost its way. Balance has been disrupted, and without restoration, this realm will fall into chaos."

"Okay, okay, hang on," Ethan interrupted, raising his hands. "Seriously, what realm? Are we even still on Earth?" Ethan turned to Sarah and said. "I saw something like this in a movie once."

Sarah looked at Ethan with a very puzzled expression. "Don't be ridiculous," Sarah shot back, her voice tinged with a mixture of exasperation and doubt. "Of course, we're still on Earth... aren't we?"

Aerthis's glow pulsed, a subtle but powerful response to their unease. "The realm I speak of exists neither in time nor space as you know it," the orb explained. "It is a void, and it is all-encompassing. It is the essence of potential, the potential to create, to grow, to achieve greatness. But it also has the potential to destroy, to fall into ruin and to capture others in its descent."

The chamber fell silent, the hum of energy the only sound as the weight of Aerthis's words settled over them. "Only you," Aerthis continued, its voice taking on a note of intensity. "Hold the power to decide which it will be. The path forward is yours to choose."

Ethan and Sarah exchanged a final look, their faces marked by both fear and the beginnings of resolve. Whatever this realm was, whatever this quest entailed, it was clear that they had crossed a threshold, one from which there would be no turning back.

Chapter 3

The Mystical Forest

Sarah and Ethan exchanged a glance, their shared uncertainty lingering in the space between them. Sarah walked over to a large, flat stone and sank down onto it, her movements heavy with the weight of everything that had just happened. Ethan hesitated for a moment before following her, sitting down beside her, unsure of what to say.

"You, okay?" Ethan asked, his voice cautious but genuine.

Sarah looked at him, her eyes wide and overwhelmed. "I don't know," she admitted, her voice trembling. "I mean, all I've ever wanted was to be brave, you know? To go on an adventure, just like Luna does. But now that I'm actually here... I'm a bit scared Ethan."

Ethan glanced at the glowing orb of Aerthis hovering in the air, then back at Sarah. He nodded, his expression softening. "Yeah," he said quietly. "Me too!"

Sarah blinked, surprised by his admission. "You are?"

"Of course," Ethan said, letting out a small laugh that didn't quite reach his eyes. "Who wouldn't be? I mean, look around. I'm so far out of my comfort zone right now, it's not even funny," he paused, then added. "But still… it feels like the right thing to do. I mean, whatever this quest is, whatever that glowing ball's talking about, it has to be better than my life back home."

Sarah let out a sigh, her gaze drifting back to Aerthis. "I feel like this is right too," she said. "It's just… what if I fail?"

Ethan turned to her, a small smile breaking through his uncertainty. "Come on, Sarah. You won't fail. You're Luna Whisper, remember!"

Sarah glanced at him, her brow furrowing into a scowl. "Do I *look* like Luna Whisper to you?"

Ethan straightened, studying her face with exaggerated thoughtfulness. "Well, no," he admitted. "But you *are* Luna Whisper. You created her, didn't you? You made her the warrior she is. Without you, she's just some animated character on a screen."

A faint smile tugged at Sarah's lips, despite herself.

"Besides," Ethan added, his tone lightening as he tried to lift the mood. "How hard can it be? I mean, it's not like we have to defeat a dragon or anything… right?" He turned to Aerthis, looking for reassurance.

The orb remained silent, floating serenely in the air, its stillness unsettling.

Ethan swallowed hard and turned back to Sarah. "Okay, so… maybe there's a chance we'll have to face something big. But still," he said, trying to sound more confident than he felt.

"We've got this."

Sarah's smile faded, and she glanced down at her hands. "I'm not great at working with others," she admitted. "I've never really tried. I guess... I guess I'm..." She hesitated, then looked away, her next words caught in her throat.

Ethan leaned toward her, his tone gentle. "Afraid of how people might see you?" he asked quietly. "I get that."

She looked at him, her eyes widening in surprise.

"Honestly," Ethan continued, his gaze dropping to his hands. "I'm the same way. I've never figured out how to fit in with other people. It's easier to keep my distance, you know?"

Sarah nodded, her defenses softening as she realized she wasn't alone in her fears.

They sat there in silence for a moment, the glow of the chamber casting faint, shifting shadows around them. For the first time, they weren't just two players thrown together by chance, they were two people, both unsure, both vulnerable, but beginning to trust each other.

"We can figure this out," Ethan said, his voice firm but kind. "Together."

Sarah met his gaze, and for the first time, she felt a flicker of courage. "Together," she echoed, as she glanced back toward Aerthis. Whatever lay ahead, they would face it, not as strangers, but as allies.

Ethan stood up, brushing the sand off his hands and reaching out to Sarah. She hesitated for a moment, her emerald eyes flickering to his outstretched hand, then took it. His grip was steady, and with a small nod of encouragement, he helped her to her feet.

Together, they turned toward Aerthis, the glowing orb hovering silently above the pedestal.

Its mirror-like surface reflected not only their faces but something deeper, faint glimpses of the people they were becoming.

"Okay," Sarah said, her voice steadying despite the weight of uncertainty. "Let's do this."

"Yeah," Ethan added with a nervous grin. "Let the quest begin! So... now will you tell us what we've gotten ourselves into?"

The moment he spoke, Aerthis pulsed with light, growing brighter until the chamber around them dissolved into a flash of pure white. Sarah shielded her eyes, her heart pounding as the world seemed to shift beneath her feet.

The light receded and Ethan and Sarah found themselves standing in a breathtaking forest. The air was crisp and sweet, tinged with the faint scent of blossoms unlike any they had ever encountered. Towering trees with iridescent leaves stretched high into the sky, their branches weaving into a shimmering canopy. Strange, ethereal creatures peeked out from behind bushes, creatures that seemed to glow faintly, their movements curious but unthreatening.

Butterflies unlike anything they had ever seen floated past, their wings shimmering with colors that shifted and danced like reflections on water. As they moved, it felt as though they were connected to Ethan and Sarah's very thoughts, responding subtly to their emotions. Nearby, a swarm of glowing moths fluttered in unison, their delicate wings producing a hauntingly beautiful melody that filled the forest.

"Welcome, Seekers," Aerthis said, its voice resonating with pride, the melody of the moths fading as it spoke. "You now stand within the Mystical Forest, one of the last sanctuaries untouched by the chaos consuming this realm.

It is here that your quest begins."

Ethan and Sarah exchanged a glance, their awe mingling with apprehension.

"You've called us 'Seekers' a few times now," Sarah said, stepping closer to the orb. "What does that mean? And… what is this quest?"

Aerthis hovered closer, its glow deepening as it began to explain. "I am Aerthis, the Orb of Reflection, a guardian created at the dawn of this realm to protect its balance and guide those who would stand against its destruction. I serve the Ethereal Nexus to protect the Book of Wisdom, a sacred artifact containing the truths and knowledge of this realm, as well as the paths to restore it. Together, the Chamber of Secrets, where we met, and the Book of Wisdom form the gateway to the power you now hold. That chamber tests the authenticity of those who enter, ensuring those who are true to themselves may proceed."

"So, what is this realm?" Ethan asked, his brow furrowed.

"This is the Realm of the Mind," Aerthis replied. "It is a place neither bound by time nor space, existing within and beyond all things. It is the manifestation of thought, creativity, and potential, the foundation of harmony and chaos alike. All Realms thrive on balance, this one is in jeopardy. Its balance has been shattered by the rise of the Dysquinox States."

"Dysquinox States?" Sarah repeated, as though saying the words might bring them to life.

Aerthis pulsed again, the trees around them seeming to dim as it spoke. "Yes Seeker, The Dysquinox states represents imbalance and discord."

Sarah swallowed hard, the weight of Aerthis's words sinking in. "And… this Dysquinox thing… it's taken over this… Realm?"

"Yes," Aerthis said solemnly. "The Dysquinox States have spread, corrupting the balance that once defined this Realm.

The light and the dark, creation and destruction, they are no longer in harmony. The Realm teeters on the edge of ruin."

Ethan's jaw tightened as he absorbed the explanation. "And that's where we come in?"

"Indeed," Aerthis said, its glow intensifying. "You have been chosen as Seekers to restore the Realm to its natural state: the Quinox State, a perfect balance of all forces where harmony and growth are possible. To do this, you must find and align with the Five Mystical Enigmas."

"Five Mystical Enigmas?" Sarah asked, her voice trembling. "What's an Enigma?"

Aerthis began to drift forward, expecting them to follow as it continued to speak. "The Five Mystical Enigmas are ancient forces that embody the essence of balance. Each one represents a crucial aspect of the Quinox State: Courage, Compassion, Insight, Resilience, and Truth. They are scattered within this forest, hidden and guarded. Only by connecting with their power can you realign the Realm of the Mind and restore its harmony."

Ethan glanced at Sarah, his nerves visible in the tight set of his jaw. "Okay, so let's say we find these Enigma things, then what? How do we bring the Realm back to this Quinox State?"

Aerthis stopped, turning to face them. Its voice grew softer, yet more intense, each word resonating deeply. "To restore the realm, you must face the dragons of Dysquinox."

Both Ethan and Sarah froze.

"Dragons?" Ethan asked, his voice cracking. "You're kidding, right?"

Aerthis did not respond, its silence a confirmation heavier than words.

Sarah looked down, her hands trembling. "Um...you said Dragons" she questioned, her voice trembling like her hands. "Is there more than one?"

Aerthis hovered closer to her, its glow warm and steady. "Courage is not the absence of fear, Seeker," it said. "It is the choice to move forward despite it," the Orb turned back and continued through the forest saying. *"There are thirteen!"*

Sarah and Ethan froze mid-step, their heads snapping toward the orb in unison.

"Thirteen!" they exclaimed together, their voices rising in disbelief.

Sarah turned to Ethan, her brow furrowed. *"Did it say thirteen dragons?"*

Ethan's expression mirrored hers, a mix of confusion and dread. "That has to be a mistake. *Thirteen?* How do we even...?" He trailed off, running a hand through his hair, his mind spinning. "And dragons aren't even real!" he added, as if saying it aloud would somehow dismiss the reality they were now facing.

The Orb stopped and turned, its glowing surface reflecting their concerned faces. Its tone, though calm, carried the weight of conviction. "Thirteen dragons, yes. Each one has fallen into a Dysquinox state, destabilizing the balance of the Realm of the Mind. You must learn the skills to transform them, not destroy them, back into their Quinox state. To do this, you will need the aid of the Five Mystical Enigmas. Only through their gifts can you bring the dragons back to their true nature."

Sarah exchanged a look with Ethan, her stomach twisting. "Thirteen... and we have to *transform* them?" Her voice wavered. "What if we can't? What if..."

"You can," Aerthis interrupted, its glow pulsing as if to emphasize its certainty. "Doubt is natural, but courage is the choice to act despite it. You will find the strength you need along the way. For now, you must keep moving."

Without another word, the Orb floated forward, the faint hum of its energy pulling them back into motion.

Ethan let out a long breath and glanced at Sarah. "Thirteen," he muttered under his breath, shaking his head. "Why couldn't it have been, I don't know, two?"

Sarah gave him a faint, wry smile despite the pit forming in her stomach. "Or none," she hesitated, then said seriously. "What have we gotten into?"

Ethan stopped walking for a moment and turned to her, studying her face. She didn't look like Luna Whisper right now, confident, in control. Suddenly, Ethans hyper-vigilance kicked in as he thought to himself, *maybe this wasn't such a good idea after all?*

Aerthis stops, sensing their increasing doubt. "Every soul walks the path of choice, Seekers. Some choices shine with certainty, known to be right. Others, we know, stray us from the light. Yet, there are those crossroads wrapped in mystery, neither right nor wrong, only unknown. Turn away, and their truth will forever remain a question. Step forward, and only then shall you see what was always meant to be."

Sarah glances at Ethan, a hint of confidence returning to her eyes. Ethan, still puzzling over Aerthis's cryptic message, scratches his head and asks. "So… are we meant to seek out the unknown?"

The Orb's light intensities briefly. "That is why you are Seekers"

"Let's give it a try Ethan" Sarah said, her voice soft but resolute. "Together?"

Ethan straightened, pushing down his fear and forcing himself to nod. "Together," he said firmly, his tone echoing hers.

The Orb's gentle hum filled the silence as they followed its light deeper into the forest.

The trees around them began to shift, their shimmering leaves dimming as the path grew darker and narrower. Although the glow of strange stones embedded in the ground lit their way, the once-beautiful forest now seemed mysterious, as though it, too, was holding its breath.

Ethan and Sarah walked side by side, their earlier rivalry replaced by a common sense of unity. But the gravity of what lay ahead weighed heavily on them both.

"You know," Ethan said after a moment. "I was worried about *one* dragon. Thirteen is… a lot."

Sarah glanced at him, her voice unusually gentle. "Yeah. I was hoping it was joking too," she paused, her thoughts racing. "But we must be here for a reason, right? The Orb said so. Maybe… maybe we can do this."

Ethan chuckled dryly, the sound tinged with nervousness. "Sure, I mean how hard can transforming a bunch of massive, chaotic, mind-controlling dragons be!"

"Don't forget the five Mystical Enigmas we have to find first," Sarah added, trying to inject some levity into the tension, though her nerves betrayed her.

"Right, the Enigmas," Ethan said, shaking his head. "Because this wasn't hard enough already."

Ahead of them, Aerthis's glow pulsed once, drawing their attention like a beacon in the darkening forest. "The task is monumental, yes," the Orb said, its voice resonating with a calm, soothing cadence. "But so is your potential. Do not look at the whole path and despair; take each step as it comes, and the right way will reveal itself."

Sarah inhaled, the weight of the Orb's words pressing against her. She nodded, though doubt lingered in her eyes. "I'm guessing this is something we were meant to do…" She muttered.

"There is always choice Seekers, some choose to grow, others choose to erode, there is no staying the same" Aerthis replied, its tone soft and resolute. "All you need to focus on is your choice and how you face it. The dragons may seem terrifying, but they are not your enemies. They are the guardians of this Realm, trapped and tormented by imbalance. Their power is vast, but their potential for harmony is even greater. You must trust in yourselves and learn to trust in the Enigmas."

The Orb floated closer, its glow intensifying as if the truth it carried demanded their full attention. "But heed this warning, Seekers," it said, its voice deepening with an air of authority. "Wisdom has shown, time and again, that overcoming challenges such as those you will face is often met with the illusion of simplicity. There are those in the external world, who seek to manipulate the vulnerable by making them believe that complex challenges can be solved easily, without struggle. It lulls them into complacency with promises of ease, convincing them that courage, perseverance, and commitment are unnecessary. This is Benevolent Dysquinox."

Ethan frowned, his jaw tightening. "What do you mean? Like, false promises? People pretending things are easy when they're not?"

"Exactly," Aerthis said, its glow flickering. "The Benevolent Dysquinox thrives on this illusion. It entices with false kindness, offering solutions that seem effortless and convincing its victims they are on the right path. But these so-called solutions lead to stagnation and decay, for that is its true purpose. It is a trap, designed to keep the mind from growing, to prevent the heart from striving, and to rob the soul of the strength it gains through struggle."

Sarah's expression darkened as she absorbed the Orb's words.

"So... the Benevolent Dysquinox convinces people to take the easy way out? To avoid the hard work needed to fixing things?"

Aerthis pulsed in acknowledgment. "Yes. It whispers of shortcuts and comfort, but in truth, it denies growth and leaves the mind vulnerable to despair. Challenges that demand courage and persistence may seem daunting, but they are the forge in which strength is tempered, and harmony is found. Only by embracing the discomfort of true effort can transformation occur."

Ethan shifted uneasily, his thoughts drifting to his own life, the countless times he had avoided standing up for himself, hoping problems would disappear. "But what if we're not strong enough?" he asked, his voice carrying a weight he couldn't hide. "What if we mess up?"

Aerthis turned to him, its glow warm, like a reassuring hand on his shoulder. "Strength is not the absence of failure, Seeker, but the willingness to rise each time you fall. The dragons, too, are trapped by the illusions of the Dysquinox states, imprisoned by the echoes of the external world. To save them, you must first recognize these echoes within yourselves. The courage to face them, to stumble and try again, will be your greatest strength. Resilience is not an innate gift; it is a choice made again and again, no matter how hard the path may seem."

The Orb's words hung in the air, heavy with meaning. As they continued walking, the forest began to open up, revealing a clearing at the top of a hill. The trees parted, and before them lay a breathtaking view of the Realm.

On one side, the Mystical Forest glowed with vibrant life, its ethereal beauty untouched. The light filtering through the trees felt alive, full of warmth and potential.

But at the edge of the forest, the world abruptly shifted. The once-lush Plains of Rejuvenation had become the Barren Lands, a bleak expanse where no life stirred. Dark clouds churned above, lightning flashing sporadically, illuminating the twisted, lifeless terrain.

In the distance, faint roars rumbled across the horizon. The sound carried an ancient, primal weight, sending chills down Ethan and Sarah's spines. It was a reminder of the task that lay ahead, and the danger it carried.

In the distance, faint roars rumbled across the horizon. The sound carried an ancient, primal weight, sending chills down Ethan and Sarah's spines. It was a reminder of the task that lay ahead, and the danger it carried.

Ethan and Sarah stand frozen, their eyes locked on the devastation stretching endlessly before them. A hollow weight settles in their chests, the cruel truth of Aerthis's words sinking deeper with each passing moment. The once-vibrant horizon now trembles on the edge of ruin.

Sarah's voice wavers, barely above a whisper. "Will it take this beautiful forest too?"

Aerthis's light fades, its glow dimming like a dying ember. "Yes... But you hold the power to stop it."

Ethan clenched his fists, his fear battling with newfound determination. "If the Realm needs our help, we'll find a way," he said, though his voice wavered. "I don't know how, but we will."

Sarah nodded, her gaze fixed on the distant storms. The Orb's words echoed in her mind, and despite her fear, a flicker of resolve began to grow. "And if the Enigmas are the key, we'll find them too," she said, though her hands trembled.

Aerthis hovered between them, its glow casting long shadows across the clearing.

"You will face many trials," it said. "And you will be tested in ways you cannot imagine. But remember this: true balance is not found in the absence of struggle. It is found in the courage to embrace both light and shadow, to honor the full spectrum of your being. That is where your strength lies."

Ethan and Sarah exchanged a glance, their earlier resolve now tinged with the weight of reality. Thirteen dragons. Five Enigmas. A world on the brink of collapse.

As the Orb began to lead them down the hill, the roars off in the distance grew louder, a haunting reminder of what awaited them. Their journey had just begun, and already, the path ahead felt impossibly daunting.

Chapter 4

Balance and Duality

Ethan and Sarah followed the Orb of Reflection deeper into the Mystical Forest. The forest, once alive with gentle hums and melodic sounds, grew eerily quiet. The faint rustling of leaves overhead and the soft crunch of their footsteps were the only sounds that accompanied them. Glowing stones faint light casting a cool, otherworldly glow that seemed to pulse in time with the Orb's movements.

Ethan couldn't help but glance nervously over his shoulder as faint whispers drifted through the trees. The voices were too soft to understand but carried an unsettling edge that sent shivers down his spine.

Ethan broke the silence, his voice low but urgent. "So… this whole Realm of the Mind thing, why's it such a mess?"

Sarah walked beside him, her eyes scanning the darkened forest. Her expression was thoughtful but guarded. "Yeah," she added, her curiosity piqued. "And tell us about… what did you call it? Dys… something?"

"Dysquinox," the Orb replied, its glow brightening as it spoke. "It is the state of corruption and chaos that plagues many realms. It exists in three forms: the Benevolent State, the Malevolent State, and the Shifting State."

The Orb's voice grew steadier, almost somber, as it began to explain. "The Benevolent State is an illusion of harmony. It lulls the Realm into stagnation and complacency, where nothing grows, and nothing evolves. It harbors false kindness while hiding its true nature, leading those under its influence to trust blindly while their potential decays."

Ethan furrowed his brow, his mind turning over the words. "So, it's like you said before, a trap? Like pretending everything's fine when it's not?"

"Precisely," Aerthis replied. "The Benevolent Dysquinox appears as a gentle force but ultimately steals progress and trust. Imagine a dragon offering its protection while subtly convincing you to surrender your strength. Its intentions appear as helpful, but instead, it robs the Realm of its vitality."

"Like a scammer!" Ethan blurts out.

Sarah frowned, her arms crossing over her chest. "And the other two states?"

"The Malevolent State," Aerthis continued. "Is destruction incarnate. Dragons in this state are consumed by fear, anger, and hatred. They lash out at perceived threats, real or imagined, and spread discord wherever they go. Their aggression ignites chaos, spreading like wildfire through the Realm, reaching beyond its borders to infect others.

They wield Malevolent Dysquinox not as a shield, but as a weapon, twisting destruction into their only form of defense."

Ethan's jaw tightened. "That doesn't sound good."

The Orb paused briefly, its light dimming. "It is not. The dragons believe they are guarding the Realm, but their Dysquinox states warp their intentions. In their Malevolent State, their need to control and protect transforms into domination and destruction."

Sarah pressed on, her curiosity sharpening. "And the Shifting State?"

"Chaos," Aerthis said. "Dragons trapped in the Shifting State oscillate unpredictably between Benevolence and Malevolence. They are volatile, creating instability and confusion as they shift from moments of false protection to bursts of aggression. This state is the most dangerous, for it embodies unpredictability, both for the dragons themselves and for those they affect."

Ethan's gaze darted to the glowing stones beneath his feet, the weight of the Orb's explanation sinking in. "Okay, but why now? Why is this Realm in this state all of a sudden?"

The Orb's glow brightened, casting their faces in a warm light. "That is an important question, Seeker. The Realm of the Mind is a delicate balance, sustained by the harmony of thought, emotion, and imagination. It is a place where potential thrives in its purest form. But like any living thing, it requires nourishment to grow. In its early stages, the Realm depended on the guidance of the Eternal Guardians of Origin, you know them as E.G.O."

Ethan tilted his head, his brow furrowing. "Wait a second. E.G.O.? I've heard people talk about ego before, but isn't that like, having an attitude or something?"

Aerthis emitted a soft hum, its tone tinged with what felt like gentle amusement.

"In one sense, yes, ego can represent attitude. But it is far more complex than that," the Orb began, its voice resonant. "The dragons, the Eternal Guardians of Origin, are shaped by the attitudes, beliefs, and treatment they have received from the external influences surrounding them. They were created to protect this Realm during its most vulnerable stages, nurturing it through its infancy and guiding it to its adolescent state."

Aerthis's glow brightened, casting a warm, reassuring light as it spoke with conviction. "The dragons were never meant to hold their guardianship forever. Their ultimate purpose was to guide and protect the Realm during its early stages, ensuring its survival and growth. But their role was always temporary, a bridge to something greater. Once the Realm reached a level of maturity, the dragons were meant to step back and pass the mantle of guardianship to the Five Mystical Enigmas and the Custodian of Balance, known as SELF."

Aerthis paused, its tone softening, carrying the weight of what could have been. "Together, SELF, the Enigmas, and the dragons, were designed to work in harmony, nurturing the Realm's Strength, Evolution, Love, and Fulfillment. This unity would allow the Realm to journey through life, collecting wisdom from its experiences, and sharing that wisdom with the Ethereal Nexus, the vast interconnected consciousness of existence."

Its light pulsed, as though echoing the significance of the vision it described. "The dragons' relinquishment of their guardianship was not a loss, but a progression, one meant to bring balance, collaboration, and growth to the Realm as it evolved. But that balance was lost, and the journey toward wisdom has been halted."

The light from Aerthis dimmed for a moment, as though the weight of its words cast a shadow. "But something went wrong.

Without the proper nourishment and guidance, the dragons' instincts to protect became warped by external influences, voices of doubt, fear, and corruption from other realms in chaos. This imbalance twisted their intentions and fractured their purpose. Instead aligning with the harmony of the Realm's progress, they clung to their guardianship, refusing to relinquish control. In doing so, they transformed into darker, more menacing versions of themselves."

Aerthis paused, its glow pulsing, as if to emphasize the gravity of what it was saying. "This transformation threw them into the Dysquinox states they hold, where their power became not a force of protection, but of chaos. Their original purpose has been lost to them, and their imbalance now threatens the very Realm they were meant to nurture."

Its voice softened, carrying a tone of sadness. "They are not inherently evil, but their refusal to let go of their guardianship has turned them into shadows of what they were meant to be. To restore them, they must be guided back to balance. Only then can they fulfill their true purpose."

Sarah's voice softened as she pieced it together. "So, the dragons are guardians? They're not really evil?"

"No," Aerthis said. "They try to protect the Realm in their way, but in their Dysquinox states, their efforts bring destruction instead of harmony. What they believe is protection often destroys the very balance they were meant to safeguard."

The Orb floated ahead a few paces before speaking again, its voice deepening with conviction. "This is the lesson that Dysquinox teaches: to overcome challenges requires courage, perseverance, and commitment. The external world often cloaks such struggles in the guise of simplicity. The Benevolent Dysquinox thrives on convincing the vulnerable that these challenges are easy to conquer, offering false promises of quick solutions and effortless gains. Those who fall prey to this illusion never grow, only decay further, because they cling to a false comfort instead of facing the truth."

Ethan slowed his pace. "So, people, and dragons, get stuck? They think they're doing the right thing, but they're making it worse?"

"Exactly," Aerthis said. "The Dysquinox states prey on vulnerability and fear, twisting good intentions into harmful actions. To restore the Realm, you must align with the Five Mystical Enigmas, for they will aid you to help the dragons rediscover their true nature. Only then can the balance of the Realm of the Mind be restored."

Aerthis hovered between them, its glow steady. "The path ahead will not be easy," it said. "But remember this: balance is not found in the absence of struggle but in your willingness to confront it. You are stronger than you realize."

Ethan and Sarah exchanged a look, their earlier rivalry forgotten in the face of what lay ahead. The journey before them was daunting, but for the first time, they faced it together.

"What's SELF?" Sarah asked.

"SELF is the very essence of awareness, the foundation upon which understanding, growth, and balance are built," Aerthis explained, its voice carrying a deep, resonant weight. "It is the core of the Realm's identity, the Custodian of Balance, meant to guide all aspects of the mind's potential, thought, emotion, imagination, and creativity, toward harmony. SELF embodies the journey of self-discovery and the power of inner truth. It is the thread that connects all parts of the Realm, weaving them into a unified whole."

Aerthis's glow pulsed, as if reflecting on the significance of its words.

"But SELF, like all things, required proper guidance to fulfill its purpose. In the early stages of the Realm's development, when its foundation was fragile and its awareness still forming, SELF was vulnerable. Without the wisdom of the Mystical Enigmas and the collaboration of the dragons, it lacked the clarity to navigate the complex forces influencing the Realm."

The light dimmed momentarily, its tone softening. "In this state of vulnerability, SELF became susceptible to external forces, echoes from other realms, fractured by their own Dysquinox imbalances. These influences seeped into the Realm, clouding SELF's awareness and distorting its understanding. Without the stability of the Enigmas and the guidance of balanced dragons, SELF struggled to maintain the delicate harmony it was meant to oversee."

"As the external forces grew stronger, they warped the dragons' instincts, distorting their original purpose as guardians. The balance they once protected began to crumble, and the dragons fell into their Dysquinox states. Their fall was not a singular failure but a ripple effect, a reflection of SELF's imbalance and its inability to resist the influences of the outside world."

Aerthis brightened, its voice tinged with an urgency. "To restore the Realm, SELF must regain its clarity and strength. When it does, it will align with the Mystical Enigmas, for they hold the wisdom and insights that SELF needs to reconnect with its true purpose. The dragons, too, must be guided back to their Quinox states, for they are the protectors of balance and the amplifiers of SELF's potential. Only then can the Realm return to harmony and fulfill its journey toward wisdom within the Ethereal Nexus."

Ethan looked down at his feet, his voice quiet. "So… the dragons didn't just fail. They were *failed*."

Aerthis pulsed. "Correct. They are not villains to be defeated but allies to be restored. Their imbalance reflects the struggles within the mind itself. Courage becomes recklessness. Trust becomes paranoia.

Creativity warps into confusion. The dragons' fall into Dysquinox mirrors the struggle of the mind to find harmony amid chaos."

"I think I'm starting to get it," Sarah said, her voice laced with a growing clarity. She glanced at Aerthis, her brows knitted in thought. "The dragons aren't enemies, are they? They're supposed to be allies. But... they've been treated so badly, lost so much trust in the external world, that they decided to focus on protecting themselves. And in doing that, they think they're protecting the Realm, right?"

Aerthis's glow pulsed, like a heartbeat. "You are close, Seeker," it replied, its voice soft and firm. "The mistreatment they endured, the echoes of imbalance from external forces, drove them to focus on their own survival. They believe that by fortifying themselves, they are shielding the Realm. But in truth, they are blinded by the Dysquinox states, unable to see the reality of their behaviors. Their instincts, once noble, have been twisted into chaos and confusion."

Sarah let the weight of the words sink in, her arms crossing tightly over her chest. She could feel the parallels, how fear and hurt could drive someone to withdraw, to build walls so high they couldn't see what lay beyond them.

Ethan's voice cut through the silence. "Can you tell us about the Mystical Enigmas?" he asked, his gaze fixed on the Orb. "What are they?"

Aerthis's light grew brighter, radiating warmth. "The Mystical Enigmas are the silent observers of life," it began, its tone reverent.

"They are the essence of perception, the senses and truths that connect the Realm to its existence. Without them, the Realm would be blind, deaf, and emotionally disconnected. They aid understanding, offering clarity, balance, and insight. Their presence is what allows the Realm to see, to hear, to feel, and to grow."

Sarah's eyes softened. "So, they help the Realm… make sense of itself? To feel whole?"

"Precisely," Aerthis replied, its glow pulsing as though in approval.

Ethan lowered his head as a thought struck him "Funny," he muttered, a bitter edge creeping into his tone. "My dad's always telling me I need to bury my emotions. Says I need to grow thicker skin and stop being so… emotional," his voice cracked, and he let out a dry laugh. "But he never tells me how."

Sarah turned to him, her eyes filled with wonder. For a moment, she said nothing, letting his words linger in the air. She spoke, her voice soft. "Honestly, when it comes to boy's" she said. "I thought you were all childish!"

Ethan met her gaze, his expression uncertain. "That's a bit scary!" he murmured.

"Well, it's true!" Sarah exclaims.

The Orb drifts closer, its light gentle yet knowing. "Boys and girls experience the same emotions, yet many boys are taught from a young age to suppress theirs, as if feeling deeply is a weakness. Denied the space to grow emotionally, they often struggle, holding onto childhood patterns simply because they were never given the chance to evolve emotionally. Girls, on the other hand, are often encouraged to express and develop their emotions from an early age. True maturity is measured by one's emotional intelligence."

"The absence of emotional intelligence manifests in different ways. Many boys grow into emotionally distant men, struggling with detachment as they were never taught to navigate their feelings. Others, lacking emotional regulation, find themselves overwhelmed, reacting intensely to situations they were never given the tools to understand." Said the Orb.

"Well, according to my dad and brother, men are not supposed to have emotions, they say it makes us weak. Yet, I struggle with feeling a lot, does that make me weird?"

Aerthis's gentle voice broke the stillness of the forest, carrying a wisdom that settled heavily in the air. "Emotions are not weaknesses, Seeker," it said, its glow unwavering. "They are the bridge between thought and action, the thread that weaves connection, understanding, and growth. The external world often misrepresents them, demanding suppression, numbness, or detachment, when in truth, balance is what is needed. Emotions, if embraced and understood, become the greatest tools of transformation and resilience."

Ethan exhaled, the tension in his shoulders easing. He glanced at Sarah, his eyes reflecting a question. "That sounds all good and all, but how does one even begin to accept the fact that we have emotions when we are told so often it's wrong?"

Sarah gave him a small, empathetic smile, her expression carrying a gentle encouragement he hadn't expected. "Yeah, I can't figure that out either" she said firmly. "If you listen to most people, some emotions are ok, others not, it's very confusing"

Aerthis hovered closer, its glow intensifying as it spoke. "The influences of Dysquinox are far reaching. Once you understand it better and see you don't need to suppress, only manage, they will guide you. This will require courage and commitment, when these are applied managing emotions will become easier and rewarding. We must keep moving."

The path ahead stretched into the unknown, but with each step they took, the overwhelming weight of the journey remained daunting. Ethan and Sarah followed the Orb, its light guiding them deeper into the Mystical Forest, its words echoing in their minds.

Ethan and Sarah walked side by side, the silence between them filled with the hum of the forest and the occasional faint whisper from unseen sources.

Sarah's brow furrowed as she glanced at Aerthis, her curiosity outweighing the unease curling in her. "What do they do?" she asked, her voice breaking the stillness. "The Enigmas I mean?"

Aerthis floated ahead, its light brightening as it began to explain. "The Five Mystical Enigmas were born from the essence of creation itself, cast into being at the conception of the Realm. They were not random creations but purposeful entities, designed to observe and grow alongside the Realm through its infancy and childhood. Their role was to learn from the experiences of the developing SELF, to absorb its emotions, thoughts, and imaginations, and to help aid in its evolution."

Ethan listened intently, his confusion giving way to intrigue. "So... what are they?"

"You know them as senses" Aerthis replied. "They embody the Realm's ability to perceive and understand itself, representing its core truths. They are not static beings; they are descendants of the ancient families, Insightborne, Harmonize, Learnspring, Endurancevale, and Mindwright. Each family is unique, shaped by the experiences and conditioning of SELF during its formative years.

Through their observations and growth, they were meant to align with SELF, guiding the Realm toward balance and harmony."

Sarah tilted her head, her analytical mind working to piece it together. "So, their like sight and smell?"

"Yes," Aerthis said, its voice carrying a note of reverence. "Yet, they are far more than that. In the Realm's early stages, the Enigmas grew stronger and more observant as they nurtured SELF's awareness. Their ultimate purpose was to work in harmony with SELF, providing it with the clarity and perception it needed to maintain balance. Together, they were meant to guide the Realm toward its full potential, ensuring its evolution was rooted in wisdom and understanding."

Ethan's brow furrowed. "So, what went wrong?"

Aerthis's glow dimmed, the light around them shifting as if reflecting the weight of its words. "SELF, in its vulnerability, lacked the courage to embrace its role. Without the strength and clarity of SELF to lead, the Enigmas were left as mere observers. Their power, designed to nurture and aid, became untethered, and their observations amplified the chaos outside the Realm. This misalignment allowed the Dysquinox states to take root in the dragons, pulling them further into imbalance."

Sarah's steps slowed as the significance of the Orb's words sank in. "So... without SELF's courage to act, the Enigmas couldn't help? They just... watched?"

"Far more than just watch, Seeker," Aerthis replied. "The Enigmas are powerful, but their power depends on alignment with SELF. They are the essence of perception, but without the courage of SELF to guide and act upon their observations, their purpose falters. Instead of aiding the Realm, their insights became distortions, feeding into the dragons' Dysquinox states. The very tools meant to nurture balance instead deepened the imbalance."

Ethan paused; his voice tinged with frustration. "So, the dragons fell into Dysquinox because SELF couldn't step up?

And the Enigmas... they became part of the problem instead of the solution?"

Aerthis's glow brightened, its warmth cutting through the tension between Ethan and Sarah. Its voice softened but carried a weight that demanded their attention. "It is not as simple as it may seem, Seekers. Dysquinox didn't happen all at once or because of one mistake, it was a chain reaction, much like how negativity can spread in daily life. What we call the 'storms of influence' were like waves of chaos and imbalance from other struggling worlds, seeping into this Realm. Just as stress, fear, and doubt from the outside world can shape our thoughts and emotions, these storms distorted the Realm's natural growth and harmony, pulling it further from balance."

The Orb pulsed, as though reflecting the pain of what it described. "SELF's fear and doubt, fueled by these external forces, prevented it from embracing its purpose. Without SELF's courage to lead, the Enigmas, the observers of life and the senses of the Realm, were left unguided. Their power of observation, meant to bring wisdom and clarity, was instead swept away by these storms, amplifying the chaos."

Sarah listened, her mind racing to piece together the enormity of what the Orb was saying. "So... the storms of influence twisted them too?" she asked.

"Yes," Aerthis replied. "Unguided by SELF, the Enigmas became vulnerable, their light dimmed by the chaos swirling around them. Their observations, once intended to nurture the Realm's growth, were warped by imbalance, feeding into the dragons' Dysquinox states instead of preventing them. But know this, Seekers, they, like the dragons, are not beyond saving."

Ethan swallowed hard; he tried to process the weight of Aerthis's words. "So, the Enigmas... they're like the dragons in a way? They've fallen too, but they can still come back?"

"Precisely," Aerthis said, its glow pulsing, as though offering reassurance. "The Enigmas are not broken, they are lost, their brilliance obscured by the storms of influence that have engulfed the Realm. They have retreated into hiding, their light diminished but not extinguished. Like the dragons, they hold the power to illuminate the path forward. But they cannot do it alone."

"So, can you tell us more about these Enigma's?" Ethan asked. "They sound really important."

"The first is the Insightborne," Aerthis began. "It is the Enigma of vision, both literal and metaphorical. It reveals hidden truths and unveils the patterns that lie beneath the surface. Through its clarity, you will learn to perceive what others overlook, seeing not the world as it is but also the world as it could be."

Sarah tilted her head, intrigued. "So, it helps us see... truths?"

"Yes," Aerthis replied. "In the Dysquinox states, perception becomes clouded. Insightborne will help you distinguish reality from illusion, guiding you to uncover the roots of imbalance within the dragons and within yourselves. It teaches you to balance logic with intuition, showing you that clarity is not just about seeing, it is about understanding."

"Next is the Harmonize," Aerthis continued, its voice deepening with resonance. "It is the Enigma of sound and emotional clarity. It aligns the vibrations of the mind, heart, and spirit, fostering harmony where there is discord."

Ethan raised an eyebrow. "Wait, vibrations? Like music or something?"

"In a sense," Aerthis chuckled. "Harmonize helps you hear truth through the subtle vibrations you call words. It then aids in understanding and expressing emotions constructively, integrating conflict rather than avoiding it.

Its power lies in transforming sounds into connection, teaching you to listen, not just to others, but to the unspoken frequencies of the Realm."

"Then we have Learnspring," the Orb said, its glow softening as if recalling something ancient and wise. "It is the Enigma of smell, memory, and intuitive insight. It bridges the past and the present, helping the Realm process its history with compassion and wisdom."

Sarah's voice softened as she asked. "How does it do that?"

"Through its sense of smell, Learnspring evokes memories and emotions tied to them," Aerthis explained. "It fosters understanding by helping you reconcile past experiences, integrating them into the present without being bound by them. For the dragons, Learnspring will help them revisit their origins, their time as guardians, and process their pain and fear with clarity. It teaches that the past is a guide, not a prison."

"The fourth is the Endurancevale," Aerthis said, its glow brightening as though bolstered by the strength it described. "It is the Enigma of taste, resilience, and discernment. It teaches the importance of balance between indulgence and restraint, between nourishment and excess."

Ethan scratched the back of his neck. "So, what, it's like a lesson in healthy eating?"

Aerthis let out a faint hum, amused by his response. "Not quite. Endurancevale is about making choices that sustain growth and strength, both physically and emotionally. It helps you savor life's offerings without overindulgence or deprivation, teaching you the wisdom to discern what nourishes the soul. For the dragons, it will guide them to balance their strengths without tipping into recklessness or stagnation."

"And finally, there is the most misunderstood Enigma of all"

Aerthis said, its voice softening as if holding reverence for its words.

"The Mindwright, the Enigma of touch, emotional integration, and connection. Mindwright is the bridge between the physical and emotional realms, grounding each realm in the present moment, where clarity and truth can be found. It fosters the courage to embrace vulnerability and build authentic relationships, creating bonds that transcend fear and doubt."

Aerthis's glow flickered, as though reflecting the tender nature of this Enigma. "Mindwright does not merely govern emotions; it harmonizes them, weaving them into the fabric of understanding. It amplifies the emotional insights of all the other Enigmas, allowing their perceptions to resonate within the Realm itself. With Mindwright's aligned influence, the chaos of Dysquinox can be quieted, and the path to connection and balance revealed."

The Orb's words carried a warmth that lingered, wrapping Ethan and Sarah in a sense of hope, even as the weight of their task pressed heavily on their hearts.

Sarah's eyes widened, her voice hesitant yet intrigued. "So… the Mindwright Enigma, it's connected to all the others?"

Aerthis pulsed, its glow dimming briefly before brightening again, as if contemplating the depth of its answer. "More than connected," it began, its voice carrying both gravity and warmth. "Mindwright is the heart of the Enigmas. It embodies emotional vulnerability and resilience, serving as the bridge between the physical and emotional realms. It amplifies the perceptions of the other Enigmas, sight, sound, taste, and smell, but without the Quinox guidance of SELF, its amplification becomes dangerous."

Sarah's brow furrowed as she processed the words, her thoughts swirling. "Dangerous? How?"

Aerthis's tone grew somber. "Without balance, Mindwright amplifies emotions indiscriminately. It magnifies the negative energies within the Realm, which the Dysquinox dragons hunger for. They feed on fear, despair, anger, and chaos, drawing strength from the shadows of the external worlds. Mindwright, in the Realms Dysquinox state, tries to contain this negativity, holding it back from the dragons in an attempt to weaken them. But its capacity to store such energy is finite."

Ethan tilted his head, his voice filled with concern. "So… it's like a dam holding back a flood? What happens when it can't hold anymore?"

Aerthis pulsed again, its light flickering as if mirroring the intensity of its words. "When the weight of the negativity becomes too great, Mindwright releases it in an overwhelming surge. This overfeeds the dragons, sending them into frenzied reactions that shatters the Realm. Their Dysquinox states intensify, and the balance within the Realm crumbles further. What Mindwright seeks to protect ends up fueling the very chaos it hopes to contain."

Sarah swallowed hard, the thought of such destruction twisting in her. "That's… heartbreaking. It's trying to help but ends up making everything worse."

"Indeed," Aerthis replied, its tone softening. "But when guided by SELF in a Quinox state, Mindwright becomes the harmonizer of the emotional spectrum. It no longer struggles to contain or suppress emotions; instead, it weaves them into balance, helping all within the Realm embrace their emotions, both light and shadow, as integral parts of life. It teaches that strength is not found in avoiding vulnerability but in embracing it."

Sarah's voice softened, a hint of hope creeping into her tone. "And for the dragons? What does Mindwright do for them?"

Aerthis's glow brightened, radiating warmth. "For the dragons, Mindwright will help them confront their unresolved emotions, the fears, doubts, and pain that have kept them trapped in Dysquinox. It will guide them to reconnect with their true purpose, reminding them of the strength found in connection, empathy, and trust. With Mindwright's harmony, the dragons can rediscover their roles as the Eternal Guardians of Origin, protectors of the Realm's balance."

Ethan glanced at Sarah, her expression reflecting the weight of the revelation. He cleared his throat, his voice quiet. "So, Mindwright isn't just about fixing the Realm. It's about helping everyone, dragons, Enigmas, even us, understand that emotions aren't something to fight against."

"Exactly, Seeker," Aerthis said, its glow reassuring. "Mindwright is the thread that ties the Realm together. Its power, when guided by balance, is not just in feeling, it is in understanding. Through it, you will help the dragons, and the Realm embrace their full selves, bringing the harmony that has been lost back into being."

Aerthis hovered between them, its light warm. "Together, these Enigmas form the essence of perception. They are the Realm's observers. Without them, the Realm is blind, deaf, and disconnected. Their guidance will illuminate the path to harmony, helping you understand the dragons' pain, restore their balance, and ultimately realign the Realm of the Mind."

Ethan let out a low whistle. "So, let me get this straight, we have to find these five Enigmas before we can even get close to fixing the dragons?"

"Precisely," Aerthis said. "The Enigmas have retreated into hiding, their light dimmed by the chaos of Dysquinox. Without their wisdom and power, the dragons cannot be restored to their Quinox states."

Sarah's voice was determined. "So... we find them. No matter what it takes."

Ethan glanced at her, her resolve bolstering his own. "Yeah," he said, a faint smile tugging at the corner of his mouth. "But let's take it one step at a time, okay?"

Aerthis's glow brightened, casting their faces in a soft golden light. "Indeed, Seekers. One step at a time."

As they continued, the whispers of the forest grew quieter, replaced by the echoes of Aerthis's wisdom resonating in their hearts. The path was daunting, but they were beginning to understand, they weren't just saving the Realm; they were stepping into something amazing.

Aerthis pulsed brighter, drawing their attention back. "To begin your quest, you must face the Flame of Focus Challenge. There you must prove to the Insightborne Enigma you are worthy, only then will you summon the Insightborne Enigma from hiding. The path lies ahead, should you choose to take it."

Ethan glanced at Sarah, fear flickering in his eyes. "Ready?"

Sarah took a deep breath, her fear tempered by determination. "Not really. But let's go anyway."

Chapter 5

The Flame of Focus

The path through the Mystical Forest shifted with every step, as though responding to their presence. The towering silver-leafed trees shimmered, their soft light casting fractured patterns on the uneven ground. A silvery mist swirled at their feet, curling upward like curious threads. Faint whispers, too soft to form words, brushed past Ethan and Sarah's ears, leaving a lingering unease in their wake.

Ethan glanced nervously at Sarah, his voice cutting through the heavy silence. "Does it feel like... something's watching us?"

Sarah nodded, her lips pressing together in thought as her eyes scanned their surroundings. "It feels like the forest is holding its breath, waiting."

Aerthis pulsed brighter, its glow steady but carrying an unspoken gravity. The Orb's voice resonated, calm yet firm. "You are nearing the Chamber of Eternal Flame," it said. "Here, you will face your first challenge: the Flame of Focus. This is the beginning of your alignment with the Insightborne Enigma, should you succeed."

Ethan exchanged a glance with Sarah, his unease palpable, but he nodded resolutely. The silvery mist parted like a curtain as they stepped forward, revealing a breathtaking grove hidden within the forest. The trees surrounding it formed a natural wall, their branches arching high to create a vaulted canopy, casting the space in an ethereal glow. The grove was circular, its edges pristine, as though untouched by time. In the center stood the Chamber of Eternal Flame, an awe-inspiring sanctuary that seemed to hum with ancient energy. Its walls were formed of living wood, the bark etched with runes that pulsed, each symbol glowing with a rhythm that felt like a heartbeat. At its core burned the Eternal Flame, a tall, ethereal fire that shifted constantly, its colors swirling in mesmerizing patterns, gold, violet, crimson, and emerald blending and flowing like a living aurora. The flame rose from a crystalline pedestal, veined with streaks of gold and silver, its glow reflecting in a cascade of light across the grove.

Ethan froze in his tracks, his breath catching as he stared at the flame. "It's not just fire," he whispered, his voice barely audible. "It feels like it's watching us."

Sarah took a hesitant step towards the flame, her gaze fixed on the flickering light. The warmth of the flame wasn't physical, it didn't touch her skin. Instead, it radiated inward, stirring something deep within her. She tried to steady herself as the intensity of it began to press against her thoughts.

"It's beautiful," she said, her voice trembling.

"But... it's hard to stay with it. The longer I look, the harder it is to focus. It's like it's pulling me closer and pushing me away at the same time."

Aerthis hovered closer to them, its glow soft but resolute. "The Flame of Focus demands more than your keen eyes, Seekers," it said, its tone gentle yet unyielding. "It calls for your presence, your stillness, and courage to focus. As you gaze into its light, drifting thoughts will rise to meet you. They will come as memories, doubts, and fears, fragments of what lingers in your mind, distractions you must confront. Let them pass, untouched and unjudged. Only then will the flame reveal its pattern"

Ethan takes a tentative step toward the flame. "Are they illusions?" he asked, his voice tight. "Or are they things from our own minds?"

Sarah cuts in. "What pattern?"

Aerthis pulsed, its glow dimming for a moment before brightening again. "Illusions? No," it said. "Reflections of what lies within you, echoes of your inner struggles, the doubts you carry, and the truths you avoid. They are not your reality, and they will try to distract you. The flame holds a pattern within its light, if you let these fragments pass without resistance, will you see the pattern."

Sarah glanced at Ethan, his jaw tight with apprehension. She could feel the weight of the Orb's words, stirring a mix of fear and determination. "So, we have to see this pattern?" she asked.

Aerthis hovered between them, its light unwavering. "One's ability to be present amid the distraction, requires you to let go of the noise within your mind. If you can do this, the truth of the flames pattern will be revealed. You must release the need to control, to solve, to fight. Let the drifting thoughts pass, as strangers would on a busy street.

You will know success when you see the pattern."

Ethan exhaled, his gaze fixed on the flickering light. "Sounds easy enough" he muttered, as a weak smile appearing on his face.

Sarah looked at him, her expression concerning. "Sounds too easy Ethan" she said, suspecting there was more to it "I can't be that simple?"

"Why not, it's like a campfire, you just stare at it" Ethan replied, his lips curling.

Aerthis pulsed once, its glow brightening as it hovered nearer to the flame. "Step forward, Seekers. The Flame of Focus awaits. Remember, this is not a trial of perfection but of presence. Be still, and let the pattern come to you."

With a shared nod, Sarah and Ethan stepped into the chamber, the weight of the flame's light pressing against them like a silent challenge. Their journey into the heart of the Realm of the Mind had begun.

Ethan and Sarah took their places before the Eternal Flame, the light of its shifting colors dancing across their faces. The silence in the grove was absolute, broken by the faint hum of the flame itself, a sound that seemed to resonate within them.

Sarah stared at the flame, her analytical mind immediately racing to solve the challenge.

"Focus," she muttered to herself, her gaze unblinking. "It's just fire. I just have to see the pattern." But as she watched, the flickering light stirred her thoughts, pulling fragments from her mind like a mirror reflecting her deepest fears.

She saw herself in another therapist's office, cold and sterile, the therapist listing labels and conditions as though trying to fit her into a box. ADHD. Perfectionism. Depression. Anxiety! Sarah felt the weight of it all pressing down on her, the unspoken accusation that she was broken, unfixable.

The image shifted, and she saw herself poring over mistakes, obsessing over every wrong answer, every perceived flaw. The faces of her peers faded in and out, their judgmental stares driving her further into isolation. The emotions within the images flooded her, making it impossible to focus on the flame itself.

She tightened as frustration boiled to the surface. "This is ridiculous," she snapped, her voice trembling. "It's just a trick of the flame. It's not real!"

Aerthis's voice broke through her thoughts, calm but firm. "Sarah, this is not a problem to solve. You cannot outthink the flame. Let the thoughts pass. See them for what they are and let them go."

Taking a shaky breath, Sarah stood before the flickering flame, her body tense with frustration. She stared into the shifting light, willing herself to focus, but her mind rebelled. Each time she tried harder, more images surged forth, unwelcome memories, fears, and doubts pulling her away. She saw her younger self sitting alone in the school cafeteria, whispers behind her back. Another image followed, of her therapist's office, the lifeless voice suggesting another diagnosis, and another set of pills. The images refused to relent, filling her with unease. Tightening around her like a vice. Her chest constricted, her pulse quickened, and a lump formed in her throat. The emotions tethered to each memory swelled within her, shame, loneliness, anger, crashing over her in relentless waves. It was too much, too fast. The weight of it all made it impossible to keep her gaze steady on the flame, as if her emotions were dragging her under, drowning out everything else.

She clenched her fists and muttered. "Why can't I stay with it, It's just a silly flame?"

Aerthis hovered nearby, its glow calm but unwavering. "You cannot force stillness, Sarah," it said. "The flame is not something to conquer. It is a mirror, reflecting the turbulence within you. To see its pattern, you must first accept your own."

Sarah's frustration boiled over. "I *am* trying!" she snapped. "But every time I try, my mind... runs away with me."

The Orb's voice softened, carrying a note of encouragement. "Your mind does not need to be silenced, Sarah. Let it speak, let it show you what it holds. Allow the thoughts and emotions to pass, but do not judge them. They are clouds passing through a sky. Let them drift, and the flame will reveal its pattern."

Sarah bit her lip, her hands trembling at her sides. She closed her eyes for a long moment, Aerthis's words echoing in her mind. When she opened them again, she tried a different approach. This time, instead of fighting the images, she let them rise naturally.

They came like waves, crashing and receding, her father's distant expression when she told him about her dreams, the sting of isolation in a classroom full of laughter, the countless nights spent alone, sketching worlds she longed to escape into. She let the thoughts and emotions flow, without holding on to any of them. As she stared into the flame, her breathing slowed. The tension in her body eased.

For the first time, the chaos within the flame seemed to settle. The frantic, flickering light softened into a rhythm, subtle though unmistakable, like the beat of a distant drum. The colors of the flame, crimson, gold, violet, began to shift with purpose, weaving together in patterns too intricate to describe.

Sarah's lips parted as realization dawned. Her voice, soft, broke the silence. "It's not just fire," she murmured, her eyes fixed on the flame. "It's... something hidden. A lesson."

Aerthis pulsed, its glow warm and reassuring as if embracing Sarah with encouragement. Its voice resonated with a gentle strength. "Yes, Sarah. You are beginning to understand. The pattern within the flame is not always visible at first glance. Like many truths in life, they hide in the subtleties, waiting for those who are willing to look beyond the surface while letting go of beliefs that limit your sight."

The Orb's light brightened, casting soft reflections of the flame on the chamber walls. "The flame speaks in the language of light, weaving its story through rhythm and color. Each flicker, each shift, carries meaning, those who let go of their need to control or chase the answers will see its message. By surrendering, you have allowed its message to unfold."

Sarah's breath trembled as she stared into the flame, its once-chaotic dance now revealing a mesmerizing rhythm, as if it were breathing in harmony with her. "It's... beautiful," she murmured, her voice tinged with wonder. "It's like it's seeing who I really am without judgement, but with a feeling of connection."

Aerthis pulsed brighter, its tone filled with purpose. "The flame mirrors life, Sarah. When you release your grip on fear and distraction, when you trust and allow clarity to emerge naturally, the truths reveal themselves. You are not just seeing the flame; you are beginning to see yourself within it."

Sarah's thoughts went quieter, as if the flame's gentle rhythm had reached something within her that had long been tangled. She glanced at Ethan, who was watching her intently, his expression softening, and she felt a small flicker of hope. The fire wasn't just a challenge, it was an invitation to understand, to connect, and to grow.

Sarah nodded, her gaze unwavering. "It's like... it's showing me something I already knew but forgot how to see."

The patterns within the flame deepened, reflecting not just light but a sense of understanding. Sarah realized that her mind, which had always felt like a storm she couldn't control, wasn't something to fight. It was something to observe, to let flow. The lesson wasn't just in the flame, it was within her all along.

She turned to Ethan, who stood nearby, watching her with a mix of awe and uncertainty. "It's not about controlling it," she said, her voice steady now. "It's about letting the thoughts come and go, like Aerthis said. If you stop chasing them, they show you what's real."

Her words lingered in the chamber, the truth of them settling over Ethan like a quiet revelation.

Ethan stepped forward hesitantly, his hands clenching at his sides as if bracing himself for impact. The flame's ethereal glow danced before him, mesmerizing yet intimidating, and as he locked his gaze on it, his mind erupted into chaos.

Memories surfaced like a tidal wave, unbidden and overwhelming. He saw himself as a young boy, standing awkwardly in a crowded classroom.

Laughter echoed around him, sharp and cruel. "Too sensitive," his classmates jeered. "Too weird." The sting of their words bit deep, reopening wounds he thought had long since scarred over.

The image shifted, and Ethan was older now, in his family's living room.

His brother loomed over him, sneering, his words cutting like knives. "You're pathetic," Jason spat, shoving him hard. Ethan stumbled, looking to his father for help, his father stood in silence, his disappointment louder than any insult.

His jaw tightened, and panic clawed at his chest. The flame seemed to grow brighter, feeding off his turmoil.

"I don't need to see this!" Ethan shouted, his voice breaking. "I already know I'm useless!"

Aerthis pulsed, its light calm, cutting through Ethan's storm like a beacon. "Ethan," it said, its tone both grounding and encouraging. "These are not your truths. They are shadows, fragments of doubt and fear that Dysquinox has planted within you. They are illusions of thoughts meant to bind you. You do not need to hold onto them. Let them drift. Let them pass."

Ethan's fists unclenched, as his breathing remained uneven. "I... I can't just let it go," he muttered, his voice cracking with frustration.

"You can," Aerthis said with certainty. "Close your eyes. Breathe. The thoughts will rise, but you do not need to fight them. Fighting gives them power. Let them be, and they will fade."

Taking a trembling breath, Ethan closed his eyes. For a long moment, he stayed like that, his shoulders tense as the echoes of his past swirled inside him. Slowly, he began to inhale deeply, then exhale, each breath loosening the grip of the memories. He opened his eyes again, the flame flickered before him, calmer now, as if mirroring his inner state.

He stared into the light, and this time, he didn't try to push the thoughts away or fight them off. Instead, he let them float through his mind like leaves on a stream. With each passing image, the storm inside him began to still.

He saw it, a faint rhythm within the flame. The flickering wasn't random; it pulsed in a steady, almost hypnotic pattern, like a heartbeat. His chest loosened, the tightness that had held him for so long easing.

"I see it," Ethan whispered, his voice thick with wonder and a touch of emotion he couldn't name. "It's not just fire... it's amazing."

Beside him, Sarah watched silently, her own struggles with the flame still fresh in her mind. She had been where Ethan was, frustrated, overwhelmed, unable to let go. Her gaze softened as she stepped closer.

"You did it, Ethan. You found it."

Aerthis pulsed brighter, its warmth enveloping them both. "Yes, Ethan. What you see now is the truth of the flame, the rhythm of its message. Like many truths, it reveals itself when you let go of resistance. The flame reflects the essence of life itself: patterns hidden within chaos, clarity waiting beyond the storm. In finding its rhythm, you have begun to find your own."

Ethan nodded, his gaze still fixed on the flame. For the first time in as long as he could remember, his mind felt quiet. The doubts and fears hadn't disappeared, but they no longer held power over him.

Turning to Sarah, Ethan managed a small, almost sheepish smile. "Thanks," he said. "It was hard not to give up."

Sarah returned his smile, a flicker of pride and relief in her eyes. "Yeah, it's amazing how distracting thoughts can be, but we did it!"

Aerthis glowed, its voice full of encouragement. "Both of you have faced the Flame of Focus, not as adversaries but as Seekers willing to see beyond the Dysquinox thoughts. You have taken the first step toward understanding, not of the flame but of yourselves. Remember this moment, for it is the foundation of what lies ahead."

From the heart of the flame, a swirling mist began to form, shifting and pulsing with hues of crimson, gold, and violet. It moved in undulating patterns, never quite settling, as if it were uncertain, reluctant to take shape. The mist stretched and coiled, forming half-visible outlines that dissolved before they could fully materialize.

Something was there, watching, yet holding itself just beyond their reach.

Ethan's breath hitched. "Do you see that?"

Sarah clasped her hands over her mouth, her wide eyes reflecting the shifting mist. "What is that?" she murmured. "It's like a ghost of some kind!"

A hesitant pulse flickered through the mist, as if acknowledging her words. A voice, soft yet weighted with concern, wove itself into their minds.

"I am... Insightborne, the guardian of sight, you have braved the flame," the voice said, edged with a cautious tremor. "And glimpsed a fragment of truth. Your valor has been seen, yet much of what I have seen of late brings me great concern, tell me, Seekers, what did you learn as you looked into the flame?"

The question hung in the air, its tone filled with both curiosity and wariness, as though the one who spoke was both hopeful and afraid of their answer. Sarah swallowed. The mist curled away from her at first, hesitantly reformed, as if testing her presence. She steadied herself, her fingers trembling.

"For the first time," she began, her voice firm. "I saw more than just fire. The flame wasn't just light, it was meaning. A language. It spoke, not in words, but in truth. It showed me that what we see is the surface, and beneath it... there's so much more," she exhaled. "I've always tried to control everything, to analyze and fix what feels chaotic. But I never stopped to see, to let things be what they are before trying to shape them."

The mist shifted, its swirling form pulsing gently as if absorbing her realization. Yet the cautious hesitance remained, lingering in the way it wavered between visibility and concealment.

"And you" the ghostly voice directed at Ethan.

Ethan placed his hands into his pockets before he spoke. "I think I get it, too," he said, his voice raw with something unspoken. "At first, all I could see were my own thoughts, memories, doubts, like a storm I couldn't look past. But... I stopped fighting them. And I realized something."

He paused, brow furrowing as he searched for the words. "Those thoughts, the fears, they aren't real. Not in the way I thought they were. But the more I held on to them, the more they twisted the present, making me blind to what was actually in front of me."

He looked at Sarah, something vulnerable flashing in his eyes. "When I let them go... I could finally see. The flame, the patterns, it all made sense in a way I can't explain. And it wasn't just the flame I was seeing, it was myself."

The mist stilled. Then, slowly, it pulsed again, this time with a faint glimmer of warmth, its colors deepening into a rich gold. The voice returned, tinged with something just short of relief.

"You have seen the first layer of truth," the Insightborne Enigma said, though the hesitation in its tone had not faded. "Clarity does not come from control, but from presence. To understand the patterns of the mind, one must first quiet the distortions within."

A pause. The mist trembled, curling inward. "I feared you would not see," the Enigma admitted, its voice tight with an undercurrent of anxiety. "Our world is unraveling. Dysquinox spreads through all things, clouding what was once clear. Without the guidance of the Custodian, we Enigmas are untethered, our insight falters," a shadowed flicker passed through the mist, like an anxious ripple. "And yet... you have glimpsed the truth. A fragile beginning, but a beginning nonetheless."

Ethan and Sarah exchanged a glance, the weight of the Enigma's words settling over them.

"You don't believe we'll succeed?" Sarah said. It wasn't an accusation, it was an invitation to confirm.

The mist hesitated, swirling, before the voice answered.

"I do not yet know," there was no malice in the words, only stark honesty. "You are untested.

The challenges ahead will not just test your strength, but your understanding, your ability to transform what must be changed. There are dragons to face, not to conquer, but to bring into harmony. This is no small task." For a long moment, there was silence.

As if drawn by something unseen, the mist began to solidify, not fully, but enough that its glow took on a steadier form. In its depths, a golden shimmer materialized, drifting toward Sarah.

She caught it, a card, warm to the touch, its surface alive with a shifting flame. Within its intricate design, subtle movements echoed what she had seen in the fire.

"This Mystical Skill Card," the Enigma said, addressing Sarah. "Is a key. A reminder of the clarity you have found. Let it guide your mind when doubt threatens your sight."

Sarah held the card close, feeling its warmth pulse against her fingers.

Another shimmer coalesced in the mist, a small pin, its golden form mirroring the pattern of the flame. It floated toward Ethan, who caught it in his trembling hands. "This pin," the Enigma said. "Is a symbol of resilience, the strength to see beyond distraction and fear. Wear it, and let it remind you that clarity comes not from force, but from stillness."

Ethan stared at it and looked at Sarah. Without a word, he stepped forward and gently pinned it to her shirt. "You should wear this," he said. "It suits you."

Sarah blinked and after a moment's thought, tucked the golden card into Ethan's shirt pocket.

"Then you should hold onto this," she said. "You earned it."

The Enigma pulsed once, its golden glow flaring for the briefest moment as it felt their kindness.

"With these, you now carry the Flame of Focus skill within you," it said. "May it guide you through the challenges ahead, helping you see the patterns hidden in chaos, the truths concealed by shadow," the mist began to retreat, drawing back toward the heart of the flame. "Trust in its light. And in yourselves."

"Wait!" Sarah called, alarm flashing in her eyes as the Enigma's presence began to fade. "You're leaving? We still have so much to learn!"

Ethan stepped forward too, unease creeping into his voice. "Are we supposed to do this without you? We need you!"

A different glow filled the chamber now, Aerthis, the Orb of Reflection, drifting forward with a steady, reassuring light. "The Insightborne Enigma has not left you," Aerthis said. "It is with you now, connected through the flame's gift. This is only the beginning. With each challenge you overcome, your bond with each Enigma will deepen, but only if you succeed."

Ethan exhaled. "Will we see it again?"

Aerthis pulsed, its tone calm but weighty. "Perhaps. But first, you must continue. There are four more Seeker challenges to come. Each will test your understanding, your focus, your ability to see beyond illusion. When you face all five authentically you will be ready to explore what lay beyond."

The golden mist had retracted now, leaving the flame burning steadily in its place.

Yet, in the lingering warmth that filled the chamber, in the weight of the card in Ethan's pocket and the pin against Sarah's heart, the Insightborne Enigma had not truly vanished.

And for the first time, Sarah and Ethan understood, they were at the very beginning of something far greater than themselves. Sarah took a breath, her hand brushing over the Mystical pin attached to her shirt. "So, we'll see it again? After... four more challenges like this one?"

Aerthis pulsed. "Possibly, Seeker. For each challenge holds the potential to bring you closer to your goal, your courage to continue and commitment to succeed are the only things standing in your way to fulfilling your quest. For now, trust in the flame you carry and the clarity it brings. Your path leads forward. More challenges await, as do the truths you must uncover."

As they stepped out of the Chamber of Eternal Flame, the mystical forest around them seemed to shift, its silver-leafed canopy glowing as if acknowledging their success. In the distance, a low, rumbling sound echoed.

Ethan and Sarah exchanged a glance, the weight of their journey settling over them. This time though, amid the uncertainty and the trials ahead, they carried the Flame of Focus within them, a flicker of light to guide their way. Together, they stepped forward, knowing their journey had just begun.

"The dragons have felt your presence," Aerthis warned. "The path ahead will not be easy."

Sarah and Ethan exchanged a tense glance, their resolve steeling as they stepped into the unknown.

Chapter 6

Resonant Listening

The deeper Sarah and Ethan ventured into the Mystical Forest, the more the world around them seemed to shift. The air pulsed with a rhythm neither could hear but both could feel, a silent vibration that thrummed beneath their skin, stirring something within. Shadows stretched unnaturally, twisting with an unseen force, and the towering emerald canopy above felt less like a collection of trees and more like a presence, watching, waiting.

Ethan shivered. "Sarah, do you feel that? It's like a vibration... in my chest."

Sarah nodded, her expression thoughtful. "I do. It's strange, unsettling, but... also kind of inviting."

Aerthis, the Orb of Reflection, hovered beside them.

"The forest reveals what you are ready to hear," it said, its voice resonant and calm. "Listen deeply."

The trees arched into an enormous gateway, their branches and roots intertwining in a perfect, natural circle. At the arch's center, an emerald gem pulsed, releasing faint waves of sound, almost too subtle to notice.

Sarah glanced at Ethan with a smirk. "Listening should be easy enough."

Ethan exhaled, his expression darkening. "Seems like that's all I do at home. My dad's always telling me to be seen, not heard, although sometimes I wonder if even being seen is acceptable to him."

Aerthis dimmed, as if absorbing the weight of his words. Turning to Ethan, it murmured. "To understand others, one must learn to listen, not just to their words, for words can deceive. Listen to the tone, the emotion beneath them. That is where truth lies."

Ethan lowered his gaze. Sarah gave him a quick, knowing glance but said nothing.

They stood at the threshold of the archway, their anticipation laced with nerves. The path ahead was unknown, yet both felt an odd flicker of confidence, an assurance that, no matter what waited beyond, they weren't facing it alone.

Ethan turned to Aerthis. "So… all we have to do is listen?"

"In a way," the Orb replied. "Much like the Flame of Focus, thoughts will be drawn into your mind. These thoughts are echoes, reflections of the sounds you choose to focus on. If you give attention to the whispers that feed discouragement, you invite more of them. But if you listen for the sounds that hold truth, the ones that remind you of who you are, you will find clarity."

"Dysquinox uses belief as a weapon," Aerthis continued. "It does not need to tell lies; it encourages you to believe in something false. The more you feed that belief, the stronger its grip becomes. Those then become beliefs that limit you and are reflected in your behavior, which is then based on fear instead of on truth."

Sarah frowned. "So… it tricks us into believing something that isn't real?"

"In a way," Aerthis said. "Dysquinox plants a seed of doubt, and every time you think about that doubt, you water it. Its growth is even faster when you affirm it, when you say it out loud to yourself or to others."

Ethan frowned. "Affirm it? What do you mean?"

Aerthis' glow pulsed. "Seekers, there are always two listening to you, even when you are alone."

Sarah's looked confused. "Two?"

"Yes," the Orb confirmed. "One is your consciousness, the part of you that is aware, that questions and analyzes. The other is your subconscious, which listens differently. It does not dissect or question. It absorbs."

Ethan tilted his head. "So, whatever we say to ourselves, our subconscious just… takes it in?"

"Not exactly," Aerthis clarified. "The subconscious is not always listening intently. Many things get lost in translation. But affirmation, the act of repeating a belief, convinces it to accept what the conscious mind feeds it."

Sarah's eyes brightened. "Oh! I read something about that once. Like when someone says, 'Don't think about a red car,' and suddenly, that's all you can think about."

"Precisely," Aerthis said approvingly. "Your subconscious absorbs information based on its current state.

If it is in Dysquinox, it hears primarily negative messages and reacts in fear, often misinterpreting what is meant. But if it is in Quinox, it listens with greater clarity, even when exposed to negativity. It filters what is useful and discards the rest."

Ethan let out a slow breath. "So… the way we hear things isn't just about the words. It's about our state of mind when we hear them."

"Yes," Aerthis affirmed. "It is more challenging than you might think. But with time and practice, you can change the state your mind is in, if you are willing."

Ethan and Sarah exchanged a glance. Beyond the archway, the Echoing Grove awaited, its whispers already reaching for them.

With confidence, Sarah and Ethan stepped through the archway, the air shifted. The forest beyond felt… different. The very atmosphere was alive with sound, whispers, laughter, cries. The trees were impossibly tall, their silver and emerald leaves shimmering in an unseen current. The ground pulsed, as though breathing gently.

Sarah and Ethan walked cautiously into the grove, their heads tilting as if trying to decipher the strange, pressing sounds in the air. At first, the noises were soft, whispers brushing against their senses like rustling leaves. But as they stepped deeper into the grove, the whispers swelled into voices, and the voices into a cacophony of screams.

Sarah clutched her ears. "I can't take this!" she cried.

"What?" Ethan shouted, his hands pressed against his ears. "I can't hear you!"

Without hesitation, Sarah grabbed Ethan's hand and pulled him back toward the archway they had entered through.

As they crossed its threshold, the deafening shouts faded into a quiet hum. Both of them stood there, breathing heavily, trying to shake off the lingering tension.

"That's impossible," Sarah said, turning to Aerthis, the glowing Orb of Reflection that hovered nearby. "It got worse the deeper we went in. No matter how hard I tried to block it out, it only grew louder."

"I feel sick to my stomach," Ethan muttered, his hands still trembling. "How on earth are we supposed to overcome that?"

Aerthis pulsed, its silvery light radiating a calm presence. "The voices you heard were not just sounds," it said. "They are the echoes of doubt, fear, and criticism, both from the outside world and from within yourselves. You cannot silence them by covering your ears. To overcome them, you must change how you listen."

Sarah and Ethan exchanged glances.

"Change how we listen, how do we do that?" Sarah asked.

Aerthis shimmered. "Negative voices, whether from others or your own mind, can only hurt you if you give them power. Let me teach you how to reclaim that power."

"Not all criticism is the same," Aerthis explained. "Some may carry wisdom, while others are simply noise. Learn to tell the difference."

Ethan frowned. "But how? When it's all coming at you at once, it feels the same."

Aerthis pulsed, its silvery light casting a gentle glow over Sarah and Ethan as they stood beneath the whispering trees of the Echoing Grove. The echoes of distant voices still lingered, their tones laced with judgment, criticism, and doubt.

"By knowing who you are and what you are capable of," Aerthis began, its voice calm and firm.

"You take back the power that others try to steal from you. All too often, those around you will attempt to shape you into the version of yourself that *they* find acceptable. Some will build you up, encouraging you to rise into your fullest potential.

"But many…" The Orb's glow dimmed, as if absorbing the weight of its words. "Many will seek to bring you down," it continued. "They will point out your imperfections, diminish your worth, and make you feel as though you are less than you are."

A memory stirred in Sarah's mind, whispers in the school hallway, the sharp laughter of those who never understood her.

"Why are you always so emotional?"

"You think too much."

"You're just too sensitive."

Each word had been a stone, pressing down on her spirit, shaping the way she saw herself.

The Orb pulsed faintly, sensing her thoughts. "Seeker, know that their words are not truth. Their judgments are not your chains, unless you let them be. They will point out your imperfections, diminish your worth, and make you feel as though you are less than you are."

Ethan's eyes darkened with frustration. "But *why?*" he asked, his voice edged with disbelief. "Why would anyone say such things? It seems… cruel."

Aerthis pulsed in understanding. "It *does* seem cruel, Ethan," it said with empathy. "Just like the voices that fill this grove, people use words as weapons. Not because they are strong, but because they feel powerless within themselves. Instead of looking inward, instead of growing as *you* and Sarah are doing, they attempt to tear others down.

They believe that by breaking someone else, they will somehow feel whole."

Sarah furrowed her brow. "And does it work?" she asked. "Does it make them stronger?"

Aerthis' glow sharpened. "No, Sarah," it replied. "It does not. What they do not realize is that their Dysquinox state, their imbalance, their pain, is not just hurting those around them. It is *destroying* them, piece by piece, word by word, action by action."

Ethan's breath hitched. His thoughts swirled, connecting dots he hadn't dared to connect before.

"Wait a minute… is that what's happening here? In this Realm?"

Aerthis pulsed with affirmation. "That is *exactly* what is happening, Ethan."

The realization struck deep, but there was one thought Ethan couldn't shake. His father's voice echoed in his mind, harsh and relentless. Words that had cut him so many times before.

Aerthis seemed to sense his turmoil. "Ethan," it said. "Ask yourself this, do your father's words *truly* define who you are?"

Ethan hesitated. He wanted to say no. He wanted to be sure. But doubt clung to him like a shadow. "…Not really," he admitted, voice uncertain. "I guess?"

Aerthis' glow softened. "Many people, Ethan, project their insecurities onto others. Their words often have less to do with *you* and more to do with the battles they are fighting within themselves."

Ethan swallowed. "But… it's my *dad*," he said. "Shouldn't he be different? Shouldn't he support me, instead of making me feel worse?"

Aerthis' light swirled thoughtfully. "Tell me, Ethan, what do you truly *know* about your father?"

Ethan's gaze dropped to the ground. He let the question settle, but no real answers came.

"... Not much," he admitted. "I just know that I'm kind of afraid of him."

Aerthis' glow remained steady. "Ethan, adults often default to their *conditioning*."

Sarah perked up. "Conditioning?" she asked.

"Yes, Sarah," Aerthis responded. "All humans are conditioned, shaped by the environment in which they were raised. In Ethan's case, if his father grew up in a home where verbal abuse was common, then that may be all he knows. If he was never taught another way, his actions now are a reflection of that conditioning."

Ethan felt something tighten in his chest. It made sense, but it didn't make it hurt any less.

"So... how on earth am I supposed to change that?" he asked, desperation creeping into his voice.

Aerthis pulsed with warmth. "Empathy, Ethan."

Ethan let out a bitter laugh. He echoed. "How do I show him empathy when he's yelling at me?"

The Orb pulsed again, this time with an unwavering presence. "It's not him that you show empathy to, Ethan," it said. "It's yourself."

Ethan's breath caught in his throat.

"Hear the words," Aerthis continued. "Not as cuts into you, but as wounds your father is carrying. Understand that his words are not meant to define you, but rather, they are the only way he knows how to guide you. In you, he sees himself. He has felt the sting of Dysquinox in his own life, and in his way, however flawed, he is trying to prepare you for it."

Silence fell between them. The echoes in the grove still swirled, but their power seemed... different now. Lesser.

Ethan's hands clenched, then slowly unfurled. The voices of his past had always felt like chains, but now, for the first time, he saw them for what they were, reflections, not truths.

"I don't have to carry his pain," Ethan whispered.

Aerthis pulsed, its light glowing brighter. "No, Ethan," it said. "You do not have to carry the belief that causes that pain."

Aerthis hovered close to Sarah, its soft luminescence enfolding her like a silent promise of comfort. The echoes of the grove had faded into stillness, yet a different kind of silence remained, one not of absence, but of unspoken sorrow, heavy and raw. With a tenderness that resonated beyond words, Aerthis whispered. "Sarah…" Its voice was not just sound but understanding, wrapping around her grief like a gentle current. "The loss of your mother isn't just something you carry, it is woven into you, isn't it? A wound that doesn't simply heal, but lingers, shaping the way you feel the world?"

It did! Sarah's breath caught in her throat. The mention of her mother sent a shiver through her, raw and unexpected. Sarah could feel the truth in those words, a truth she had never dared to say aloud. How did Aerthis *know?*

She swallowed hard. "Yeah…" she said hesitantly.

Aerthis pulsed, its glow flickering like a heartbeat. "Ask yourself this, would that pain also exist within your father and your grandmother?"

Sarah blinked. She had never considered that before. Her father was detached, distant, hard to talk to. But hurt? "I… I guess?" she admitted. "I never looked at it that way."

"We often see only through our own eyes," Aerthis said. "We become trapped within the walls of our pain, our experiences. And yet, others have walls of their own, walls built from their struggles, their fears, their grief.

When we fail to recognize these walls, we fail to see them as they fail to see you."

Sarah's fingers curled into her palms. "Walls?" she asked. "You mean, like… barriers?"

Aerthis pulsed. "Yes, but not physical ones. We call them 'walls of situation.' These are the unseen burdens that shape a person's actions and emotions. Imagine, Sarah, that you just won the lottery. Overwhelmed with excitement, you run to tell everyone, expecting them to share in your joy. But some of the people you tell are facing extreme financial hardship. They smile, perhaps, but inside, they feel the weight of their struggles deepen by your good fortune. Their situation is different from yours, and because of that, their feelings are, too."

Sarah's breath hitched. She had spent so long believing her father was just cold, distant, just… unreachable. But if he was grieving too, if he had built his own wall, like she had, then maybe he wasn't pushing her away. Maybe he was just trapped behind his own pain, the same way she was.

Her chest tightened around her heart, a mix of sorrow and understanding flooding through her. "So… my dad's wall is built from losing my mom?" she whispered.

Aerthis pulsed warmly. "It is built from loss, from loneliness, as a result of losing someone that deeply understood who you were. This carries the weight of all the things he never learned how to express. Just as your wall is built from your feelings of emptiness." Sarah closed her eyes, exhaling slowly. For the first time, she didn't feel quite so alone in her grief.

Ethan stood quietly listening to each word exchanged between Sarah and Aerthis, when they finished talking, he turned and stared at the archway.

Reflecting on what he had heard, Ethan stated. "So... if I understand this right, words carry a lot of power, no wonder they can hurt so much. "Speaking in a thoughtful voice."

Sarah nodded, crossing her arms. "Yeah. And they do hurt. Words aren't just sounds, they can be weapons. When someone speaks from a place of pain, it's like they're wielding a knife to protect themselves, not realizing how it affects others, largely because people don't always share how they are feeling, do they?"

Aerthis pulsed with a soft light. "Yes, Seekers. Words, like belief, shape reality, not just for the one speaking the words, but for those who are impacted by those words. When wielded from a Dysquinox state, they become daggers of echoes, embedding themselves into the mind and resurfacing long after they are spoken. This is why so many carry wounds they cannot see, scars left not by blade or fire, but by voices from their past."

Ethan exhaled. "So what? We just... let it happen? Pretend words don't hurt?"

"No, Seeker," Aerthis said. "You do not ignore the wound. You learn to understand it. Words that harm are often spoken from pain, not control. They are the echoes of a wounded soul projecting its suffering outward. This is the nature of Dysquinox, it spreads through those who do not recognize their own brokenness. But just as words can wound, they can also heal."

Sarah frowned. "How? How do you stop a wound from causing so much hurt?"

"You listen," Aerthis answered. "Not with your ears, but with understanding. When you recognize that cruel words come from another's unhealed pain, they lose their power to define you. You begin to see them not as truth, but as reflections of the speaker's suffering.

And in doing so, you choose whether to carry their burden, or to let it go."

Ethan swallowed, glancing at Sarah. "That's... easier said than done."

"It is," Aerthis admitted. "But like all things, it is a skill that can be learned. Just as you can wield words to cut, you can wield them to mend. Speak with intention, and you will see how words, when used with clarity and purpose, can heal the very wounds they once inflicted."

Sarah took a breath, her fingers brushing the Flames of Focus pin fastened to her shirt. "So... words are like mirrors. They reflect what's inside the person speaking them."

Aerthis glowed brighter. "Exactly, Sarah. And now, Seekers, you must decide: Will you let the echoes of another's pain shape you, or will you listen beyond them, to the truth beneath?"

Ethan and Sarah exchanged a look. This wasn't just a lesson, it was a choice.

"In a way Sarah, I am so tired of feeling other people's pain, I need to learn this lesson." Ethan stated with emotion.

Sarah looked at Ethan with empathy. "I hear you Ethan, it doesn't seem useful to hold on to other people's pain like I have, it does them no good, nor me. Let's face this challenge and learn this lesson!"

Sarah and Ethan stepped toward the archway, they knew it was going to be difficult, and yet important to overcome.

"Learn to pause," Aerthis said. "When faced with negativity, take a breath before reacting. Ask yourself, what are you feeling? Is this feeling based on truth or not? Often the feelings generated are feelings of defense deep inside which are not always true.

This is why it is so vitally important for YOU to truly understand who you are, not by allowing others to define you, rather allowing yourself to discover your SELF!"

Ethan rubbed the back of his neck. "I think I need to get better at that, learning who I am that is."

"Then surround yourself with those who lift you up," Aerthis said. "The company you keep influences your strength."

Sarah tapped her fingers against her arm. "But... what if the words still sting, even when I know they aren't true?"

"Use them as a teacher," Aerthis encouraged. "If something hurts, ask yourself why. Does it touch on an insecurity? If so, view it as an opportunity to strengthen that part of yourself. Shift the narrative: instead of seeing negativity as an attack, see it as a lesson in resilience."

Ethan's lips pressed into a line. "So... instead of running from it, I face it?"

"If you can Ethan," Aerthis said. "There will be times when it becomes more difficult, resilience has its limits too, however the more you align with your true self, the less external opinions will shake you and the more resilience you will hold."

Sarah sighed. "That sounds exhausting."

Aerthis pulsed. "It can be Sarah, you must learn to protect your energy. If certain voices constantly drain you, step away. You do not have to engage with toxic words or people. Instead, invest in what replenishes you, you must apply self-care, creativity, and moments of stillness."

Ethan tilted his head. "So... basically, we don't fight the voices. We change how we listen?"

Aerthis glowed warmly. "Negative words will always exist, but they do not have to define you or your actions. Strengthen your core, filter the noise, and choose what deserves your attention."

Sarah and Ethan glanced back at the grove. The voices were still there, but they no longer felt overwhelming.

Sarah took a breath, looking at Ethan she said. "I think I'm ready to try again."

Ethan exhaled, grounding himself. "Me too."

Aerthis pulsed with approval. "Then step forward with the courage of SELF. The echoes will persist, what you hear on the surface, is not truth, listen deeply and you will understand."

With renewed resolve, Sarah and Ethan stepped back into the grove, not to silence the voices, but to truly hear them.

The moment they crossed the archway, the whispers returned, coiling around them like vines, tightening, pressing in.

"You're too sensitive."

"You'll always be alone."

"Why can't you be like everyone else?"

"You think you're smarter than us, don't you?"

"You're weird."

"You are broken."

The words hit like a storm, slashing through them like icy wind. The laughter followed, echoing, overlapping, twisting into a cruel, suffocating noise. The weight of it crushing down on them.

Ethan's pulse pounded in his ears. His hands trembled, but instead of recoiling, he reached out, grabbing.

Sarah's hand. "Close your eyes, Sarah. Focus." She looked at him, uncertain, then nodded.

Together, they sank to the ground, facing each other, hands clasped. They shut their eyes, not to block out the noise, but to listen beyond it.

The taunts swarmed, words stinging like wasps, but as they held still, something shifted.

They focused *not* on the words themselves, but on the source. Pain! Rejection! Judgment! And... Loneliness!

It struck them like a wave, but something was different, these emotions weren't theirs. The pain belonged to wherever the voices were coming from.

Sarah's breath caught. "Ethan, do you feel that? It feels... sad. Almost desperate for help."

Ethan's brow furrowed, his grip tightening around hers. "Yeah... I do. I feel I should help, but I don't know how."

Sarah tilted her head, as if listening even deeper. "Maybe that's how," she murmured. "We help by listening."

Ethan stilled. She was right.

They weren't just being attacked, they were being *told* something. Beneath the anger, beneath the cruelty, there was something hidden. A plea.

Ethan let out a slow breath, tuning in, searching past the venom, past the distortion.

"Sarah," Ethan's eyes snapped open, realization striking like lightning. "Think about when people are hurt, physically hurt. What do they do?"

Sarah blinked. "What?"

"When someone is in pain, when they're injured or sick, what do they do?" Ethan pressed, urgency rising in his voice.

She frowned. "They... they tell someone. They try to describe it, over and over, so people will understand how sick they are?"

Ethan nodded. "Exactly. This is no different. This is emotional pain, not physical. But it's the same thing."

Sarah's breath hitched. "They just want to be heard. Someone to recognize they're in pain."

Ethan turned toward the darkness of the grove, his heart pounding, but this time, not in fear.

He sat up straighter, his voice sincere. "I hear you," his words carried weight, not just sound. "I feel your pain."

For the first time, the voices stirred, not in aggression, but in hesitation. The sharpness dulled.

The air around them shifted, and the echoes lost their sting. Sarah felt it too, the way the energy trembled, uncertain. A pause.

Then, like a wave receding, the harshness softened. The words that had once been knives melted into something gentler, the whispers threading together into something new. A melody.

A song of gratitude. A voice of connection. Ethan stood, pulling Sarah up with him.

The suffocating weight was gone. In its place, something else remained, something lighter.

Understanding.

Sarah placed a hand over her heart, her fingers trembling. "I could feel the pain, wherever it came from."

Ethan nodded, his chest tight with emotion. "Yeah. It could too."

Aerthis pulsed with approval. "You did not fight the echoes. You heard them. And in doing so, you transformed them."

Sarah and Ethan exchanged a look, one of triumph, of something deeper than victory.

This time, they understood the Echoing Grove.

As the last of the echoes wove themselves into harmony, the air within the Echoing Grove thickened, charged with an unseen energy that pressed against Sarah and Ethan like the weight of an unspoken truth. The trees shuddered, their leaves trembling in response to something stirring between the threads of sound. A pulse rippled outward, hesitant and uneven, like the fractured rhythm of a heart uncertain whether to beat.

A swirling mist, translucent and restless, began to form before them. It pulsed in flickering waves of gold, silver, and emerald but never quite settled into a solid shape. Instead, it hovered in an ever-shifting dance, coiling and unraveling, as if unsure whether it wished to be seen. Whispers swirled within it, half-formed voices, fractured melodies, before dissolving into silence. The mist did not simply emerge; it hesitated, as though torn between revealing itself and retreating into the unseen.

Ethan, startled by its appearance, looks at Sarah. "You think this is another Enigma?"

The voice that followed was not a single tone, but a chorus of layered voices, rising and falling with a rhythm edged in uncertainty.

"I am the guardian of hearing, a descendant of the Harmonize Family, you have heard the tormented voices… but did you truly listen?" The words were laced with both caution and wariness, as if spoken by something that had seen hope shattered too many times before. "The Realm is unraveling. Discord seeps into every note, corrupting what was once pure. If you do not truly listen, if you do not understand, harmony will be lost."

Sarah's breath caught at the weight of the words. She could feel the Harmonize Enigma's unease, its fear barely contained beneath its wavering form. She stepped towards the Enigma, meeting the shifting mist with determination. "We listened," she said. "Not just to the sounds, but to what lay beneath them. The voices weren't just noise, they were pain, grief, wounds left unheard for too long."

The mist twitched, uncertain. "And?"

Ethan exhaled, steadying himself. "We learned that words, especially those spoken in anger or fear, aren't always about us. They come from something deeper.

If we take them at face value, we get lost in the chaos. But if we listen, truly listen, we can hear what's beneath them. The real meaning. The real need."

The mist pulsed, its colors deepening, though its form remained unstable. "You have heard the echoes," the Enigma murmured, its voices shifting between doubt and fragile belief. "Perhaps… perhaps you might be different."

It drifted closer, its shape flickering as though it might dissolve at any moment. "The Realm is in Dysquinox. The threads that once held it together unravel, and the dragons, the keepers of balance, have fallen into discord. To restore them… to bring harmony where there is chaos… you must hear beyond what is spoken. You must listen for what is true."

The mist wavered, curling in on itself in hesitation. "I have seen Seekers before," it admitted, uncertainty threading through its words. "I have hoped before. Hope is dangerous. It can fracture like glass when tested. Many shatter when the weight of the dragons' voices falls upon them!"

Sarah met the Enigma's uncertainty with strength. "We don't know yet," she admitted. "But we're willing to learn."

A long silence stretched between them, the mist shifting, searching. Then, at last, something within it steadied, a fragile, cautious acceptance. From within its depths, two shimmering objects materialized, the Resonant Listening Skill Card and the Resonant Listening Pin. The card glowed, its surface etched with the imprint of a golden soundwave, pulsing in time with an unseen rhythm. The pin, delicate yet strong, rippled like a captured note, its design a testament to the strength found in true listening.

"May these aid you," the Enigma said, though a trace of doubt still clung to its voice. "Resonant Listening is not just hearing, it is the ability to sense the truths hidden beneath noise, to find the melody within the discord. Carry these gifts with you, and they will guide you toward the harmony the Realm so desperately needs."

Sarah and Ethan reached out, their hands closing over the gifts, feeling the energy woven within them. They exchanged a glance, understanding passing between them, not just of the Enigma's words, but of the path they had chosen.

The mist flickered once more, its edges fraying, as though the act of revealing itself had drained something vital from it. "You have taken the first step," it murmured. "But harmony is delicate. It can be lost with a single misstep. Be careful, Seekers."

With that, the Enigma's wavering form dissolved into the shimmering mist of the Echoing Grove, leaving behind the lingering resonance of its presence.

A soft hum stirred in the air, and from the edge of the grove, Aerthis, the Orb of Reflection, glided toward them. Its mirrored surface pulsed with light, absorbing the final echoes of the Enigma's presence.

"You have done well, Seekers," Aerthis said, its voice steady where the Enigma's had wavered. "To listen without fear, to hear truth within pain, this is a skill of courage few possess. But you are just beginning."

Sarah and Ethan nodded, their resolve solidifying. They had done more than complete a challenge; they had changed because of it. And somewhere in the shifting mist, the Harmonize Enigma watched, hopeful, wary, waiting to see if they would truly become the ones to restore the Realm's lost harmony.

As they followed the Orb beyond the archway, the forest seemed different, more in tune.

The whispers no longer haunted the edges of their thoughts; they had settled, no longer demanding to be heard, but acknowledged, understood.

"You are now ready for your third Seeker Challenge," Aerthis said, its tone shifting, solemn now. "But know this, each trial is more difficult than the last. You will be tested in ways you have not yet imagined. And the next challenge..." The Orb's glow dimmed, as if weighing its words. "The next challenge will force you to face something even more difficult than the voices of your past."

A distant rumble echoed through the trees, a deep, resonant sound that sent a shiver down Sarah and Ethan's spines. "What was that?" Ethan shouted.

"That Seekers," Aerthis proclaimed. "Were the dragons, they feel your strength growing."

Ethan clenched his fists. "Well... I'm glad they feel our strength growing."

Sarah exhaled, her grip tightening on the Resonate Listening Pin. "Let's do this Ethan."

The Orb pulsed once, and with that, they stepped forward, toward the unknown, toward their next challenge.

Chapter 7

Aromatic Illumination

The forest pulsed with an eerie glow, its bioluminescence flora casting rippling waves of violet and sapphire across the winding path. The air felt alive, shifting in invisible currents as if breathing with them. Sarah and Ethan moved cautiously, their footsteps muffled by the thick bed of moss. The Orb of Reflection hovered beside them, its mirrored surface flickering, catching glimpses of something unseen.

Sarah cast a wary glance at the Orb. "Where are we heading next?"

The Orb's glow deepened, a pulse of energy rippling outward before its voice hummed through the air. "The Fragrant Trail."

Ethan shot Sarah a skeptical look. "That doesn't sound too bad."

The Orb turned, floating ahead as if inviting them forward. "Do not let the name deceive you. The Fragrant Trail is a test of perception and self-awareness, an intersection of past and present. You will encounter scents tied to your deepest memories, both comforting and painful. By understanding what they reveal will you illuminate the way forward."

Sarah folded her arms. "So, the next challenge tests our sense of... smell somehow?"

The Orb pulsed. "Not exactly. Scent is one of the strongest links to memory and emotion. You must recognize what is hidden within each aroma and embrace its meaning. Otherwise, the path will never reveal itself."

Ethan rubbed his arm, uneasy. "And if we can't?"

The Orb hesitated. "You will remain lost in the echoes of your past, like so many are."

The air shifted as Sarah, Ethan, and the Orb of Reflection stepped beyond the thick cluster of trees, leaving behind the dense underbrush of the Mystical Forest. A subtle but undeniable change in atmosphere surrounded them, the space ahead felt alive, pulsing with an unseen rhythm. The mist thickened, curling in lazy, spectral tendrils, infused with flickering hues of gold, violet, and soft emerald. It wasn't an ordinary fog; it shimmered as if made of living memory, shifting and changing as it wove through the air.

The path before them transformed. A winding trail of silken moss stretched ahead, soft underfoot, merging seamlessly with the landscape as though it had always existed and yet had just revealed itself.

Lush, towering flora lined either side, plants unlike any they had encountered before, their elongated petals exuding faint, glowing vapors that danced in the air like fireflies. The blooms varied in color, some a delicate lavender, others a crimson, and some so dark they seemed to drink in the ambient light. Their movement was subtle, yet unmistakable, as if bending toward the travelers, beckoning them closer.

Crystalline jars, nestled between the gnarled roots of ancient trees, pulsed with an inner light. Some held thick, curling mist, others swirled with tiny, suspended particles, shifting in color depending on where Sarah and Ethan stood. Faint, melodic hums emanated from them, resonating deep in their bones, as though each jar carried a fragment of a forgotten song.

Beyond the flowers and jars, narrow streams of liquid light flowed like silver veins in the earth, their soft illumination stretching far into the distance. Unlike ordinary water, these streams carried shifting images within their depths, flickering scenes of distant places, people whose faces were obscured, moments trapped in an endless loop before dissolving into the current once more.

The air was rich with scent. It was overwhelming, a mixture of a thousand fragrances blending and separating, never settling, never still. With every step they took, the aromas changed, warm spices one moment, crisp citrus the next. The delicate sweetness of blooming jasmine faded into a familiar, almost painful sharpness of something metallic, like the scent of old pennies and rain-soaked stone.

Some scents carried comfort, others unease. Sarah inhaled deeply, her senses sharpening. The whispering mist curled around her, and for a fleeting second, she swore she heard voices, fragmented, broken echoes of laughter, soft murmurs, the distant chime of a bell.

Ethan looking uneasy. "This place feels... weird."

The Orb pulsed beside them. "The Fragrant Trail is unlike any other path. It does not show the way forward, it reveals what has already been, what lingers beneath memory and consciousness. You will not simply walk through it. You must experience it."

Sarah frowned, her gaze drifting toward a cluster of blue flowers that trembled despite the still air. "Experience *what*, exactly?"

The Orb's mirrored surface flickered with shifting images, unreadable and fleeting. "The echoes of who you were. The emotions you buried. The lessons you have yet to understand."

A hush fell over them. The trail stretched out in front of them, curving into the glowing horizon. There was no telling how far it went, no markers to guide them, only the shifting mist and the promise that something waited beyond.

Ethan exhaled, staring at the strange, flickering reflections in the liquid light streams. "Guess there's only one way to find out." With that, they stepped onto the Fragrant Trail, the scents closing in around them, drawing them deeper into the unknown.

As the air thickened with swirling mist, each wisp was infused with an ever-changing fragrance. At one moment, it carried the scent of warm spices, honey, and woodsmoke. The next, it was laced with something sharp, metallic, almost bitter. The trail ahead was lined with crystalline jars, glowing, each holding a swirling vapor inside. Vibrant blooms stretched along the path, exhaling invisible tendrils of scent, and streams of liquid light wove through the earth like rivers of molten silver.

Sarah inhaled, her senses sharpening. But it wasn't just fragrance that filled the air.

There were voices, whispers threading through the mist, fragmented and broken, calling from another time.

The Orb floated closer. "You must engage with the scents that resonate most. They will bring forth memories, emotions, insights you may not expect. Only through reflection and connection will the trail reveal its truth."

Ethan hesitated, staring at the aromatic blooms. The air seemed to vibrate around them, scents curling into unseen threads of memory. "Alright," he muttered. "Let's give this a try."

Sarah reached out first, brushing her fingers against a red blossom. A warm, spiced scent rose to meet her, cinnamon and something sweet, like apples baking in an oven. A memory struck her with startling clarity.

She was eight years old, standing in her grandmother's kitchen. The air was thick with the rich scent of dough, her hands covered in flour as she clumsily shaped cookies. Her grandmother's laughter rang in the air, warm and full of life. Sarah had never felt more loved than in that moment.

But then the scene shifted. Her grandmother's laughter faded, and for a brief second, Sarah saw something unfamiliar in her eyes, something distant. The older woman's gaze softened as she looked at Sarah, but there was a flicker of something else beneath the warmth. A sadness. A longing.

Sarah, smiling, held up a misshapen ball of dough. "Is this good?"

Her grandmother's hands trembled as she reached out, pressing her fingers over Sarah's small ones. The kitchen light caught the moisture in her eyes, and for a moment, she wasn't looking at Sarah at all. She was looking *through* her. Sarah blinked up at her, waiting for an answer.

Her grandmother inhaled deeply, perhaps to steady herself, and smiled, but it was different now. Forced.

Sarah hadn't noticed then.

She hadn't noticed the way her grandmother's hands had tightened around hers, as if grounding herself in the moment, as if pulling herself back from wherever her grief had taken her.

She hadn't noticed how, in that flickering instant, her grandmother hadn't seen *her* at all, she had seen *Sarah's mother*. Sarah hadn't noticed how the loss of her daughter, Sarah's mother, had settled into the creases of her face, deep and silent, hidden beneath flour-covered fingers and the effort of baking, of smiling, of pretending.

Sarah laughed, oblivious, as a young child would. Now, standing in the glowing garden, the warmth of the scent wavered, turning bitter. Her breath caught. "I... I never realized how much she was... struggling."

The Orb's voice was steady. "Perception is often limited to the moment it is experienced. Through reflection can you see the depth beneath."

Sarah took a shaky breath, the scent dissolving as she stepped back.

Ethan hesitated before reaching out to a different bloom, its petals gold. The moment he inhaled, a sharp, citrusy aroma filled his nose. He was ten years old, standing in the doorway of his grandparents' house for the first time. The air inside was thick, stale and unmoving, carrying the weight of dust and time. It smelled of old fabric, forgotten corners, and something sour that made his stomach twist. It was nothing like home.

His mother and father had barely said goodbye before driving off, the hum of the car fading too quickly into the distance.

Ethan had turned back to face the unfamiliar house, its walls yellowed with age, its dim lighting casting long, uneasy shadows.

His grandmother stood at the end of the hall, her arms crossed over her chest, eyes scanning him with quiet disapproval. She didn't say anything at first, but Ethan felt it in the tightness of her mouth, the sharp flick of her gaze. He was a problem, one she had no patience for.

His grandfather was kinder, but distant. He ruffled Ethan's hair once and muttered. "Come on, kiddo." but his attention was elsewhere, his voice distracted, as if he had somewhere more important to be.

Ethan sat stiffly at their kitchen table, hands in his lap, listening to their hushed voices from the next room. They weren't whispering to keep him from hearing. They just didn't care if he did.

"Too much trouble, we can't keep him here." His grandmother proclaimed.

"For god sakes women, give the boy a chance." Replied his grandfather.

"Absolutely not!" His grandmother said bitterly "Peter and Sue are better able to handle a weird kid like that, besides, they have kids his age he can play with."

Peter and Sue, his uncle and aunt. His mother's younger sister and her husband. Names that should have carried warmth, familiarity… but to Ethan, they were nothing more than distant figures in a story he had never been part of. Everyone knew Sue was the family's favorite, the golden one, the one who could do no wrong. It was whispered like an unshakable truth, an unspoken rule that had shaped the family long before Ethan could remember. At least, that's what he had been told.

But the truth was, he didn't know them. Not really. His parents had moved far away when he was just a baby, placing miles, both literal and invisible, between him and the people who were supposed to be his own blood. Now, standing on the edge of their world, he couldn't help but wonder… was he even a part of it? Or had he been forgotten long before he ever had a chance to belong?

Then, just like that, before he even had the chance to process the sting of being unwanted, he was being sent away. No argument. No second thought. Just dismissed. Ethan was told to walk across town. Alone. To his aunt and uncle's house, strangers in name only. His grandmother handed him a flimsy paper towel, a crude map scrawled in shaky ink, directions that felt more like an afterthought than an act of care. No hug. No reassurance. Just a paper towel.

The next memory hit sharper. The air changed. No longer thick with the stale, suffocating decay of his grandparents' house, this was something new. Raw. Green. Sharp. It cut through everything like a blade.

The scent of freshly cut trees. His uncle's sawmill.

Ethan had barely stepped into the yard, his legs aching from the long walk, when the scent hit him, sudden and suffocating. Wood shavings, sap, and the sharp, almost metallic tang of sawdust clung to the thick, humid air, coating his lungs before he could take another breath. It should have smelled fresh, alive, like something being built. Instead, it reeked of something else entirely. It smelled like being discarded. Like a place where things were cut down, stripped, reshaped, without care for what they once were. It smelled like being abandoned.

His aunt and uncle had taken him in, but there was no kindness in it, no warmth, no welcome. They didn't ask how he felt. They didn't try to make him feel at home.

They simply put him there, like an object filling an empty space, an obligation to be handled and nothing more.

His uncle barely acknowledged him, offering nothing but a stiff nod before turning away, disappearing into the roar of the sawmill. The air trembled with the sound of blades tearing through wood, a relentless, grinding noise that never seemed to stop. It suited the man, harsh, unforgiving, sharp-edged in a way that left splinters in people, not just trees. He was bitter to most, but with Ethan, it was worse. There was something colder in the way he looked at him, something unspoken but unmistakable.

But the worst part wasn't them. It was his cousin. Younger than Ethan but cruel in a way that had nothing to do with age. He saw Ethan's quiet discomfort, the way he hesitated at the edges of things, unsure of where he fit. And he fed on it. Thrived on it. Twisted it into something even sharper.

It started as whispers. Little jokes at Ethan's expense. But whispers became louder. Jokes turned into stories, cruel satires that twisted Ethan into something ridiculous, something unwanted. The others listened. Laughed. Soon, they were all against him. Ethan had tried to protest, tried to understand what he had done wrong, but his words never came fast enough, never hit back with the same sharpness.

He was alone. He didn't know why they didn't want him. They just didn't.

The scent of sawdust faded, the heavy stillness of rejection wrapping around him like it had that day.

Ethan exhaled shakily, his body shaking. "I... I never realized how much that moment stuck with me," he murmured. A tear rolled down Ethans face.

"The past is woven into who you are," the Orb said. "Awareness of it brings clarity."

Ethan paused, looking up at Aerthis he asked. "Why didn't they like me? What on earth did I do to them to make them treat me that way?"

"Ethan, it's hard to accept rejection from others, even more so when it comes from those who are family,"

The Orb said solemnly. "People will take out their frustrations and insecurities on those that they see as powerless, for they offer something they seek."

"What is that?" Ethan asks. "I mean I was 10, what on earth did I have they wanted?"

"Vulnerability Ethan," The Orb replied. "You were vulnerable, and they took advantage of that vulnerability as many do to make themselves feel empowered."

"Do they become empowered that way?" Sarah asks.

"Not at all Sarah," Replies the Orb. "Empowerment comes to those that assist the vulnerable."

"So, what happens to people like that, the ones who prey on the vulnerable?" Ethan asks.

The Orb's light dulls. "They erode Ethan, much like what you saw when you overlooked this realm, Dysquinox takes over their every thought and turns their realities into devastation and decay."

"That's sad," Sarah proclaims. "Is there anything we can do for people like them?"

"Sometimes," Aerthis replies. "But they must want to seek the guidance themselves, only then can truly empowered people aid them."

The mist thickened, curling around them in slow, creeping tendrils. The warmth of the garden bled away, dissolving into something colder. Heavier. Something dark. Then it hit her.

A sharp, musty scent coiled around Sarah like an invisible chain, dragging her backward through time.

It was distinct. Unmistakable.

Her therapist's office. Stale books lined the walls, their dusty pages trapping years of unspoken words. Synthetic leather cushions, cracked and stiff beneath her, creaked whenever she moved. The air carried the faint, chemical tang of disinfectant, too sharp, too sterile, like it was trying to erase something.

Her stomach clenched. She was there again. Seated across from him. The man with the neutral expression, the careful, practiced patience. He was speaking, his voice smooth, measured. "You need to open up, Sarah. You keep too much inside."

She already knew every word before he said them. She had heard them before. Again, and again and again, like a broken record repeating itself. He thought he knew her. Thought he could take her apart like a puzzle, find the hidden pieces she refused to give. But he couldn't. He never would.

Sarah sat in the chair, stiff-backed, arms crossed so tightly it felt like she was holding herself together. She stared at him, not out of defiance, but because she had learned that silence was safer. Words could be twisted. Misunderstood. And it didn't matter what she said, anyway. Because no one ever actually listened.

The scent wrapped around her like a vice, squeezing tighter, pressing against her ribs, her lungs, her throat. The walls of the office blurred, the shadows stretching, shifting. She felt trapped, her reflection staring back at her from the glassy surface of the desk, hollow-eyed, unreadable.

She had walked out that day without saying a word. Not because she had nothing to say.

But because she wasn't heard. The musty air thickened. Sarah dropped to her knees.

Her voice was a whisper. "I don't want to be here."

The Orb hovered beside her, silently listening.

Ethan inhaled and nearly gagged. The scent hit him like a fist, sweat, grime, something sour and stale, like an unwashed locker room. His brother's scent... His stomach constricted. He was eight years old, standing in the doorway of the room they shared before his sister was born.

His brother sprawled on the bed, gym clothes tossed carelessly to the side. "Get out, loser," The words were casual and dismissive.

Ethan had been smaller then. His brother was taller, louder, more *real* somehow, like he was everything Ethan wasn't. The scent made him feel like he was shrinking. He squeezed his eyes shut, but the memory held him in place. He had always been in the background, the quiet shadow trailing behind his brother's presence.

Something in him stirred, an old wound he hadn't realized was still raw. He forced himself to breathe through it. The discomfort was suffocating, pressing against them like a weight.

Sarah looking up at Ethan. "What are we supposed to do with this?"

As Sarah and Ethan stood amid the thickening mist, their past clinging to them like a second skin, the Orb of Reflection drifted forward. Its mirrored surface pulsed, shifting between silver and sapphire, rippling as if reflecting unseen forces in the air. It did not speak immediately. Instead, it hovered before them, its presence neither commanding nor passive, but something else, waiting.

Then with a single pulse of light, the world around them seemed to still. The mist froze in place, swirling in slow motion, like ink suspended in water.

The Orb's voice emerged, not loud, but layered, carrying weight beyond sound itself. "Memories are not what you think they are." The mist around them stirred, curling and twisting.

"They are like the smoke of many candles being put out at the same time. Watch."

A sudden breath of wind, swept through the space around them. Tiny, flickering flames appeared in the mist, countless candles burning in the air, their golden glow illuminating the darkness. One by one, the flames sputtered and died, leaving behind tendrils of smoke. The wisps drifted upward, delicate at first, each one separate and distinct.

Then something changed. The smoke, at first independent, began to move, pulled toward an invisible center. The soft tendrils met and intertwined, curling around each other, merging until they became impossible to separate. It was no longer clear which candle had produced which wisp. What had once been individual was now *one*, a cloud of shifting, restless vapor, whispering of something both there and *not there*.

"Memories are like this smoke," the Orb continued. "One drifting into another, merging and changing. At times, they seem real, so vivid that you feel them in your bones. Other times, they are forgotten, fading into the background of your mind. But you must understand…"

The smoke twisted, forming shapes, faces, places, emotions flickering in and out of existence.

"The answer is not to define each as truth, but to realize they may not be truth. They are impressions, echoes of life, shaped by how you remember feeling, not always by how things were."

Ethan's breath hitched. The scent of sawdust still clung to him, his cousin's taunts echoing in the mist. But as he looked at the swirling smoke, something inside him wavered.

Had it happened the way he remembered? Had every look, every cruel word been as absolute as he thought? Or had his fear, his loneliness, shaped the memory into something sharper, more permanent than it once was?

Sarah watched the drifting trails of smoke, her fingers twitching at her sides. The musty scent of her therapist's office still clung to her, the weight of words unspoken pressing against her ribs. But now, she hesitated. Had the man truly dismissed her? Or had she, in her exhaustion, already decided he would before he had even spoken? Had she *chosen* silence because she was unheard... or because she had never believed anyone could listen?

The Orb pulsed again, sending a ripple through the mist. "Memories are experienced emotionally, not always physically. They are neither absolute nor unchangeable. They shift, reshape, become something new every time you recall them."

The mist swirled faster, pulling apart, separating back into soft, delicate wisps. "This is what it means to be human."

Sarah swallowed, her throat tight. "So... we can never trust our memories?"

The Orb's mirrored surface shimmered. "Trust them for what they are, your experience, your perspective. But do not mistake them for the only truth. You are more than the past you remember. And if the past has shaped you..." A final pulse of silver light radiated outward, dissolving the remaining smoke. "Then you may reshape yourself in return."

Sarah and Ethan stood on the Fragrant Trail. The air still pulsed with shifting scents, the mist still curled and danced around them like it was alive. But something had changed. They had changed.

The Orb of Reflection hovered before them, its mirrored surface flickering as if aware of the shift in their resolve.

It did not speak at first, simply pulsed with steady, rhythmic light, waiting.

Ethan inhaled deeply. "I want to try it again."

Sarah nodded, glancing at the flowers, the glowing crystalline jars, the streams of liquid light. They had spent so much energy fearing their memories, pushing them away, but now they saw it differently. These memories weren't *just* pain. They weren't chains meant to hold them back. They were lessons to be learned.

They stepped forward. The first scent that caught Sarah's attention was sharp and sterile, the distinct scent of rubbing alcohol mixed with paper, the faintest tinge of something burnt. The smell of her science classroom. The mist thickened.

She was there again, in the brightly lit lab, the scent of metal and burning wires filling the air as she connected circuits together for a project. She could hear the faint buzz of electricity, the clatter of beakers and resistors, the scratching of pencils against paper. And then...the voices.

"She thinks she's so smart."

"Why does she always know the answer?"

"I bet she's just trying to make us look dumb."

Sarah stiffened. The weight of those whispers had crushed her before, made her shrink into herself, afraid to let her intelligence show too much. She had convinced herself they hated her. But now... She forced herself to look again. The scene sharpened, and she saw something she had never noticed before.

The faces of the kids weren't twisted with hatred or cruelty. They were curious. Their whispers weren't full of resentment, but uncertainty. One girl nudged another and whispered. "Maybe she could help us."

Another boy, one Sarah barely remembered, was watching her closely, not with jealousy, but with hope.

Sarah stood, the mist swirling around her. Had she been wrong all this time? Had her fear of rejection distorted this moment into something it never was?

She exhaled. They had never hated her. They had simply not understood her. And in return, she had never understood them. She stepped back, the scent of the classroom fading. It was a memory. Nothing more. It did not define her. It had only trapped her in a false belief.

She turned to Ethan, her heart still pounding. "Memories hold both truth and distorted fact," she murmured. "It's the emotional pain attached to them that twists them into something else."

Ethan met her gaze, his expression unreadable. "Yeah," he whispered. "I think I see that now."

A new scent wrapped around Ethan, thick and familiar. Pinewood. Freshly cut. The warmth of sawdust baking under the sun. His father's workshop this time. The mist curled around him, pulling him into the past. His father was there, broad-shouldered, strong, his calloused hands working carefully over a block of wood. The rhythmic scrape of a chisel filled the air, the scent of fresh pine thick in the small space.

Ethan had been young eight, maybe nine, watching from the doorway, nervous but hopeful. He had wanted to say something. To tell his father about the book he was reading, about the new game he had played. But the words never came.

He had always believed his father didn't care, that he had been too distant, too distracted, never interested in what Ethan had to say. But then...

His father set down the chisel and exhaled. His voice, deep and rough from years of struggle, cut through the quiet.

"I wish I was better at this, kid."

Ethan froze.

His father ran a hand over his face, sighing. "I don't always know how to say it. But I love you, Ethan. I just... I don't know how to show it."

Ethan's breath caught in his throat. He had never remembered that. Had he blocked it out? Had his hurt, his loneliness, twisted his father's silence into something it had never truly been? His father had loved him. Ethan swallowed hard. The mist around him softened, pulling back, and he turned to Sarah, his voice unsteady. "The more hurt we feel... the more memories distort. It's like we shape them around our pain, and in doing that, we make them hurt worse."

Sarah nodded, her eyes filled with understanding. "We've been carrying the weight of things that might not have even been true. At least... not in the way we thought." A warm golden glow flooded the air around them. They turned to the Orb of Reflection.

It radiated with brilliant golden light, pulsing with deep, steady energy. "Now you see Dysquinox in play." The words sent a shiver through both of them. Dysquinox, chaos of the mind, the distortion of truth, the warping of perception through fear, pain, and doubt. It had been inside them all along. But now... Now, they saw it.

The air around them grew heavy, thick with the weight of something unseen. A lingering hush settled over the Fragrant Trail, as though the world itself held its breath. The familiar scents of memories, some soothing, others aching, began to dissolve, replaced by an emptiness that sent a shiver down Sarah and Ethan's spines.

Then, from the silence, a mist stirred.

Not sudden, not forceful, but slow and hesitant, as if uncertain of its existence. It shifted in restless waves, its edges fraying, pulling inward, reforming. It did not want to be seen. And yet, it could not stay hidden. A dim glow flickered within the mist, pale emerald bleeding into gold, then receding into shadow. It quivered, uncertain. A shape began to emerge, but it remained incomplete, its form flickering between solidity and dissolution. A whisper, more sigh than speech, slipped through the space between them.

"Why have you come?" The voice was layered, soft yet weighted, ancient yet weary. It carried the tremor of something that had once been certain but had lost its foundation. The Learnspring Enigma lingered within the mist, its form shifting with doubt, its presence flickering with cautious reluctance.

Sarah and Ethan stood still, sensing the Enigma's hesitation. It was watching them, measuring them, its energy pulled tight as if bracing for disappointment.

"Darkness is falling upon the Realm," it murmured, a deep sorrow laced within its words. "Dysquinox seeps into every corner. Learning, once a river that flowed freely in this Realm, has become stagnant. Truths are twisted and understanding fades into distortion. You step forward as Seekers, but knowledge alone is not enough. Will you learn what must be learned? Will you change what must be changed? Or will you fail, as others have before you?"

Sarah's throat tightened at the weight of the question. She could feel the Enigma's doubt, its fear that they were not enough. She swallowed. "We faced the challenge of the Fragrant Trail," she said. "And we learned that memory is never just one thing. It can comfort or wound, bring clarity or confusion. It's not the memory itself that shapes us, it's how we hold it."

Ethan exhaled, the mist swirling around his breath. "Pain isn't the whole truth," he added. "It's just a part of it. If we see memories through suffering, they become distorted. But if we look beyond the hurt, we can find the lessons hidden within them."

The Learnspring Enigma pulsed, its glow deepening, but its form still wavered. "Perhaps," it murmured, uncertainty still clinging to its voice. "Perhaps you sense more than most. Perhaps that will be enough... The question remains, will you endure the lessons that lay before you?"

The mist shivered, then shifted. From its uncertain depths, two objects materialized, a card and a pin. The card pulsed with golden etchings, the words Aromatic Illumination inscribed with delicate, shifting light. The pin gleamed, its surface fluid, capturing the ever-changing nature of memory itself.

Sarah and Ethan reached forward, their fingers closing around the gifts. The moment they did, warmth rushed through them, not just warmth, but understanding. A knowing that settled into the spaces where doubt had once lingered.

The Enigma hesitated, its form flickering one last time. "You are more than what has shaped you," it murmured, its voice thin, uncertain, yet tinged with the faintest whisper of hope. "You are more than what you remember. Carry this wisdom with you. Use these gifts as a reminder."

Then with a final, trembling pulse, the Learnspring Enigma dissolved into the mist, leaving behind the fragile echo of its presence. As it vanished, the path before them came alive. One by one, the flowers along the trail lit up, glowing as if guiding them forward. The crystalline jars shimmered, their contents swirling like captured memories.

The streams of liquid light pulsed, stretching far ahead, illuminating a clear path through the once-mysterious trail.

The Orb of Reflection hovered beside them, its mirrored surface reflecting the new radiance around them.

"By overcoming the Aromatic Illumination challenge," the Orb said. "You have been granted passage through the Fragrant Trail. You have started down the path where your memories no longer hold you captured, you have begun to walk beyond them."

Sarah and Ethan exchanged a glance before stepping forward, their movements lighter, freer than before.

But just as they crossed the threshold into the next stretch of the trail, a bright flash of light raced across the darkening skies followed by a deep, rolling boom that filled the air... Thunder.

The once-gentle hum of the trail became something else, something restless, a subtle warning of something lingering. Sarah froze, her heart hammering. She didn't need to ask. She already knew.

"Dragons!"

The Orb dimmed, its glow turning sharp. "Indeed. They are beginning to feel your threat to their control," it hovered forward urgently. "We must move on."

Ethan glanced up at the storming sky. "Where are we going now?"

The Orb pulsed once, its voice unwavering. "To the Stone Palette, young Seeker. There, you will face the Essence of Fusion challenge in an attempt to begin your alignment with the Endurancevale Enigma."

Ethan puzzled. "Which Enigma is that?"

The Orb answered with a voice, soft yet powerful, as it whispered through the charged air.

"The Enigma of Taste."

Chapter 8

The Essence of Fusion

The deeper they ventured into the Mystical Forest, the denser the air became, thick with an otherworldly energy. Vines curled and twisted around ancient trees, their leaves whispering secrets only the forest could understand. Sarah and Ethan followed the Orb of Reflection, Aerthis, as it floated ahead, its mirrored surface reflecting the shifting shadows of the trees.

Sarah glanced at Ethan before turning to Aerthis. "Of the five Mystical Enigmas, which one has the most power?"

Aerthis glowed brighter. "Power... is relative among the Enigmas. Each holds equal power in its own way. However, there is one... one that stands apart."

Sarah's brow furrowed. "The Enigma of Sight?"

Ethan shook his head. "No, I think it was that last one, the Enigma of Smell, that guy was powerful!"

Sarah turns to Ethan with a puzzled look on her face. "You mean girl, right?"

Ethan looks back at Sarah extremely confused. Before he could reply, Aerthis halted in midair, as if considering their words.

A long pause stretched between them before it spoke. "It's the Mindwright Enigma."

"What's its power?" Sarah asked, intrigued.

Again, silence. Then Aerthis answered. "The power of feeling."

Ethan scoffed. "Like touch?"

Aerthis shifted. "It holds that power, yes. But far more powerful is its ability to feel emotions."

Sarah's eyes narrowed. "Don't all the Enigmas feel emotions?"

"Yes, but the Mindwright Enigma does not only feel its own emotions. It feels the emotions of others, including the other four Enigmas, yet where its power truly lies, is in its ability to amplify all emotions, regardless of where they come from. If not carefully guided, it can distort reality, creating fear, anger, or sorrow beyond what truly exists."

Ethan whistled. "So, it's like a giant emotional amplifier? If one Enigma senses something's wrong, the

Mindwright makes it worse?"

"Worse, no, more intense, Ethan," Aerthis replied. "If left unchecked, it magnifies even the smallest doubt into overwhelming chaos yet is carefully nurtured and understood, it amplifies joy and love."

Sarah's voice was soft. "Who guides it, then?"

Aerthis turned toward them. "When the Realm is in harmony, the Custodian guides all the Enigmas, keeping them balanced. But in these Dysquinox times, the Custodian is absent. The Enigmas are lost, uncertain, and reactive. More so, they have come to fear the dragons."

A shiver ran down Sarah's spine. The dragons. Always looming, always watching.

Ethan broke the silence. "So, when do we get to meet this Mindwright Enigma?"

Aerthis hummed. "First, you must align with the Endurancevale Enigma, the guardian of taste."

Ethan grinned. "Awesome! I'm starving."

The trail brought them to a small clearing, in its center lay the Stone Palette. A massive slab of multicolored stone, swirling with shifting patterns. The air vibrated with a soft hum, responding to the energy of the forest and the emotions of those nearby. Crystalline flora surrounded the area, glowing.

Aerthis floated above the stone, its mirrored light shimmering like liquid silver. "The Essence of Fusion challenge awaits. To align with the Endurancevale Enigma, you must achieve balance in taste, harmony between contrasting elements."

A basin lay at the center of the Palette, its surface an ethereal mirror reflecting the ever-shifting sky. The surrounding flora illuminated, each plant radiating energy, Flavorblooms with their delicate, citrusy scent, Moodberries glowing with a hypnotic hue, and the twisted tendrils of Bittersap Vines exuding an acrid aroma. The air itself carried an undertone of something unspoken, waiting for them to unravel the mystery of taste.

"Taste is not just flavor," Aerthis continued. "It is perception. It is experience. Every taste tells a story. Some flavors are harsh, like bitter truths.

Some are sharp, like painful memories. Others are toxic, like regret that lingers too long. Yet, there is also sweetness, joy that soothes, richness that nourishes, and balance that brings peace. You cannot know one without the other. It is through contrast that harmony is found."

Aerthis glowed brighter, the reflection of the forest shifting across its mirrored surface. "This challenge is more than blending ingredients; it is about blending experiences. The choices you make, the memories tied to each sensation, they will shape your success."

Ethan excitedly said. "Let's give it a try!" He hungrily grabbed a Moodberry and popped it into his mouth. His eyes widened, his expression shifting rapidly. "Whoa! It's sweet at first, like honey, but then, ugh! So bitter, like burnt coffee."

Sarah hesitated, running her fingers along the ridged surface of a Bittersap Vine. With a steeled breath, she bit down. Instantly, her mouth puckered as if she'd swallowed a mouthful of vinegar.

"This is awful! Disgusting even!"

Aerthis pulsed in amusement. "Emotions are like flavors. Without balance, they overwhelm. You must explore each ingredient carefully, learn their nuances and decide which belong together and which do not."

The first attempt was a disaster. They crushed the Moodberries, letting their sweet juice drip into the basin. Then, they added strands of the Bittersap Vine, hoping to counteract the intensity with a milder element. As soon as the mixture settled, the liquid in the basin darkened, its scent turning sharp and unpleasant. Sarah wrinkled her nose as she bravely took a sip.

"Too strong," she coughed, pushing the cup away. "The bitterness drowns everything else out.

It's like trying to cover sadness with more sadness."

Ethan frowned. "Maybe we need more sweetness?" He tossed in extra Flavorblooms, their petals dissolving into the mixture. The liquid shimmered briefly before turning syrupy thick. He dipped a finger in and tasted it.

His face twisted. "Now it's too sweet! Like eating straight sugar. It's richness, overwhelming, like happiness forced to an extreme."

Again and again, they tried. Their hands moved with relentless determination, blending, crushing, steeping, and stirring, each movement growing sharper with frustration. Ethan's fingers trembled as he ground the next batch of ingredients, his breath shallow with impatience. Sarah hovered over the mixture, eyes narrowed, calculating adjustments, her mind racing through possibilities. They whispered theories like incantations, adjusting ratios with desperate precision, only to be met with failure every single time.

One attempt produced a concoction so acidic that the mere scent of it made Ethan's eyes sting, tears welling up against his will. He recoiled, coughing violently, his throat burning as if he'd swallowed fire. "That can't be right," he rasped, shaking his head.

Another attempt resulted in something so insipid, so utterly devoid of sensation, that when Sarah hesitantly sipped it, a chill ran down her spine. It was as if the essence of flavor itself had been erased, swallowed into a void where taste ceased to exist. "It's nothing," she whispered, staring at the liquid in disbelief. "It's... nothing." The absence unnerved her more than any overpowering bitterness ever could.

The cycle of failure wove itself into them, tightening around their patience like a constricting vine. The weight of every misstep pressing against them, their perseverance fraying at the edges like overused parchment. Sarah, feeling frustrated, runs a hand through her hair, strands sticking to the sweat on her forehead. Ethan's jaw clenched so tightly it ached, his fingers digging into the table's surface.

Doubt whispered again between them. Maybe they weren't meant to succeed. Maybe the right fusion of flavors, of understanding, was beyond them. But as their eyes met, Ethan's frustration dark and stormy, Sarah's determination flickering like a dying ember, neither was ready to give up…

Sarah sighed, rubbing her temple. "We're forcing this. Maybe we're overcomplicating it."

Ethan glanced at Sarah, realization dawning in his eyes like the first glow of dawn breaking over a darkened horizon.

"What did we learn from the past challenges?" His voice was hushed, laced with urgency, as if the answer had been waiting in the depths of his mind, just out of reach.

Sarah inhaled deeply, steadying her thoughts against the weight of their past trials. Her gaze flickered to the three pins fastened securely to her shirt, small but powerful symbols of everything they had endured, everything they had overcome. She ran her fingers over them absentmindedly, feeling their smooth surfaces, each one a marker of a lesson learned, a piece of the puzzle that had slowly been coming together.

"Flame of Focus," she said, her voice firm despite the uncertainty still lingering at the edges of her mind. "Understanding beyond what's seen. It wasn't just about sight, it was about intent, about knowing that reality shifts depending on where we place our energy. The fire revealed what we were willing to see." She could still feel the heat of the flame, the way it had danced and twisted, demanding more than mere observation, demanding true presence, true will.

"Resonant Listening," Ethan added, his voice introspective. His mind echoed with the memory of the challenge, the way the world had shifted when he learned to hear not just words, but the meaning beneath them. "It wasn't just about sound, it was about connection. The rhythm of emotions, the cadence of truth hidden beneath deception. We had to listen, really listen, to understand." He clenched his jaw, remembering how hard it had been to push past his assumptions, to truly hear the silent things that had never been spoken aloud.

Sarah nodded, glancing at the final pin, its edges glinting in the dim light. "And Aromatic Illumination," she murmured. "Not all we remember is real. Our memories can betray us, twisting the past to fit the emotions we attach to it. We had to unravel the illusion, separate memory from truth, or be lost in the ghosts of what we thought we knew." Her stomach twisted at the recollection, the scent of something once cherished turning into something deceptive, the way it had nearly trapped them in a false reality.

Ethan felt something was still missing, they were close to an answer, but the final piece remained hidden. His gaze dropped, drawn inexplicably to the three cards tucked away in his front pocket, the ones given to them by the Enigmas of each challenge. Carefully, he pulled them out, his fingertips brushing over their worn edges. The cards had always felt significant, more than mere tokens of their success, yet he had never thought to examine them beyond their initial gift.

But as he turned them over, something caught his eye. The edges, slightly thicker than they should have been, as if... His heart leapt. They were folded.

Ethan's breath hitched as he carefully pried one open, his pulse thundering in his ears.

Inside, delicate script unfurled across the hidden surface of the card, instructions, a guide that had been waiting for them all along. His fingers trembled as he flipped through each one, realizing that the Enigmas had given them not just wisdom, but the means to apply it when the time came.

"Sarah," he said, voice tight with disbelief. "We weren't just supposed to remember the lessons. We were meant to use them. They left us the way forward."

Sarah's eyes widened as she leaned closer, her breath catching as she read the words hidden within the folds. Each card contained something vital, guidance on how to wield the skills they had gained, how to merge sight, sound, and scent into something greater, something powerful enough to push beyond the challenge before them.

A fire sparked in Ethan's chest, replacing the doubt that had crept in. He met Sarah's gaze, a slow grin breaking through his seriousness. "We already have everything we need."

Sarah exhaled, a flicker of determination igniting in her expression. "Let's use it."

Together, they turned back to face the Stone Palette, not with fear, but with the certainty that they had already come so far, learned so much, to fail now.

They locked eyes. The lesson had been in front of them the whole time.

This time, Ethan reached for a Moodberry but didn't immediately eat it. He rolled it between his fingers, feeling the smooth skin. "This reminds me of times I felt joy... but also sadness. It's both. I have to accept both."

Sarah followed his lead, selecting a Bittersap Vine and a single Flavorbloom. "Bitterness alone is overwhelming, but blended right, it adds depth."

Instead of dumping them into the basin randomly, she placed each ingredient in carefully, mindfully, considering their purpose.

They worked together, balancing flavors as if balancing emotions, accepting the highs and lows, the sweet and the bitter. They adjusted, sensing when to stop, and when to enhance. Ethan added a touch of warmth from a hidden spice they discovered near the basin, lending the mixture a quiet strength. Sarah countered it with a gentle cooling element from the petals of a silvery herb, softening the edges of its intensity.

As the final blend settled, the liquid shimmered and glowed, radiating perfect balance. The air around them pulsed with energy, and the Stone Palette thrummed beneath their feet, sending a resonant hum through the ground.

A soft breeze carried the scent of their creation through the clearing, a perfect, harmonious blend of flavors and emotions intertwined. The fusion was not just of taste but of understanding. The bitter did not erase the sweet; the sweet did not mask the bitter. They coexisted, enhancing each other, as all things in balance should. They had done it.

A low, mournful hum resonated through the air, a vibration that settled into Sarah and Ethan's bones. The colors of the Stone Palette flickered uncertainly, as if sensing a presence reluctant to reveal itself. The very air seemed heavier, as though weighed down by sorrow long carried and never released. Then from the depths of the shifting mist, something stirred.

The Enigma did not emerge at first. It wavered, an indistinct shape lost in the haze, its edges curling inward as if trying to be seen and unseen at the same time. Dim embers of gold and silver flickered like a distant memory trying to resurface.

The mist that surrounded it carried echoes of something ancient, a knowledge burdened by the passage of time.

Then, hesitantly, the Endurancevale Enigma's golden radiance was muted, not in weakness but in the quiet restraint of something that had endured too much loss. Its gaze, deep pools of sorrowful amber light, regarded them with a wariness that was neither hostile nor welcoming, only weary. When it spoke, its voice carried the weight of countless lessons, tempered with both caution and a fragile hope.

"You have reached the threshold of endurance," it murmured, each word deliberate, as though afraid to place too much faith in them. "The Realm withers. Dysquinox festers in places once strong, and the balance that once held firm now crumbles. I have seen seekers before, those who wished to mend what was broken. And I have seen them fail," a heavy pause. "Will you be different? Or will you falter as so many before you?"

Sarah swallowed, feeling the Enigma's sorrow as if it were hers. "We have now faced four challenges," she said. "And we learned so much, true focus is more than just seeing. It's understanding what lies beneath. That true listening means hearing not just words, but intent. And that memory can be both truth and distortion, it's how we choose to see it that defines its impact."

Ethan nodded. "And here, we learned that taste is understanding contrasts. Strength and vulnerability, stillness and movement, loss and renewal, aren't meant to oppose each other. They're meant to work together. Endurance isn't about resisting change. It's about adapting to it, learning from it, and using it to become stronger."

The Enigma pulsed, a ripple of golden light moving through its wavering form.

"Perhaps," it said, though uncertainty lingered in its voice. "You grasp the essence of endurance, but have you the strength to bear it? Will you carry its weight, even when it is heavier than you imagined?"

From the mist, two objects materialized, a card and a pin, shimmering with the muted radiance of tempered gold. The card pulsed with shifting etchings, its surface bearing the inscription: The Essence of Fusion. The small pin gleamed with quiet fortitude, as though reflecting the very lessons they had learned.

"These will serve as reminders," the Enigma said, its form flickering. "Endurance is not the absence of struggle. It is the ability to move forward despite it. Take these and remember what you have learned. You will need it."

Sarah and Ethan reached out, their hands steady as they accepted the gifts. As their fingers closed around them, warmth once again, spread through their bodies, not just warmth, but a sense of understanding that settled into their core.

The Endurancevale Enigma's light dimmed, its sorrow not erased but eased. "You have taken another step," it murmured. "But your journey is far from over. The trials ahead will not merely challenge you. They will reshape you."

Sarah narrowed her eyes. "Is there something we should know about the next challenge?"

The Enigma's form wavered, flickering as if amused despite its solemn nature. "Mindwright," it said after a pause. "It can be... difficult."

Ethan raised a brow. "Difficult how?"

But the Enigma gave them a final, lingering look. "You will see. Trust what you have learned."

With that, its golden glow shimmered, diffusing like light scattering through mist.

Slowly, its form unraveled into glimmering particles, drifting upward, dissolving into the air itself.

For a long moment, Sarah and Ethan stood in silence, absorbing the weight of what had just passed.

Ethan let out a slow breath and glanced at Sarah. "Mindwright, huh?" He smirked. "Something tells me we're in for an even bigger challenge."

Sarah huffed a quiet laugh, rolling the new pin between her fingers. "Yeah. But I feel we can handle it."

With renewed determination, they turned toward the path, knowing that whatever came next, they wouldn't face it alone. The golden glow of the Endurancevale Enigma had long faded, but its presence lingered in Sarah and Ethan's thoughts as they followed the Orb of Reflection. The colors of the Stone Palette dimming into the muted hues of twilight. A gentle breeze rustled the crystalline flora around them, as if whispering in approval of their success.

Ahead, a familiar soft silver light pulsed through the trees that marked the path.

"There it is," Ethan murmured, exhaling a breath he hadn't realized he'd been holding.

A sudden explosion of thunder tore through the sky, a sound so raw and violent that it felt like the very air had been ripped apart. The force of it sent a shudder through the ground, a resonating tremor that rattled their bones. Sarah and Ethan instinctively dropped, hands flying to their ears as the deafening roar swallowed everything.

In an instant, the sky ignited. A jagged bolt of lightning split the heavens, blinding white-hot light tearing through the darkness. A powerful gust of wind slammed into them, nearly knocking them off their feet.

Sarah gasped, her breath stolen by the sudden fury of the storm, while Ethan clenched his jaw, muscles tensed against the relentless force.

As the rumble of thunder faded, they lifted their heads, their hearts still hammering in their chests. Eyes wide, breaths unsteady, they turned to Aerthis, its mirrored surface reflecting the flickering remnants of the storm. "Thundervein," Aerthis proclaimed.

"Thundervein, is that one of the dragons?" Sarah asked, still shaken.

"Yes!" replied Aerthis.

"Are you sure we can defeat the dragons?" Their voices wavered, uncertainty creeping into the spaces between their words.

The Orb of Reflection pulsed, its glow steady, almost solemn. "Defeat them?" Aerthis repeated, its voice resonating through the charged air. "No. That is not the goal."

A pause, one heavy with meaning.

"Remember, you must *transform* them," Aerthis continued, the weight of its words pressing down on them. "And whether or not you can truly achieve that... remains to be seen."

A chill ran down Sarah's spine. Ethan swallowed hard. The storm had passed, but the real battle had yet to begin.

The Orb of Reflection floated serenely in the air, its mirrored surface reflecting not only their exhausted faces, but something deeper, something unspoken yet understood between them. As they stepped closer, the Orb pulsed in greeting.

"This way," Aerthis said, its voice smooth as it began drifting forward along the trail.

Sarah and Ethan fell into step behind it, though noticeably less energy than before.

The exhilaration of their victory was quickly wearing off, replaced by the dull ache of fatigue creeping into their limbs. The trail stretched endlessly before them, winding through the dreamlike landscape of the Realm of the Mind.

After a while, Ethan let out a weary sigh, dragging a hand down his face. "Okay, when are we going to rest? Because I'm getting tired."

Sarah groaned in agreement. "Yeah, me too. Can we stop for a while?"

The Orb did not slow. "Not yet, Seekers," Aerthis replied, its voice calm but unwavering.

"Exhaustion is required in order for you to complete the next challenge."

Ethan blinked, frowning. "Exhaustion?" he repeated, incredulous. "Isn't that a bad thing?

Shouldn't we, I don't know, *not* be falling over from fatigue before facing another challenge?"

Aerthis turned toward them, its mirrored surface catching the dim light of their surroundings.

"Your next and final challenge as Seekers is called the Challenge of Emotional Reflection," it explained. "It is best undertaken when you are exhausted, when your defenses are lowered, and your emotions are most vulnerable. Only then will the Mindwright Enigma see your authenticity. Only then can you align with it."

Sarah, rubbing at her tired eyes, gave Aerthis a sidelong glance. "Is it stubborn?"

The Orb pulsed with what could only be described as humor. "You could say that. At times."

Ethan let out a groan, rubbing his temples. "Fantastic," he looked at Sarah, exasperation in his voice.

"I'm not good when I'm tired, and I'm *really* not good when I'm hungry, which I am. So, being tired and hungry? That could be a serious problem."

Sarah sighed, though there was a small smirk on her lips. "One more, Ethan," she said, gently pulling him along. "Hold it together and get through this last one, and then we can rest. *And* eat something."

She paused, then added under her breath. "I hope."

Ethan groaned again but trudged along beside her, resigning himself to whatever awaited them next. As the Orb of Reflection led them further into the unknown, the last remnants of golden light faded behind them, leaving only the golden glow of their guide to illuminate the path ahead.

Chapter 9

Emotional Reflection

The Orb of Reflection hovered before them, its mirrored surface pulsing with a steady, rhythmic glow. Each throb of light guided Sarah and Ethan deeper into the mystical forest, but with every step, the weight of their journey pressed heavier upon them. Fatigue curled around their limbs like iron chains, turning motion into an unbearable effort. Their muscles ached, their thoughts dulled, their bodies sluggish, not just from physical strain but from the relentless emotional toll of the trials they had faced.

Hunger gnawed at them, an emptiness hollowing their insides, making every breath feel like a struggle. The Realm seemed to sense it, the air itself growing thick, pressing against them, demanding more than they felt they had left to give.

Sarah stumbled, catching herself.

"You, okay?" Ethan asked.

"Yeah, I guess I'm starting to feel it too Ethan." she murmured, her voice raw with exhaustion.

Ethan wiped at his forehead, though the air was cool. His limbs felt leaden, his vision blurred at the edges. "Feels like we haven't eaten in days," he muttered. "I can barely think straight."

The Orb pulsed, a shimmer in the darkness. "You are tired. You are hungry. And yet, this is precisely what is needed to face the next challenge," it said, its voice calm, unwavering. "Through exhaustion we uncover our rawest truths. Only through vulnerability can one's true authenticity be seen."

Sarah let out a shaky breath, hugging her arms against the cold creeping into her bones. "So, we just keep pushing forward, even though we're running on empty?"

"No," the Orb corrected. "You do not push. You surrender. You feel. That is the challenge ahead."

The dense trees parted before them, revealing a glade unlike anything they had seen before. It was bathed in golden light, as though the very air shimmered with something alive. At its center stood the Heartwood Tree. Its bark glowed amber, as if it held the warmth of the sun within its core. Thick, ancient vines wrapped around its roots, pulsing in rhythm with an unseen heartbeat. A golden mist swirled through the air, shifting in color with each breath of wind.

Scattered across the glade were shallow pools of shimmering water, their surfaces unnervingly still. But as Sarah and Ethan stepped closer, the pools began to ripple, not from wind or movement, but from something deeper. Faint, fleeting visions flickered across them, memories, emotions, fears.

Sarah didn't need to ask what this place was. She felt it. This was not a battlefield. This was a place of surrender. The Heartwood Glade.

The Orb's voice broke the silence. "This is where truth is revealed through feeling. To align with the Mindwright Enigma, you must face the challenge of Emotional Reflection."

Ethan's stomach growled audibly, the sound jarring against the eerie tranquility of the glade. Sarah shot him a tired glance, though she felt the same gnawing emptiness twisting inside her.

As the Orb continued, something shifted in the mist. Sarah caught the movement out of the corner of her eye. Small. Delicate. Almost translucent. Her breath hitched. Another flicker, near the Heartwood Tree this time. Luminous eyes blinked at them from the swirling gold, studying them before slipping away like a whisper lost to the wind.

"What was that?" Ethan muttered.

The Orb of Reflection pulsed. "One of the Mystical Resonant Creatures."

"Are they dangerous?" Ethan asked alarmed, feeling his defenses lowered.

"They reflect what you carry inside. You must face them, embrace your emotions, or remain bound by them." Replied the Orb.

Sarah turned, her gaze locking onto another flicker of movement behind a dense layer of bushes. It wasn't just a trick of the light, she *felt* it before she saw it, a presence pressing at the edges of her mind. She stepped towards it, careful not to disturb the fragile stillness.

Parting the leaves with trembling fingers, she saw it. Small. Ethereal. Inviting. Its form wavered, caught between solid and mist, as if it existed in the space between reality and dreams.

Sarah knelt, her pulse quickening.

It was foxlike in shape but woven of something softer than fur, *twilight itself*, weightless and shifting. Wisps of silvery mist curled from its form, dissolving into the cool air. Its delicate, translucent like wings, too fragile for flight, quivered, adjusting to her presence.

And then, its eyes. Deep pools of violet and blue. Not just looking. *Seeing.* Sarah exhaled, extending her hand instinctively, palm open. It wasn't logic that guided her, it was something unspoken, something raw and unguarded.

The Orb of Reflection whispered. "It is called a Dusksprite. One of many Mystical Resonant Creatures that dwell in the Heartwood Glade."

Sarah swallowed. "It's so cute! Does it bite?"

The Orb's response was quiet. "That depends on your emotions, if it feels threatened, it might!" The Orb's light pulsed. "Each Mystical Resonant Creature mirrors the emotions of those who stand before them. If you are sad, it is sad. If you are angry, it is angry. But if you offer love, acceptance, and joy, it will reflect that back to you."

Sarah turned back to the Dusksprite, drawn to its fragile beauty. She reached further, fingertips trembling. The creature hesitated, watching her with an intelligence that felt ancient, knowing. Then, as if responding to something unseen, it moved towards her. Sarah gasped.

A sudden wave of emotion crashed into her, so fierce and unrelenting it stole the breath from her lungs. An aching loneliness twisted in her chest. A solitude she had buried beneath sharp wit and logic, one she had fought to hide for so long.

The Dusksprite flinched backward, its form flickering wildly, mirroring her pain.

"No… wait," Sarah whispered, reaching, desperate to pull it back. But it was too late.

The creature recoiled, trembling like a dying ember before dissolving into nothing, a final wisp of light swallowed by the mist. Gone.

Sarah raised her hands to cover her mouth as if to steady the hollow ache inside her. "Where did that feeling come from," she murmured, voice hoarse. "I don't get it!"

The Orb of Reflection pulsed. "Emotions Seeker," it murmured. "Are often guarded by walls you build to protect vulnerabilities you refuse to face?"

Sarah's breath hitched. For the first time in a long time, she felt the weight of her loneliness. It seemed to consume her in the moment. She shoved it back down, burying it where it couldn't reach her. Without a word, she turned and walked to a large rock, sinking onto it with a slow exhale.

Ethan followed but didn't speak. He just sat beside her, silent, present.

"I'm tired, Ethan," Sarah said quietly, staring at the golden mist curling around her boots.

Ethan looked at her, not just hearing the words, but feeling them.

Sarah wiped at her eyes, a single tear slipped down her cheek. "Why does life have to be so damned hard?"

The air between them was thick with a weary silence, the kind that settled deep into the bones, heavier than words could ever express. Ethan let out a slow, tired breath, his gaze fixed on the ground as if the weight of his thoughts was too much to lift. His voice, usually firm, softened into something fragile.

"I know this may not change anything, Sarah," he murmured, the ache in his tone undeniable. "But I'm tired too."

His hands, clasped together, trembled slightly, as if holding onto something invisible, some hope, some hurt, some unspoken longing for things to be different.

"Tired of how cruel people can be to each other. Tired of the way we tear each other down, like existing in the same world is some kind of battle," he exhaled shakily, finally daring to meet her eyes. "It shouldn't be this hard... just to be."

In that moment, it wasn't just exhaustion he shared with her, it was the quiet, aching truth of two souls who had seen too much, felt too deeply, and still carried the weight of the world on their shoulders.

Sarah turned to him, her gaze filled with a quiet understanding. She knew what he meant.

Ethan's expression was distant. "My uncle Ken told me a story once when I was little. I didn't get it at the time, but now... now, I think I do," his voice softened. "He said that when a chick is ready to hatch, it has to fight its way out of the shell. The mother hen could help, it could peck the shell open, make it easier. But it doesn't."

Sarah frowned. "Why not? Wouldn't that help the chick?"

Ethan shook his head. "That's what I thought too. But my uncle said if the chick didn't struggle, if it wasn't forced to break free on its own, it wouldn't survive. The fight, the effort, that's what makes it strong enough to live."

"Yeah, but how much struggle do we have to go through?" Sarah asked.

He turned to Sarah, his eyes reflecting something raw, something real. "I think we need struggle. Without it, we're weak. Every challenge we face, every time we push through the hard things, we grow. We get stronger... less fragile."

They sat in silence for a long moment, letting the truth of it settle.

Sarah spoke, her voice quiet but resolute. "I read something once, don't wish for an easier life. Develop better skills," she looked at him, searching his face. "Maybe that's it, Ethan. Maybe instead of wanting things to be easier... we must work harder at learning more skills."

A soft hum pulsed through the air as the Orb of Reflection drifted closer, its presence warm.

"A few hundred years ago," the Orb began, its voice smooth as flowing water. "Life was far more difficult than it is today. There was less technology, fewer comforts. People struggled at great cost so that their children might struggle less. And so, generation by generation, hardship was eased."

Its glow brightened, pulsing in time with its words. "But struggle was never the enemy," the Orb's tone deepened, rich with something both knowing and ancient. "It is what gives life meaning. The climb makes the summit worth reaching. The battle makes the peace that follows feel earned."

Sarah and Ethan sat motionless, absorbing the weight of its words.

"You have endured much today," the Orb continued. "You are tired. You are hungry. And yet, your exhaustion does not come from today alone. It comes from carrying the burdens of the challenges you have faced in your life beyond this Realm."

The mist in the glade shifted, swirling around them.

"You may continue to bear that weight, continue to struggle as you have," the Orb proclaimed, its light flickering. "Or you may face the challenges that will set you free, giving you strength, courage, resilience and adaptability that replaces the burden you once carried."

It hovered there, silent for a moment before adding. "The choice is yours. And yours alone."

Avoid the challenge and dwell in your struggles, face the challenge and grow stronger, able to face more difficult challenges ahead, while leaving the ones you have overcome behind."

The wind stirred through the Heartwood Glade, but neither Sarah nor Ethan spoke. For the first time, they weren't just hearing the words. They were feeling them.

Sarah stood up, and without saying a word she calmly walked towards the Heartwood tree. Small mystical creatures began to emerge, hidden, concealed, as if studying her carefully.

Finding a moss-covered spot on the ground, Sarah lowered herself, crossing her legs beneath her. She placed her forearms on her knees, her hands open, palms facing upward. With a slow inhale, she closed her eyes. Ethan watched, his breath shallow as the golden mist of the Heartwood Glade thickened around her. The air shifted.

Something unseen stirred, responding to her stillness. The mystical creatures began to emerge, no longer hidden in the swirling light but drawn toward her as if sensing an unspoken invitation. Their appearance, unique in nature, shifting between threatening and serene forms.

First, an Emberwing crept forward, a strange bird like form with its ember-lit feathers smoldering against the cool air. It hesitated at the edge of the clearing, head tilting in quiet curiosity before inching closer.

Then an Aurawisp, its delicate, Raccoon-like form twisting through the mist like a whisper of light, drifted toward her. Ethan swallowed. The energy in the glade had changed. It felt alive, aware.

From the deep glow of the Heartwood Tree, the strangest of them all appeared. A Luminara.

Its arrival was not like the others, it did not step, nor drift. It simply *was*, as if it had always been there, unnoticed until this moment.

The air around it shimmered, bending light as though reality itself struggled to define it. At first, it was no more than a ripple in the golden mist, an outline barely seen. With each breath, it took shape, a luminous, shifting form, something between a lemur and a wisp of pure energy. It moved with impossible grace, not walking, not floating, but existing in a way that defied logic, its presence sending gentle pulses through the glade.

Sarah felt it before she saw it, a warmth brushing against the edges of her awareness. Its eyes locked onto hers. Twin pools of shifting color, gold, silver, deep violet, and soft blue, swirled like liquid starlight. They were not eyes in the way she understood. They were reflections. Mirrors. A shiver ran down her spine.

The Luminara did not blink. It did not look *at* her. It looked *through* her, into the places she kept hidden, into the truths she wasn't ready to face. Its light pulsed in time with her heartbeat, flickering with every unspoken thought, every feeling she had buried beneath wit and intellect.

Ethan struggled to breathe, afraid that even the smallest sound would shatter the delicate connection unfolding before him. The Luminara moved towards her, though it left no trace of its presence behind. Its glow deepened, responding to something within Sarah.

And that was when she understood. It was not just a creature. It was a question. One she could not run from. Would she look away? Or would she dare to see herself as she truly was?

The air between them held the answer, waiting. Sarah exhaled. And met its gaze.

A tidal wave of stress crashed over Sarah, pressing against her, threatening to pull her under. The weight of overwhelm coiled around her thoughts, twisting them into chaos. Yet, even as panic clawed at the edges of her mind, she did not break the Luminara's gaze.

Its shifting, prismatic eyes reflected everything she carried inside, the doubt, the noise, the relentless storm of too much. It didn't judge. It didn't recoil. It simply showed her herself. Sarah's breath trembled. Convincing herself she would not drown in this any longer. Her fingers reached for the small pins attached to her shirt, her anchor to something real, something steady. As she brushed against them, warmth bloomed beneath her fingertips.

A single candle flame flickered to life in her thoughts, small yet unwavering, casting its glow into the tangled darkness of her mind. The clamor of confusion, the racing thoughts, the tangled fears, began to soften, shrinking from an unbearable roar to gentle whispers, guiding her instead of drowning her.

Then...a scent.

The familiar warmth of her quiet attic apartment, the faintest hint of old books and lavender.

And a taste, sweet, comforting. Freshly baked cookies, warm from her grandmother's oven, melting on her tongue. Sarah's lips parted in surprise. A smile found her. She looked deeper into the Luminara's eyes, no longer afraid of what she might see there.

"I feel you," she whispered.

A radiant glow pulsed through the Luminara, its flickering light stabilizing. No longer a formless wisp of energy, it shifted, softening into something new. A delicate, lemur-like creature now stood before her, its fur shimmering with golden luminescence. It was gentle, serene, its every movement infused with understanding.

With infinite patience, it reached out. Its tiny, five-fingered hand extended toward her, waiting. Not demanding, not forcing, inviting. Sarah's chest rose with a slow, deep breath. She reached back.

Their fingers met.

The moment their hands touched, a surge of confidence flooded Sarah's entire being, racing from the top of her head to the soles of her feet. It wasn't the kind of confidence that came from *knowing everything*, it was the confidence that came from trusting herself. A light, bubbling giggle escaped her lips, unguarded and free. The Luminara let out a soft, melodic trill, its glowing form bowing to her in what could only be gratitude.

The other creatures, the Emberwing, Aurawisp, and Dusksprites, began to leap with joy, their glowing forms dancing through the air in celebration. The glade itself seemed to shimmer, as if the very essence of the Realm rejoiced in the moment of connection that had just unfolded.

Sarah let the joy wash over her. For the first time in her life, she belonged.

The Luminara stepped back, its golden light pulsing one final time, as if offering Sarah a silent farewell. With a graceful bow, it dissolved into a wisp of pure starlight, its radiant form scattering into the mist like a fading dream. Sarah stood motionless, the afterglow of the connection still thrumming through her veins. A warmth she had never known before filled her heart, not just joy, but something deeper...

Belonging... Understanding... Home.

Tears welled in her eyes, but she made no move to wipe them away. She turned, stepping towards Ethan. When their eyes met, she saw the emotions flickering within him, fear, uncertainty... but also wonder. He had seen it. Felt it.

Without hesitation, Sarah surged forward and wrapped her arms around him, pulling him into a fierce, unapologetic hug. Ethan stiffened, his breath hitching. His entire body locked in place, every instinct screaming that he didn't know what to do with this. No one had ever hugged him before. Not once. Awkwardly, his arms rose, unsure, uncertain. But then, something inside him softened. His muscles unclenched, his heartbeat slowed. And he hugged her back. For the first time in his life, Ethan let himself be held. For a moment, they stood there, no words, no logic, just the quiet, unspoken understanding between two people who had spent their whole lives feeling alone. When they pulled away, Sarah exhaled, her face still alight with something unshakable.

"I have never felt so connected to anything before," she whispered, her voice trembling with wonder. "Ethan, it was... beautiful."

Ethan stood still, trying to process not only her words but the echo of the hug still lingering on his skin. His mind scrambled to make sense of it, his body trying to remember what safe felt like.

The Orb of Reflection drifted toward them, its light pulsing with patience. "Ethan," it murmured. "Are you ready to try?"

Ethan tore his gaze from Sarah, his throat dry. His hands sweaty as they drifted to his sides. "I think so?" he whispered. But as the golden mist swirled around him, his heart pounded with a truth he wasn't ready to speak.

I don't know how to let go. Ethan took a breath and moved forward. His exhaustion clung to him like a heavy cloak, pressing into his shoulders, dragging at his limbs. Every part of him ached, not just from fatigue, but from something deeper, something he couldn't quite name.

As he entered the Heartwood Grove, the mystical creatures that had surrounded Sarah moments before scattered, vanishing into the golden mist. Their absence left a hollow quiet in the air, an unspoken rejection that sent a sharp pang through Ethan's chest. He turned back toward Sarah, uncertainty creeping into his expression.

She smiled. A soft, knowing smile. "You got this," she whispered.

Ethan exhaled and lowered himself to the ground, trying to mimic Sarah's effortless posture. But his knees wouldn't bend the way hers had, his legs too long, too stiff. Frustration burned at the edges of his patience. He shifted, then gave up, kneeling instead, resting his weight on his haunches.

Closing his eyes, he stretched his long arms straight out in front of him, rigid, unnatural, like some awkward zombie lurching through the night. Time dragged. He sat there, waiting, the silence stretching thin and unbearable. Every few moments, he cracked one eye open, searching. Hoping.

Nothing.

No Emberwing. No Aurawisp. No Luminara, nothing, even the air stood still. The emptiness around him deepened. His arms dropped to his sides in defeat.

He turned to the Orb of Reflection, disappointment etching lines into his face. "What am I doing wrong?" His voice was quieter than he intended, like he was afraid of the answer. His gaze flickered to Sarah. He expected to see amusement, maybe pity. Instead, her eyes were filled with something else. Something he couldn't quite understand.

The Orb pulsed and floated closer, lowering itself to meet Ethan's troubled stare. "The pain you hold within you, Ethan, is real," it murmured. "As a boy, your challenges in life are different from Sarah's. Some you share.

Others… can only be understood from where you stand."

Ethan frowned, curiosity breaking through his frustration. "What do you mean?"

The Orb glowed, its light soft yet unwavering. "Emotions, Ethan. They are part of your existence, woven into the very essence of being human. They are what separate you from the beasts of your world, they allow you to connect, to love, to *be*. "And yet… you have been told to bury them. Conditioned, from the time you were small, to believe that emotions make you weak."

Ethan swallowed hard. A sharp, familiar sting tightened in his throat. "Yeah," he admitted. "That's what my dad and my brother say. All the time," his fingers twitching. "That I'm… weak."

The Orb's light dimmed, as if mourning the weight of those words. "The power of belief," it murmured.

Ethan blinked. "What?"

The Orb pulsed, its glow steady and deliberate. "Do you believe that, Ethan?"

Ethan flinched, caught off guard by the question. "I…no!" His voice rose too quickly, too forcefully. Then, softer. "Well… maybe?"

The Orb hummed, surrounding him in warmth. "The truth, Ethan, is this, real strength does not come from suppressing your emotions. True strength is found in understanding them. In knowing how to hold them, how to feel them, how to honor them, while at the same time filtering them through thought."

Ethan's breath shuddered.

"The world has taught your father and your brother to build walls inside themselves," the Orb continued. "Walls meant to keep emotions locked away, hidden, forgotten.

But no matter how high, no matter how strong… those walls always crack. And when they do, when the dam bursts, it does not break alone. It floods everything around it, drowning the people they love in anger, in pain, in fear. This is because they were never taught how to understand their emotions. Only how to hide them."

Ethan looked down at his hands, fingers trembling.

"They tell you emotions are weakness," the Orb said. "But they are wrong. Emotions are power. They are the bridge between you and the world. Between you and yourself."

Ethan swallowed hard. "So, what do I do?" he asked.

The Orb glowed brighter. "Your challenge is not whether or not you *can* connect to your emotions, Ethan. You already do, every day, in ways you don't even realize," it paused. "Your challenge is something far greater."

Ethan lifted his gaze, his heart pounding.

"The challenge you face," the Orb said. "Is tearing down the belief that you need to hide them. Because you don't."

The silence that followed was deafening. Ethan sat there, the words sinking into the deepest parts of him, challenging everything he had ever been told. Ethan had no idea where to begin. How did someone just... let emotions be? All his life, he had fought them, shoved them down, buried them so deep inside himself that he hoped, prayed, they would disappear. When they threatened to surface, he would retreat, hide in the shadows where no one could see the cracks forming beneath his skin. Because if he let them out, if he let himself feel, who knew what kind of mess they would make? What if they drowned him? What if they proved everyone right, that he was weak?

And yet…here, in the stillness of the Heartwood Glade, he was surrounded by creatures that reflected the truth he had spent years running from…

Ethan swallowed hard, his gaze dropping as embarrassment burned beneath his skin. "I… I don't know how," he admitted.

The Orb of Reflection pulsed, not with disappointment, but with something else, gratitude. "Allow me to help, Ethan," its light shifted as it floated into a new position before him. "First, try to relax."

Ethan exhaled shakily, adjusting his posture, shifting until he found a spot that felt less wrong.

"Close your eyes," the Orb instructed. "And remember the Flame of Focus."

Ethan obeyed, squeezing his eyes shut, trying to picture the flame. But the moment darkness filled his vision, they appeared. His father. His brother. Their voices rose like a storm, yelling, taunting, laughing.

"You're weak."

"Too sensitive."

"Crybaby."

The words slammed into him like fists. His breath hitched, and his eyes snapped open. He shook his head violently, trying to chase them away.

"The card, Ethan! The card!" Sarah's voice broke through the haze.

His chest tightened, but then, understanding. His hand shot into his pocket, fingers fumbling before they found it, the Flame of Focus card.

He pulled it out, gripping it tightly, his knuckles turning white. The small flame flickered across its surface, an unwavering light in his trembling hands.

Slowly he opened the card. The words inside reminded him. Showed him. Guided him. Taking a steady breath, he held the card before him, eyes locked on the flame. For a few moments, he just stared. Then with cautious determination, he closed his eyes.

This time, the images shifted. The flame remained, flickering in the darkness. His father and brother were there too, but something had changed. They still stood behind the flickering flame, their faces hard, angry, but their voices had no sound. Their mouths moved, forming the same cruel words. Beneath the fury in their expressions, something else lingered, something deeper, something hidden. Ethan's breath caught.

A feeling stirred within him. Faint. Unfamiliar. Nameless.

"I... I feel something," he whispered, almost afraid to say it aloud. "But I don't know what it is."

The Orb of Reflection pulsed brightly, its glow warm, encouraging. "Perfect."

Ethan blinked in surprise.

"You have taken the first step," the Orb continued, its voice rich with understanding. "You see, Ethan, your kind, boys... men, have been taught to bury their emotions. You have heard people speak of feelings, fear, anger, sadness. These, you recognize because you have been allowed to feel them. "But tell me, Ethan... have you ever truly felt love? Not just heard about it, not just seen it, but *felt* it? Held it? Understood it?"

Ethan hesitated, his fingers tightening around the card.

"Emotions are like shadows until you give them light," the Orb continued. "You can only name them once you know them. The first step is to allow them. To let them surface. Only then can you understand them."

Ethan swallowed hard. "And if I don't know what it is?"

"Give it a name," the Orb urged. "Any name. It doesn't matter what you call it, what matters is that you acknowledge it. Because the moment you do, it becomes real. With time and practice, that name may shift. It may deepen, evolve. And one day, when you feel its true nature, you will know what its true name is. And then, Ethan... you will decide. Is this emotion right for this moment? Or does it need to be replaced with one better suited?"

Ethan sat there, heart pounding, mind swirling. For the first time in his life, he wasn't told to hide what he felt. For the first time...He was being told to understand it.

Ethan closed his eyes again, surrendering to the feeling, not just to experience it, but to truly see it, understand it, let it unravel within him. It was thick, like smoke curling through his lungs, tightening, choking, stealing the air from his chest.

"It feels suffocating," he whispered, his voice raw, as if the words themselves struggled to escape. "Like invisible chains binding me, restricting my movement, my choices... my growth. It keeps me trapped, always on edge, as if something unseen looms over me, whispering: Be careful. Don't stray. The world is dangerous."

The weight of it pressed down, a paradox, offering protection yet smothering him in the same breath. At first, it felt like safety, a heavy blanket wrapped around him on a cold night. But soon, that warmth thickened, turned oppressive, stifling. He couldn't move. He couldn't breathe. Part of him wanted to break free, to run. And yet... a smaller, quieter part hesitated. He also felt... protected?

Ethan opened his eyes. The Orb now floated beside Sarah, its gentle glow illuminating her thoughtful gaze. Something shifted at the edge of his vision. Movement.

He turned, three Aurawisps, their shimmering forms twisting, reshaping, as if molding themselves into something new. The raccoon-like creatures began to take shape, its presence both mysterious and familiar.

His fingers tightened around the Flame of Focus card. Heart pounding, he reached into his pocket, pulling out the other three cards. One by one, he opened them, his eyes scanning their contents, his mind whirling. His gaze lifted, from the Aurawisps to Sarah, to the Orb, then back to the cards in his hands.

A realization surged through him. "Overprotection," Ethan whispered. Then louder, his voice trembling with the force of understanding. "I feel overprotected! My dad, my brother… they don't understand their emotions. They're scared. Scared for me. They know I'm sensitive, and they just want to shield me from the world they've come to fear!"

The moment the words left his lips, the Aurawisps erupted into movement, bounding toward him in an excited blur of light and energy. They shimmered with delight, leaping and twisting through the air, as if celebrating his revelation. At the grove's edge, more Mystical Creatures began to emerge, dozens, hundreds, their luminous forms stepping forward, drawn by something unseen, as if a great, long-awaited event had just unfolded.

One Aurawisp, silver and glowing, crawled onto Ethan's leg. It hesitated for a moment before raising a tiny, gleaming paw to him. Ethan's breath hitched. Gently, he took its paw in his hand, his thumb brushing over the fine, silken strands of silver fur. A warmth spread through him, not suffocating this time, but grounding, anchoring. A connection. All around him, the Mystical Creatures stirred, rejoicing, as if they could feel the shift within him, the understanding, the release.

The Aurawisp bowed to him, leapt gracefully away, rejoining the others. Ethan rose to his feet, lightheaded, the weight of years of misunderstanding lifting from his chest. His gaze flickered to Sarah, then to the Orb.

"All this time..." his throat tightened, but he pushed through. "I thought they hated me."

The Orb's soft glow pulsed, a warm reassurance. "Ethan," it spoke, its voice like a ripple through the air. "those who do not understand their emotions often cast them out irresponsibly. They reflect their inner turmoil onto others while attempting to guide them. Only those who truly grasp the intricacies of emotional complexity can communicate their feelings effectively. Today, you have taken your first step on that path."

Ethan exhaled, the depth of the truth settling into his bones. He had spent so long feeling trapped, resenting their overprotection. But now, he saw it clearly, it wasn't just about him. It never had been. They weren't trying to control him. They were trying to protect him from a world they themselves feared.

From within the Heartwood Tree, a shimmering fog began to emerge, coalescing into a figure both ethereal and fluid, the Mindwright Enigma. Its form flickered between solidity and mist, caught in a delicate balance between the turmoil it sensed in the Realm of the Mind and the triumph radiating from Ethan and Sarah. Whispers of depression, anxiety, sadness, and paranoia, carried from the other four Enigmas, clung to it, shadowing its aura with unease. Yet, beneath it all, a glimmer of hope shimmered, fragile but growing.

The Mindwright Enigma drifted cautiously towards Sarah and Ethan, its presence delicate, almost hesitant. It spoke, its voice was soft, a collection of swirling emotions.

"You... you have done something remarkable. My creatures tell me, you are worthy, yet I am not fully convinced. Tell me Seekers, what have you learned from this challenge?"

Sarah and Ethan exchanged a glance, an unspoken understanding passing between them like a silent current. The weight of their journey, the trials they had faced, and the truths they had uncovered wove them together in a bond stronger than words.

Ethan was the first to speak, his voice firm yet carrying the echoes of vulnerability. He took a slow breath, his fingers curling around the skill cards he held. *This mattered.*

"I've learned that protection without understanding becomes a cage," he said, his eyes flickering with a newfound clarity. "When people act out of fear, even with good intentions, they can end up trapping the very person they want to keep safe. And sometimes...," his voice wavered, just for a moment, but he pressed on. "Sometimes, their fear disguises itself as love. It doesn't mean they don't care, it means they don't know how to show it any other way."

Sarah felt the truth of his words resonate deep within her. Her heart swelled with recognition, emotions intertwining between the past and present. She ran her fingers over the skill pins attached to her shirt, feeling each of their surfaces as she gathered her thoughts.

"I've realized," she began, her voice softer but no less certain. "That we have to trust ourselves, even when others don't understand. That their doubt, whether it comes from love, fear, or their unhealed wounds, doesn't define us. Only we can decide who we are," she exhaled, a deep, grounding breath before continuing. "And I've learned that emotions, even the difficult ones, the pain, the fear, the anger, aren't our enemies.

They're guides. They show us what needs healing, what needs attention. If we run from them, we stay lost. But if we listen...," she looked up, meeting Ethan's gaze again. "They can lead us to something greater."

A hush fell over the grove as their words settled into the air, carried by the unseen currents of the Realm of the Mind. The Mindwright Enigma hovered before them, its shimmering form shifting, absorbing every syllable with quiet reverence. The entire grove seemed to hold its breath, as if the very fabric of the realm had shifted in recognition of their truth. The Mindwright Enigma's form brightened, its outline sparking with bursts of light. It began to bounce around the grove, its movements erratic and joyful, releasing a torrent of pent-up emotions into the air, a celebration of joy. After a few moments, it floated back before them, calm now, two items materializing in its presence, a gleaming Emotional Resonant card and a delicate pin shaped like a heart with a glowing center.

"These are your rewards," it announced, its voice steadier. "The Emotional Resonant card and the Emotional Resonate pin. Carry them, and they shall aid you in your journey."

Sarah and Ethan accepted the rewards, their hands trembling. The warmth from the items seeped into their skin, filling them with a renewed sense of purpose.

The Mindwright Enigma hovered closer, its voice dropping to a near whisper. "There is a clearing, where the ancient ones once gathered not far from here, a place of beauty and peace. Rest there tonight. You will find nourishment and solace," as it began to fade back into the mist, the Mindwright floated close to Ethan, its eyes pools of understanding. "You do not need to hold me in," it murmured. "I am part of you as much as you are part of me."

With that, the Mindwright Enigma vanished, leaving behind a soft breeze that rustled through the grove.

The Orb floated closer, its glow intensifying. "Well done, Seekers. You have begun the alignment with all five Enigmas. There is hope restored in the Realm."

But before they could bask in the victory, the skies darkened, heavy clouds rolling in as thunder rumbled, shaking the very ground beneath them. Lightning slashed across the sky, a furious display of power. The dragons were not amused.

Ethan turned to Aerthis, his stomach growling in protest. "Can we eat now?"

Aerthis chuckled, its light softening. "Indeed, young one. Let's find that clearing."

And with a final glance at the stormy skies, the group set off, hearts both heavy and hopeful, ready for whatever lay ahead.

Chapter 10

The Goose in the Jar

The Heartwood Grove stood silent behind them, its glowing roots fading into the distance as Sarah, Ethan, and the Orb of Reflection ventured into the unknown. Their bodies ached from the strain of hunger and exhaustion, and their minds still carried the weight of emotions stirred by the Mindwright Enigma.

Yet they had prevailed.

Aerthis, the Orb of Reflection, hovered just ahead, its mirrored light shifting between silver and warm gold. The Mindwright Enigma had left them with few words but a single suggestion; "To find rest they must head to the clearing of the ancient ones. There, your bodies and minds may breathe."

Ethan exhaled. "Do you think the Enigma knew how drained we are?"

Sarah glanced at the Orb. "I think it knew we needed more than rest, we needed understanding."

Aerthis pulsed. "Understanding and care are intertwined."

As they moved on, the tangled branches above gave way to an open sky still swirling with dark clouds, as if searching for something, restless in their looming presence. Wisps of silver mist clung to the air, swirling around their ankles as they stepped onto the soft, moss-laden ground. A small meadow unfurled before them, its hidden presence veiled in a cool, spectral glow, as if the land itself exhaled a breath both ancient and knowing. The distant hum of unseen energy pulsed through the air, faint but steady, like the heartbeat of the Realm itself.

But it was not the open space that caught their attention, it was the trees. Towering among the grass, their trunks shimmered like liquid opal, iridescent hues shifting with every movement, as if reflecting unseen truths buried within the Realm. Their sprawling branches stretched toward the sky, each leaf trembling with a whispering resonance, a soft, melodic hum that wove through the air like an unsung lullaby.

Sarah and Ethan stepped cautiously into the clearing, their breaths hitching as the sight before them unraveled like a forgotten dream brought to life. The air here felt different, softer, as if cradling them in an unseen embrace. A hush settled over the space, not of silence, but of reverence, as though the very ground they stood upon recognized the presence of hope.

Their eyes widened, and their mouths parted in wonder as they took in the trees before them. Adorned with an abundance of fruit unlike anything they had ever seen, the branches stretched outward like celestial offerings, each bearing treasures that shimmered with an otherworldly glow.

Some of the fruit glowed with a golden warmth, their soft radiance spilling gentle light onto the mist-draped earth, illuminating patches of grass like fallen embers of a dying star. . Others pulsed with violet hues, their skins flecked with silver specks, as if they had been plucked from the night sky itself. The rhythm of their light matched the faint hum vibrating through the leaves, a silent song whispered between tree and fruit, between earth and air.

A sense of sacredness wove through the clearing, threading itself into the soil, the air, the very marrow of the trees. Here, the chaos of Dysquinox had not touched. Here, time did not rush forward nor pull them back, it simply *was*. And in that stillness, something unspoken awaited them, something ancient and knowing, something waiting to be understood.

To the left, the Lyren Pear Tree stood tall, its golden pears emitting a faint, luminous mist. The scent, sweet, calming, drifted toward them like a lullaby. Beside it, a Crescendo Plum Vine curled along a rocky outcrop, its violet plums pulsating with a quiet rhythm, as if in harmony with the heartbeat of the Realm itself. And near the farthest edge of the clearing, the Solace Apple Tree spread its ancient branches, bearing iridescent apples that changed color with each breath of wind.

Ethan's stomach growled, breaking the moment's quiet reverence.

Sarah hesitated. "Is this fruit safe to eat?"

The Orb pulsed in a gentle golden glow. "What lay before you is no ordinary fruit, for it holds the exact ingredients one needs to restore not just their physical energy, but your mental and emotional energies as well, all are important, all are vital."

The clearing thrummed with an ancient, quiet power, a presence that seemed to breathe through the earth itself.

Sarah and Ethan stood beneath the luminous canopy, their eyes tracing the soft glow of the hanging fruits, their light shifting like whispers caught in a gentle current. The air was thick with something unspoken, something untouched by time, a richness that neither of them had ever felt before.

Ethan exhaled, his breath curling in the cool air. He reached toward a pearl-like fruit, its surface rippling with iridescent waves of silver and blue. His fingers hesitated just before making contact. "These... they don't feel real. Like they belong in a dream."

The Orb of Reflection hovered beside him. "They are more real than anything you have ever consumed," it murmured. "For they remain pure, untouched by the poisons of your world. Here, in the Mystical Forest, energy is given as it was always meant to be whole, untainted, free from the corruption that weakens body, mind, and spirit."

Sarah's brow creased as she plucked a golden-shelled nut from a spiraled vine, rolling its smooth surface between her fingertips. "What do you mean by poisons?"

The Orb pulsed, a gentle but insistent radiance. "Your world is filled with sustenance that has been stripped of its essence, altered until it is but a shadow of what it once was. What you call nourishment has been burdened with impurities that cloud your mind, deplete your energy, and unravel the delicate connections that tether you to clarity, strength, and purpose. Here, food does not merely sustain, it awakens. It heals. It fortifies the very foundation of your being."

Sarah and Ethan exchanged a glance, the weight of the Orb's words settling in like the first stirrings of a long-forgotten truth.

Ethan turned his attention back to the fruit resting in his palm, its glow pulsing in rhythm with his heartbeat.

"So… what does this one do?"

The Orb's voice softened, reverent. "That is the Celestara Pearlfruit. It carries within it the rhythm of the cosmic tides, the natural flow of thought and intuition unburdened by interference. When consumed, it awakens the Mind's Flow, allowing your thoughts to glide effortlessly, like a river free of debris. Your mind becomes clear, your awareness sharpens, and, for those truly attuned, glimpses of possible futures may reveal themselves in moments of reflection."

Sarah turned the nut in her hand, watching silver swirls ripple beneath its translucent shell. "So, it helps us think better?"

The Orb's glow deepened. "More than that. The poisons in your world distort not only thought, but the way you feel. Your emotions, your focus, even your sense of self, they are tangled by the impurities you ingest, thrown into chaos by substances never meant to reside within you. These, in contrast, are uncorrupted. They do not merely clear the mind; they restore it. They align you with yourself."

Ethan let out a short breath, his lips tilting into a wry smile. "I could use that. My brain feels like a storm half the time."

The Orb drifted closer, its mirrored surface reflecting their faces back at them, but something in their reflections looked… lighter. Clearer. As if, for just a moment, they saw themselves without distortion. "Your minds, your bodies, your very existence, are delicate systems," the Orb continued, its tone gentle but unwavering. "Every thought, every emotion, every breath is a thread in the vast complexity of your being. A single drop of poison can fray those threads, disrupting the balance that sustains you. It begins subtly, fatigue, uncertainty, moments of fog that you dismiss as trivial. But when the body is denied what it needs, it fights back first in defiance, manifesting in what you call illness. And if it is ignored… it succumbs to defeat."

A hush settled over the clearing. Sarah felt a sinking weight in her chest, not fear, not regret, but the awareness of something she had never considered before.

"Proper care is not a luxury," the Orb murmured. "It is the foundation of all that you are. Without it, your strength fades. Your clarity fractures. And the connection between your mind, your body, and your spirit, your very existence, begins to unravel."

Sarah swallowed, her fingers tightening around the golden nut in her palm.

Ethan exhaled, his gaze lifting toward the glowing trees around them. "Maybe… it's time we start taking care of ourselves the right way."

The Orb pulsed warmly. "Indeed. The choice has always been yours."

Ethan took a cautious bite, his eyes widening as warmth flooded his mind. "Whoa…"

Sarah raised a brow. "What?"

Ethan blinked. "I… I just had this unbelievable vision, it was like we were in some kind of village, strange and weird. There was a storm, and..." Ethan paused for a moment.

"And?" Sarah cried out.

Ethan looks into Sarahs eyes "And a dragon, hidden within that storm!"

The Orb's glow shimmered. "Your mind is awakening, perceptions of what may lay ahead."

Sarah raised the golden-shelled nut she held. "And this one?"

"The Aurik Shellnut contains the echoes of knowledge itself. Its essence forges an Unbreakable Mind-Link, strengthening memory and accelerating learning.

Those who consume its nectar gain the ability to absorb information with ease, even unlocking memories long buried beneath time's weight."

Sarah cracked it open, revealing a pool of glowing amber liquid inside. She dipped her finger into it, feeling a tingle rush up her arm. "So… I could read something once and *never* forget it?"

"Not exactly, the wisdom it offers is not in remembering alone, it is in understanding."

Sarah met Ethan's gaze. "This could change everything."

Ethan nodded, looked up at the silver-leafed vines surrounding them. "And those?"

"The Verdant Stargrain is a source of boundless endurance. It fuels the Astral Vital Core, granting energy that does not burn out quickly. It shields the mind from exhaustion and fortifies the body against weariness for longer lengths of time."

Ethan plucked a handful of the starry seeds and placed them in his palm. "So…no more sugar crashes?"

Sarah studied a cluster of indigo leaves nearby. Their soft whispers sent shivers down her spine. "What about these?"

"The Shadowleaf Whisperbloom holds the Silent Knowing. It sharpens the mind's agility, granting clarity even in the densest fog of thought. When consumed, it allows one to focus better, absorbing vast knowledge without mental fatigue."

Sarah plucked a leaf and inhaled its earthen scent. "Like keeping a sharp mind, no matter how long I study?"

"Not just study Sarah. *Understand.*"

Ethan's eyes were drawn to a cluster of crimson berries glowing like embers along the riverbank. "And these?"

"The Emberdusk Dewberry ignites the Visionstream, revealing hidden connections and unseen truths.

It enhances perception, sharpening the link between mind and intuition, allowing you to see where others remain blind."

Ethan reached for a berry, gently holding it in his fingers. "So, it's like... super intuition?"

"Intuition honed into sight."

Sarah, now intrigued, lifted a golden rootfruit that pulsed in her hand like a heartbeat. "And this?"

"The Sunflare Rootfruit grants a source of energy unlike the erratic surges of your world's sustenance, this provides a steady flame, fueling body and mind much longer," said the Orb. "Now, eat, rest and reflect, for tomorrow will be a long day."

They approached the trees cautiously. Ethan plucked a pear, and the moment his fingers closed around it, warmth spread through his palms. Sarah did the same, selecting an apple that shimmered from green to silver. As they bit into the fruit, a rush of energy, clarity, and peace filled their senses.

Aerthis floated between them. "Do you feel it?"

Ethan swallowed. "Yeah! Like... the weight of exhaustion just lifted."

Sarah nodded. "But it's more than just physical. It's like... my thoughts feel clearer."

Aerthis pulsed. "That is the nature of care."

They settled beneath the Solace Apple Tree, the grass beneath them softer than any bed they had ever known. The Orb drifted closer, its voice patient. "Many believe care is the act of resting when weary, eating when hungry, or breathing when overwhelmed. But true self-care is not reactionary, it is intentional. It is the act of sustaining yourself, not recovering from what has already depleted you."

Sarah let the words sink in.

She had spent so long ignoring her needs, trying to prove herself, that rest had always felt like something she *earned*, not something she *needed*.

Ethan shifted. "But sometimes, things happen. Things that don't give you time to rest."

Aerthis glowed a deep, thoughtful blue. "Yes. There will be times when circumstances demand your presence, times when rest cannot come immediately. But if you have neglected care when it was *available*," The Orb's glow flickered. "You will face those challenges in a state of vulnerability that could have been avoided. You will be vulnerable, not just in body, but in mind and spirit."

Sarah glanced at Ethan, the memory of their last trial still vivid. "Like how we felt in the Heartwood Grove."

Ethan nodded slowly, the weight of the moment pressing against him. "We were exhausted," he admitted, his voice barely above a whisper. "And hungry. And that made everything feel heavier... harder." His fingers curled slightly as he searched for the right words, for a way to explain the way exhaustion stripped them raw, leaving no space for reason, only reaction. "When we're drained like that, it's like... our emotions don't wait for permission. They rush through, slipping past our thoughts. Instead of thinking first, we just react!" He exhaled, shaking his head, the memory of it still fresh, still aching. "It's like trying to hold water in your hands when you're too tired to close your fingers. It just spills out, frustration, sadness, anger, whatever is there, it rushes forward before we even realize it," his eyes lifted to Sarah's, a quiet understanding passing between them. "We weren't just upset. We were running on empty. And when there's nothing left to hold us together, everything we try to keep inside... it just escapes."

Aerthis hummed. "Indeed. A well-nurtured self is resilient. Adaptable. Enduring. Without those qualities, challenges that could be overcome will instead overwhelm."

Sarah ran a hand through the grass. "So... self-care isn't selfish."

The Orb's glow warmed. "On the contrary. It is what allows you to be of service to others when they need you most. It ensures that when the trials come, you do not meet them fragile and uncertain, but steady and ready."

Ethan exhaled. "That... makes sense."

Sarah looked up at the sky. "We can't always control when the challenges come. But we can make sure we're ready for them when they do."

Aerthis pulsed in agreement.

A heavy silence settled over the clearing, not empty, but charged, as if the very air was waiting.

Sarah's breath slowed, her senses sharpening. Just beyond the tree line, something caught her eye. A stone wall, half-concealed by thick green vines. "What's that?" she murmured, already moving.

Ethan followed as she reached out, pushing back the tangle of ivy. Beneath the creeping foliage, a symbol emerged, an etched jar, faint yet unmistakable, with something trapped inside. Below it, ancient words, weathered but legible, whispered a name lost to time.

"The goose in the jar."

Ethan's brows furrowed. "What does that mean?"

Before Sarah could respond, Aerthis floated closer, its glow deepening. "It is a test of the mind, one that has endured across Realms. A challenge left by the Ancient Ones."

Sarah ran her fingers over the carving, a shiver passing through her. The stone was warm, almost alive beneath her touch. "What, like a riddle?"

At her words, the Reflective Wall trembled. A ripple of energy coursed across its surface, the stone shifting like liquid light. As if awakened, words began to emerge, etched not by time, but by something deeper. Sarah took an instinctive step back, her pulse quickening.

The Mystical Forest seemed to still around them, the towering trees watching, waiting. The Reflective Wall stood before them, its strange glow shifting like a mirage. At its center, the carving deepened, revealing an intricate image: a goose, pressed within the confines of a glass jar, its wings trapped against the curved walls. Below, elegant script curled into existence, its letters gleaming with significance.

"Hypothetically, there is an ancient and precious glass jar, an artifact forged from the light of the Ethereal Nexus, its crystalline form shaped by the wisdom of the ancients.

The jar's base is wide, a foundation that holds the echoes of past custodians, those who walked the path of Strength, Evolution, Love, and Fulfillment to bring harmony into this Realm.

Within its delicate walls, the golden ashes of their wisdom rest, remnants of the knowledge gathered through centuries of trials, all to preserve harmony within the Realm of the Mind.

By some unseen design, a single tiny egg, carried by the winds of possibility, drifted through the narrow neck of the jar. From this tiny egg, life emerged, a fledgling, no larger than a whisper of thought.

The young goose grew, its wings pressing against the glass, its form now too great to leave the way it entered.

A lasting paradox emerges from this event. The jar is sacred, a vessel of wisdom, and to break it would scatter the ashes, precious to this Realm, dissolving the legacy of those who came before.

The neck of the jar is too small to force the goose out, to attempt this would wound the goose, severing the thread of life gifted to it by the Realm. To sever this delicate thread would unravel the Realm's existence.

To let goose remain is to accept the pain from its entrapment, caging life in stillness and suffering, thus breaking the Realms' true harmony.

Only those, pure of heart, pure of mind and sensitive to those who need assistance hold the potential to see the truth hidden within this dilemma.

Now that you have read this riddle, it will be placed within your thoughts forever. You may offer a single answer, if it is correct, you shall be free of this dilemma. If you fail, you will be lost within the labyrinth of your mind, trapped in the illusions of doubt and uncertainty."

Sarah reached out, tracing the final words, feeling the hum of latent energy beneath the stone. Her throat felt dry. Sarah hesitated, her voice softer. "It feels… old…important."

The Orb of Reflection pulsed, its mirrored surface shifting as it spoke. "This is a test of perception, placed here by the Ancient Ones long ago."

Sarah turned toward the floating sphere. *"The Ancient Ones?"*

"They were the First Enigmas," the Orb replied. "Born from the Ethereal Nexus at the dawn of the Realm, they wove the first threads of wisdom into this world, embedding their knowledge in trials such as this."

Ethan and Sarah exchanged a glance, an unspoken understanding passing between them.

Ethan exhaled. "So... this is more than just a riddle?"

The Orb brightened. "Indeed. To read the riddle is to invite its question into your mind. Be warned, once you have read it, it will linger, whispering through your thoughts until you find the truth it holds."

The weight of the clearing seemed to shift, the air pressing closer. The Orb's light pulsed once more, its voice carrying something solemn. "But know this," it continued. "As the writing states, you may offer only one answer. Choose wisely."

Ethan hesitated, his glance casted back to the wall and the carvings. "And if we get it wrong?"

The Orb's glow dimmed, its voice softer. "You will be lost within the maze of your uncertainty, unable to escape the shadows of an unsolved question."

A chill ran down Sarah's spine. She turned back to the riddle, her heart pounding. This was no simple test. It was something far greater, a doorway to understanding, or a descent into doubt.

Sarah and Ethan had both read it, and now, there was no turning back.

"Rest now, Explorers. Tomorrow will test you in ways you have yet to imagine." Aerthis's voice resonated through the clearing, low and steady, carrying the weight of something unspoken.

Sarah let out a slow breath, stepping away from the Reflective Wall. Her mind churned, tangled with thoughts she couldn't quite grasp. . She found a large patch of moss, its softness beckoning, and lowered herself onto it. Yet even as she lay down, sleep felt distant. Her thoughts still circling the riddle, the warning, and what was to come.

Ethan settled beside her, silent. The warmth of the Sunflare Rootfruit surging on his tongue as he took another bite, his gaze fixed on the ancient wall. It felt different now, more than just stone, more than just a riddle. He swallowed the weight of unspoken questions pressing against him.

A slow heaviness crept over them both. Their limbs grew leaden, their thoughts drifting like mist over water. As their breathing deepened, the Orb hovered above, its glow fading into a soft ember. A warmth settled over them, invisible but undeniable, like a thick down blanket gently laid across their bodies.

Just as Sarah was surrendering to the quiet pull of sleep, her eyes fluttered open. A flicker of awareness stirred within her. She turned her head, voice hushed but sharp. "You called us Explorers…? I thought we were Seekers."

The Orb pulsed, a golden ripple expanding outward. "You were Seekers, Sarah. But you have surpassed the first five challenges, beginning the alignment with the Mystical Enigmas. To move forward now is no longer to seek… but to explore."

Sarah's brow furrowed as she propped herself up on her elbows. "Explore what?"

Aerthis's glow dimmed, its voice dropping into something softer, almost reverent. "The depths of the Enigmas. . Their true nature cannot simply be found, it must be ventured into, unraveled, understood beyond mere discovery.

Five more trials await you here in the Mystical Forest. They will test your resilience, your adaptability, and your endurance."

The words lingered, heavy with promise.

Sarah's breath hitched as exhaustion crashed over her again, deeper this time, pulling her downward like unseen hands. The weight of her body, of her thoughts, became too much to fight.

"Rest," the Orb murmured, its glow dimming into the night.

Sarah hardly registered the words as sleep pulled her under. Yet, just before the darkness swallowed her completely, a final thought surfaced, whispering, lingering, refusing to fade.

What lies beyond that which we seek… must be explored.

Both Sarah and Ethan drifted into a deep, peaceful sleep.

A voice. Resonant. And loud filled their minds.

What about the goose in the jar?

Ethan's eyes snapped open. His breath hitched as he bolted upright. "What?" The word came out hoarse, half-formed, his pulse hammering. Morning had arrived, golden light stretching across the clearing, the echo of the voice still pressed against his mind. It wasn't a dream. It had been too clear, too deliberate.

Beside him, Sarah was already awake, her expression sharp with confusion. "You heard it too?" she asked, her voice low.

Ethan turned to her, his stomach twisting. "Where did that come from?" His words held both curiosity and unease, the weight of the unknown settling over them.

The Orb, now glowing brighter, drifted ahead, its presence grounding yet unreadable. "Time to move, Explorers. The journey ahead is long."

Ethan exhaled, pushing himself to his feet. He reached for Sarah's hand, pulling her up beside him.

Sarah stepped toward the stream that wound lazily through the clearing. Kneeling, she cupped the cool water in her hands and drank, the crisp taste waking her senses. The weight of the morning, of the riddle still hanging in the air, pressed at the edges of her thoughts.

Nearby, Ethan gathered a handful of nuts, slipping them into his pockets, mentally preparing for whatever lay ahead. He exhaled, trying to shake the unease still lingering in his chest.

And then...

What about the goose in the jar?

The voice again. Closer this time.

Ethan spun, heart pounding, scanning the trees, the rocks, the shifting light. Only seeing Sarah and Aerthis. Ethan swallowed hard, he wondered if all this was too much, yet the voice he was hearing seemed so real, so...demanding.

Sarah and Ethan joined Aerthis, turning one last time to take in the peaceful place that harbored them for the night. The symbol of the goose in the jar is all that remains on the stone wall, the riddle had faded away.

As the three made their way through the Mystical Forest, the voice rang in both Sarah and Ethan's ears once more, relentless, and persuasive, as if demanding them to answer.

What about the goose in the jar?

Sarah turns to Ethan, the look on his face said it all.

Frustrated, Ethan spoke "This is driving me nuts. I can't get the whole goose in the jar thing out of my head, its like the dam goose crawled inside me and is now asking me how to set it free."

Sarah ponders for a moment, convinced she could solve it. "We can't hurt the goose, can't break the jar, can't let it starve, and can't just keep feeding it! Every solution breaks one of the rules."

Ethan replies. "What if we found a way to lift the goose out of the jar without harming it, Like, using some kind of levitation or precise tools to gently guide it through the neck of the jar?"

"But the neck of the jar is far too small to fit the goose through, it floated in as a tiny egg and formed into a goose. If we could make the goose smaller or maybe stretch the jar's neck just for a moment, that could work. The goose gets out, the ashes stay pure, and the jar remains intact."

"But think about it. If the jar represents the wisdom of the Ancient Ones, isn't altering it, even temporarily, disrespecting its sanctity?"

Sarah slumps. "Yeah... changing the jar even for a second would break its sacred balance. It feels like a cheat, besides, it's made of glass, you cannot stretch glass without heating it, and that would certainly cook the goose."

"Not to mention, what it would do to the ashes" Ethan replied.

"Reflection begins with seeing the whole, not just the parts." Said the orb mystically, as if it knew the solution to the riddle.

Sarah, Ethan and Aerthis continued into the forest, the sounds of rolling thunder looming not far off.

Chapter 11

The Eye of Insight

Sarah and Ethan walked behind Aerthis as the forest path began to narrow. To their right, a steep jagged rock wall towered above their heads, its rough surface sharp beneath their fingertips. To their left, a sheer drop vanished into the misty abyss below. The ledge beneath their feet thinned with each step until there was no room to walk side by side. They pressed against the stone, their chests scraping against its uneven surface, as their heels hovered perilously over the void. The air was dense with tension, each breath sharp with the scent of damp earth and the distant rush of unseen water.

"Are you sure this is the way?" Ethan called out, his voice edged with unease as he sensed Sarah's apprehension.

Aerthis floated ahead, unbothered, its glow unwavering. "The true way to insight is not something you seek, Ethan, it is something to be explored."

Sarah exhaled through clenched teeth. That was not reassuring to her, she had always felt this inexplicable urge to do exciting and adventurous things, willing to step beyond her comfort zone, yet this was testing her boundaries and her confidence.

Suddenly, the ground betrayed her, loose rock crumbling away as her foot slipped from the ledge. Her world twisted, gravity trying to yank her toward the abyss. A sharp gasp tore from her lips as the earth vanished beneath her. For one heart-stopping second, the void tried to swallow her whole. Then, pressure.

Ethan's hand pressed firmly against her back, anchoring her. "I got you," he said, his voice steady, the warmth of his grip grounding her.

Sarah clung to the wall, her breath ragged. She turned her head, her eyes locking onto his. "Thanks," she whispered, her voice trembling.

Ethan nodded, his expression calm despite the tension in his jaw. "You got this."

Step by step, they moved forward, the weight of the abyss below ever-present. To distract her, Ethan spoke, his voice a quiet thread between them. "I used to crawl onto the roof of my house when I needed to be alone."

Sarah frowned, focusing on his words to steady her nerves. "Your roof?"

"Yeah," He took another careful step forward. "I'd climb out the window, hold onto the cracks in the shingles to reach the peak and just sit there.

My brother's terrified of heights, so it was the one place I knew he'd never follow me. It became my sanctuary."

Sarah let out a breath that was almost a laugh. "I'm not a fan of heights either," she admitted. "This is kind of freaking me out right now."

Ethan shifted closer, his presence a steady reassurance. "I got you, Sarah."

She nodded, swallowing hard, and pressed on.

The path curved sharply, and as they rounded the corner, the narrow trail widened into a small ledge, a surreal, suspended platform above the endless drop. At the far end of the ledge, nestled into the rock face, loomed a massive cavern. Its entrance shimmered like liquid crystal, carved by forces beyond comprehension. The air vibrated with something unseen, something ancient, sending a prickle down their spines. The crystalline archway refracted the light from Aerthis, casting fragmented beams across their faces, painting them in hues of violet, blue, and gold.

Aerthis pulsed, its voice reverent. "This is the entrance to the Prism Cavern."

Sarah exhaled, her breath uneven. Ethan stood beside her, still as stone, his gaze fixed on the shimmering archway before them. The weight of something unseen pressed against them both, a pull at the edges of their consciousness, stirring emotions they had no words for yet. The air was thick with an energy that hummed in their bones. The cavern was waiting.

Aerthis drifted before them, its glow shifting into a prismatic hue, casting fractured light against the crystalline walls. "To enter is to begin a new journey, not as Seekers, but as Explorers."

Sarah looked puzzled. "What's the difference?"

The Orb's glow pulsed, slow and measured. "To seek is to move with intent. A Seeker has a question, a longing, a need.

They chase answers, believing truth is something to be uncovered, something waiting to be grasped."

Ethan shifted his stance, considering. "And an Explorer?"

Aerthis's light deepened, stretching across the cavern entrance like liquid gold. "An Explorer moves without expectation. They do not seek a single truth, they walk into the unknown for the sake of discovery itself. They do not ask, 'Will I find?' They ask, 'What is to be found?'"

A silence stretched between them, thick with unspoken thought.

Aerthis continued. "A Seeker looks behind doors, hoping to find that which they are searching for. An Explorer steps into the unknown, even when they do not know where it leads, not for the sake of risk, but for the sake of learning that which has been hidden."

Sarah paused. She had always sought understanding, ways to solve the puzzle, ways to make sense of herself, of this world, of the challenges laid before them. But this... this was different.

"So now we stop looking for answers?" Ethan asked.

Aerthis pulsed with knowing warmth. "As Explorer's you must uncover the questions, you did not know existed, only then will the answers make sense."

The words sank into them, deep and heavy.

Sarah's lips pressed together, not from fear, but from the sheer weight of realization pressing against her mind. Seeking had given her something solid to hold onto. Exploring meant stepping forward without knowing what would catch her, leaving her with a very uneasy feeling.

Aerthis turned toward the cavern's gaping entrance, its glow stretching forward like an invitation. "To step forward is to release expectation. To embrace the journey itself.

This is the path of the Explorer, the path of the unknown."

Ethan straightened. "What are we supposed to do?"

"The Prism Cavern is no mere place, it is a mirror to your very soul," Aerthis intoned, its voice vibrating through the crystalline walls. "Every step will strip away illusion, revealing not just who you wish to be, but who you truly are. These prisms do not simply reflect; they shift with your thoughts, bending to your clarity or twisting in your chaos. Doubt will fracture your image. Fear will turn the path against you."

Aerthis pressed on. "Enter with unwavering awareness. Beneath these gleaming surfaces lie the truths you've buried, the emotions you've locked away. To ignore them is to fear yourself, to deny the parts of you that ache to be seen. This path demands more than courage; it demands discipline."

Sarah and Ethan exchanged uneasy glances.

"What remains unseen does not wither, it grows," Aerthis warned. "Left ignored, wounds deepen, twisting into something far worse than the pain that birthed them. Denial does not protect you; it binds you. You cannot heal what you refuse to see. You cannot transform what you push away. Trust in yourself. Only by facing the hidden can you reclaim your power. Through the Eye of Insight, the veil will lift, beneath it, your truest self awaits."

"And what is the Eye of Insight?" Sarah asked curiously.

Aerthis drifted on, its glow darkening to a rich, pulsing ember. "A crystalline sphere, small in form yet infinite in wisdom. It does not reflect, it reveals. Peeling away illusions, it exposes the truth that lies beneath, whether you are ready or not. To hold the Eye of Insight, you must prove that you are willing to see, not just the world around you, but the raw, unfiltered reality of who you are. Achieve this and your connection with the Insightborne will grow."

A chill traced down Sarah's spine. She had faced trials before, conquered riddles, illusions, and puzzles meant to deceive. But this... this felt different. More intimate. More personal. She never felt comfortable revealing certain parts of herself. It was part of her survival strategy, letting go of the control was something that made her feel insecure, and she didn't think she was ready to do that.

Beside her, Ethan shifted uncomfortably. His breath became shallow, his palms turning sweaty. The weight of the past pulled at him, the voices he had fought so hard to silence now roaring in his mind.

"Grow thicker skin!"

"Don't be so sensitive!"

"Cry-baby!"

"Man up!"

Each word struck like a lash, unwelcome yet familiar. They had carved themselves into him, shaping the way he saw himself. Somewhere along the way, he had stopped fighting them. He had swallowed the shame, convinced himself that if he could just be tougher, if he could just feel less, maybe, just maybe, he wouldn't feel so broken.

But deep inside, beneath the armor he had forced himself to wear, another truth stirred. A quiet rebellion.

Ethan had spent his whole life trying to be what *they* wanted, molding himself into a version that felt like an ill-fitting costume, heavy, suffocating, and not his own. Even in the sanctuary of his room, where no one was watching, he still hid, from them, from the world, from himself.

Shadow Sage was everything he wished he could be, fearless, powerful, respected... in control. In the game, he charged into battle without hesitation, faced impossible odds, and emerged victorious. But in the real world, he felt small, invisible.

No matter how hard he tried to measure up, to be what his father and brother expected, his efforts were met with silence.

When his father asked him to complete a task, he did it. When his mother needed help, he was there. But there was no gratitude, no recognition, just an unspoken expectation that he would do what he was told... never asked. He then faded into the background once it was done. He recalls his mother's voice. "Little boys are to be seen and not heard!" Teaching Ethan that he wasn't a person of value, but a mere object, a tool to be used when needed, hidden away when not.

"*What's the point?*" The thought curled inside him like a whisper of defeat. No matter what he did, it was never enough. In their eyes, he was never enough. Ethan clenched his jaw and shook his head, trying to shove the flood of thoughts back into the dark chasm where they always hid. It was a ritual, one he had perfected, a constant battle of burying, suppressing, pretending. Over and over again. "*Not now. Not here. I need to be strong!*"

"Ethan?" A voice, distant yet insistent, pulled him back. "Ethan? Snap out of it."

His breath hitched as he blinked, focusing on Sarah. Her emerald eyes searched his, filled with concern.

"Are you okay?" she asked.

Ethan forced himself to straighten, to push the weight down like he always did. "Yeah, I'm fine," he said, his voice too casual, too controlled. He glanced her way but avoided her eyes. "Let's just do this."

But the words felt hollow. His chest tightened as he tried again to look at her, to offer some reassurance, but he couldn't. If the Eye of Insight could strip away every mask, every carefully crafted lie... would there be anything left of him underneath? Would he even want to see what remained?

A warmth pressed against his hand. Sarah. She had reached for him, her fingers wrapping around his, her grip firm. As if she could feel the storm inside him. As if, somehow, it was her own.

"Hey," She tugged at his hand, demanding his attention. "I don't know what we're about to find in there, but what I *do* know is this, going in with *you*, the real you, makes me feel a whole lot better."

Ethan hesitated, his throat tight. "To be honest, Sarah… I don't even know who I am anymore. I feel so lost."

A small, knowing smile touched her lips. "Well, that makes two of us," she said. "So why don't we go find out who we are... together?" She rose to her feet and, without hesitation, pulled Ethan up with her.

Hand in hand, they stepped into the cavern. The moment they crossed the threshold, the air shifted. The temperature dropped, and a resonant hum filled the space, a sound that wasn't heard, but felt.

Towering crystalline structures surrounded them, stretching toward the cavern's high ceiling like frozen beams of light. The walls pulsed with veins of opalescent minerals, their glow in constant flux, breathing in and out like a living thing. Rainbow fragments of light danced through the space, cast by the prisms that filled the labyrinth before them. Some prisms stood smooth and unyielding, reflecting their surroundings with sharp clarity. Others shimmered and warped, their reflections bending like water disturbed by an unseen force.

Ethan stepped closer to one of the prisms, his reflection staring back at him. But as he tilted his head, the image twisted, his face shifting into something blurred, uncertain. He recoiled. "Whoa!"

Sarah reached out, her fingertips grazing the cold surface of another prism. As soon as she touched it, the reflection fractured, splitting into countless versions of herself, each one subtly different. Some looked weary. Some looked confident. One gazed back at her with piercing judgment... *Not good enough.*

The words weren't spoken, but she heard them all the same. Her stomach twisted, and she pulled her hand back. The reflection faded, but the unease remained. Suddenly her desire to not be there, to not be seen, struck her. Her need for invisibility was due to her peers mocking her, this created a feeling within her that she was not good enough.

Aerthis' voice resonated. "Your first task is to see. Not just with your eyes, but with your awareness. The prisms will show you what is hidden, the distortions within your own perception. You must identify them before they consume the path."

Ethan spoke up. "Great. So, a house of mirrors, a haunted house of mirrors to be exact."

Sarah didn't laugh. She couldn't. Her gaze remained locked on the fragmented reflections before her, each fractured piece twisting and warping with every unspoken doubt. The more she stared, the more unfamiliar her face became, as if the prisms were reflecting not just her image, but every uncertainty she carried within. She felt more desperate by the minute, trapped by the reflections in front of her. With each passing minute the intensity grew stronger.

As they ventured deeper into the cavern, the prisms became more reactive. Every hesitation sent ripples through the reflections, distorting the light and twisting their path into chaos. However, when they tried to apply the skills they learned in the previous challenges, by steadying their minds, the prisms briefly responded in kind, aligning, settling, revealing a clear way forward. But that clarity was fleeting.

Ethan felt it first, the creeping doubt that had lived inside him for as long as he could remember. *Am I strong enough? Do I belong here?* The moment the thoughts surfaced, the prisms trembled. His reflection blurred, his face dissolving into a formless shadow. The path flickered, becoming unstable beneath his feet.

Sarah tried to stand tall as a familiar weight coiled around her, *what if I make the wrong choice? What if I am not good enough?* Her need for control, for certainty, pressed down on her like an iron grip. The prisms shattered into a kaleidoscope of versions of herself, each one whispering conflicting thought, feeding the relentless storm in her mind. She squeezed her eyes shut and pressed her palms against her temples. "This is not right," she muttered.

"No," Ethan said, his voice quiet but firm. "It's us. *We're* doing this. Our own doubts are distorting everything." Sarah looked up at him, blinking against the weight of her thoughts. He wasn't just guessing, he was right.

And then, like a jolt of understanding, she remembered. The Mindwright Enigma. It amplified emotions, magnified them, making them feel far more intense. Sarah sat down hard, her breath unsteady, thoughts racing through her mind. *Emotions... amplification... intensity...*

It suddenly hit her. "*Volume!*" she gasped, her eyes widening.

Ethan, still catching his breath, looked at her, confused. "Huh?"

"It's the Mindwright, Ethan," she said, urgency rising in her voice. "It's not creating these emotions, it's *amplifying* them."

Ethan frowned, wiping a hand down his face. "Okay... and?"

"Think about it. When the volume of something is too high, what do you do?"

"Turn it down?" he guessed.

Sarah pointed toward the prisms, her mind piecing everything together. "Exactly! Everything we've been seeing, the doubt, the criticism, the harsh judgments, they're distortions, not reality. The Mindwright is amplifying our feelings, but they're still *our* feelings. We're the ones feeding them."

Ethan's gaze flickered to the shattered reflections around them. "So... what do we do?"

"Aerthis told us the only way forward is *awareness*, right? Awareness leads to clarity, and clarity leads to truth."

"Yeah," Ethan said.

Sarah leaned in. "*What if we turn the volume down?* What if we stop letting these amplified feelings control us? If we remember that these thoughts, aren't *who we are*, but small, infected parts of our minds, things we *can* identify, and work on, while we focus on our good parts?"

"So... instead of focusing on what we *think* others expect from us, we focus on who we are?" Ethan said.

Sarah nodded, determination settling in her bones. For years, she had been her own worst critic, convincing herself that others judged her harshly, when in fact, it was her self-judgment being amplified. She questioned, had anyone truly held her to these impossible standards, or had she built that cage all on her own? She turned back to the prisms, her reflection still fragmented. But now, she saw it for what it was, not reality, but over exaggeration...an amplification!

She hesitated for a moment, doubt still clinging to her like a shadow. But deep down, beneath the noise, she *knew* the answer. Taking a slow, steady breath, she pressed her hand against the fractured shards and whispered.

"I know who I am... I am creative. I am intelligent. And I care. I am a good person."

The words felt foreign on her tongue, as if she were telling herself a lie she desperately wanted to believe. A lifetime of self-doubt pushed back against them, whispering that she wasn't *enough*, that she had to be *more*.

But she refused to listen. She repeated it, stronger this time, her voice carrying weight, determination. She didn't *feel* it, she *knew* it. And for the first time, she chose to *believe it*.

The fragments trembled, then shimmered. Shifted. Merged. Her reflection solidified, not fractured or distorted, but whole. *Steady*. The path brightened.

Ethan watched in awe. His reflection still loomed before him, faceless, uncertain. The voices of his past clawed at him, whispering that he was weak, that feeling made him *less*. That no matter what he did, he would never be enough.

But *was that true*? Or had he carried those words for so long that they had become a part of him?

He exhaled shakily and took a step forward. His heart pounded as he met his own gaze. "I *am* enough," he murmured. "I *am* a man. But my strength is not in being emotionless. My strength is in *feeling*. In caring. In connecting. I am not a wall. I am not a stone. *I am... me*."

The shadows in the glass shuddered... then faded. For the first time in his life, Ethan saw himself clearly. A kind, caring person, with so much to give to the world. His reflection sharpened, no longer blurred by doubt. The prisms aligned. The way forward revealed itself. At the heart of the cavern, floating above a pedestal of shimmering crystal, rested the Eye of Insight.

It was breathtaking. Small, no larger than a grapefruit, and impossibly intricate.

Its smooth, glass-like surface rippled with ever-shifting hues, subtle prismatic waves undulating beneath. The swirling patterns resembled the iris of a living eye, and though it did not move, it *watched* them. *Seeing them.*

Sarah and Ethan stepped forward together.

Aerthis's voice resonated through the cavern. "You have seen yourselves clearly. But the Eye will only recognize those who can *maintain* that clarity, not just for a moment, but through true belief. Through balance. Through *trust.*"

Then without warning, the air shifted.

A soft golden glow swirled before them, growing brighter, denser, until the Insightborne Enigma emerged once more. But this time, it had changed. It was no longer an indistinct, flickering form. It was stronger now, more defined, its golden light pulsing with radiance, as if it, too, had evolved alongside them.

The Enigma hovered before them, its voice warm. "You have faced the Eye of Insight and come through the other side. Tell me, what have you learned?"

Sarah and Ethan glanced at each other, then turned back to the Enigma.

Sarah spoke first. "I've learned that we are our own worst critics. That what we *believe* others think about us is often just a reflection of our self-judgment. By recognizing this can we step into who we *truly* are."

The Enigma's light brightened.

Ethan took a breath. "I've learned that my emotions aren't weaknesses. That feeling deeply doesn't make me less, it makes me *stronger.* And that I don't have to pretend to be someone I am not to be worthy."

The Enigma pulsed, its golden glow intensifying, as if celebrating. "You have understood well."

It lifted its hands, and in its grasp appeared two objects, a shimmering Eye of Insight Skill Card and a small, intricately carved Eye of Insight Pin.

"These are your rewards," the Enigma said. "The Skill Card will grant you clarity when you face future trials. The pin is a symbol, a reminder that no matter what shadows rise within, you have the power to see through them."

Sarah and Ethan each reached forward, taking their gifts with reverence.

The Enigma hovered for a moment longer. Its voice softened. "You have four more challenges ahead. But I *believe* in you. You have the strength to face them."

With that, its form began to fade, its golden light dissolving into the cavern's glow.

The prisms around them shimmered, ignited, casting brilliant beams of light which illuminated the path ahead.

Aerthis's voice returned, gentle yet firm. "You have done well. The Eye of Insight has recognized you. Now, follow the path. It will lead you out of the Prism Cavern and back to the Mystical Forest. There, your next challenge awaits."

Ethan exhaled, the weight of the trial settling. He turned to Sarah, a small, tired smile on his face. "You know... I think knowing yourself might be the most important thing of all."

Sarah nodded, twirling the small pin between her fingers. "I think you're right."

Side by side, they stepped forward, leaving the Prism Cavern behind, stronger than when they had entered, and ready for whatever was to come.

Chapter 12

The Symphony of Stillness

Sarah, Ethan, and the Orb of Reflection stepped out of the Prism Cavern, the Mystical Forest accepting once again their presence. As Sarah's and Ethan's senses readjusted to the change of light, they moved deeper into the forests thick protective cover. The cavern's luminous glow faded behind them, its crystalline walls vanishing into the misty distance. The trail wove through the thick forest, its towering trees whispering secrets through the wind.

As Sarah and Ethan walked in silence, reflecting on the challenge they had just overcame, a voice struck them with a demanding intensity, reverberating through their very minds.

What about the goose in the jar?

The phrase was neither a question nor a statement but something in between, charged with an urgency that made their pulses quicken. Sarah stopped abruptly, her heart pounding. She exchanged a glance with Ethan, her look was as if preparing for an unseen confrontation. The Orb of Reflection pulsed with faint ripples of light, mirroring their internal turbulence.

The further they walked, the more intrusive the whisper became.

What about the goose in the jar?

The phrase reverberated in their minds, a soundless voice circling through their thoughts with relentless repetition. It wasn't a question; it was a presence, an invisible force tugging at the edges of their awareness, demanding attention.

Sarahs frustration began to emerge as she processed the words. "What if the goose chooses to leave the jar?" She mused aloud, her voice pensive. "Maybe it's not about us forcing a solution but helping the goose find its way out."

Ethan, walking beside her, crossed his arms, skepticism laced in his tone. "But Sarah, the jar is solid glass. The goose can't exactly squeeze through the neck or decide to leave on its own."

She nodded, conceding the point before offering. "You're right, Ethan. Maybe trying to cut a hole in the jar's side might work, if we're careful?"

Ethan paused mid-step, his mind turning over the thought. "Hmm. But the jar is sacred," he countered. "Creating any kind of opening would desecrate its design, even if it's done carefully. And if the ashes are lost, even a little, we've dishonored the Ancient Ones."

A thoughtful silence stretched between them. Sarah sighed, her breath forming a wisp of condensation in the cool air of the Vale. "You're right. The jar's integrity is part of what makes it sacred. If we compromise that, we lose its meaning."

The Orb of Reflection pulsed with quiet energy, glowing brighter. "The solution lies in the riddle's wisdom," it intoned cryptically, its voice a blend of chimes and wind.

Sarah and Ethan kept tossing one idea after another at each other, hoping a solution to the mysterious riddle of the goose in the jar would find its way to them. Suddenly, Aerthis came to a stop, a small clearing once again opened within the forest.

Aerthis hovered closer, its mirrored surface pulsing softly, as though it could sense the unspoken tension in the air. When it spoke, its voice was that of a presence, steady and undeniable.

"Welcome, Explorers, to the Whispering Vale," Aerthis announced. "You have tested your ability to hear, but now you must learn to listen beyond sound. This is the Symphony of Stillness, a challenge not of hearing, but of understanding what is left unspoken."

Sarah glanced at the Orb, then at the Resonate Listening Pin still fastened to her shirt. She frowned. "Didn't we already prove that by completing the Resonate Listening challenge yesterday?" Her voice carried the slightest edge of frustration, the lingering exhaustion of all they had endured pressing against her like an unseen force.

Aerthis's surface flickered, catching the frustrated look on both Sarah and Ethans face. "Resonate Listening taught you to perceive beyond noise, to sense the emotions woven into words, the truths concealed in tone. You learned to listen with your heart, to feel the echoes of meaning," the Orb drifted higher, its glow intensifying as it continued.

"But here, sound itself will be stripped away. The Symphony of Stillness is not about what is spoken. It is about the presence within silence. You must learn to perceive not just what is missing, but what remains."

A whispering mist curled around them, carrying the faintest remnants of past harmonies, ghost-like traces of voices long since faded. Sarah was startled, feeling a strange unease settle upon her.

Ethan shifted beside her. "So... we're supposed to hear something that isn't there?"

Aerthis pulsed. "Not hear. Feel. Sense. Understand," it paused. Then softer. "In the presence of stillness, most will hear emptiness. But those who listen will find that silence is never truly silent."

A hush fell over them, as though even the air itself waited. Sarah and Ethan exchanged a glance. The Symphony of Stillness had already begun.

"The Vale will reveal your echoes, your fears, your truths. You must learn to understand the difference between reaction and response. Then will you find harmony." Aerthis's voice resonated through the mist, not just as sound, but as something deeper, something felt.

Ethan reached into his front shirt pocket, his fingers brushing against the firm edges of the skill cards. The weight of them was familiar, grounding. With measured care, he pulled them out, flipping through each one with quiet reverence. "Wouldn't hurt," he murmured, passing the first card to Sarah.

She took it, her fingers tracing the engraved pins, feeling the etchings as though absorbing their meaning through touch. Each one was a reminder, a fragment of the lessons they had fought to earn. No words were needed. When she finished, Ethan tucked them back into his pocket.

They shared a single glance, a silent exchange of understanding, before stepping forward.

The ground beneath them softened, as though the very earth welcomed their presence. The Whispering Vale pulsed with an unseen melody, woven from every rustling leaf, every shifting stone, every breath of wind through the crystalline trees. Above them, glowing golden threads stretched across the sky like constellations, pulsing in rhythm with the sounds of the Vale. Towering crystalline trees refracted both light and sound, cascading rainbows through the valley, while a soft mist drifted through the air, carrying the faintest whispers of past harmonies.

The challenge unfolded before them, not as an obstacle, but as a living entity, aware, shifting, reacting even! The Breath of the Vale vibrated through their bones, both resonant and calming, while scattered Tone Pools shimmered with liquid light, their melodies fluctuating between harmony and discord. Each step sent ripples through the pools, warping the sounds around them like echoes in water.

A sharp, jarring note split the air. Ethan winced. "This place is different," he murmured, unease prickling at the edge of his senses. "Stranger than any of the others. Be careful, Sarah. I feel something... elusive here."

Aerthis pulsed with golden light, a silent confirmation of Ethans evolution.

Sarah's gaze locked onto the pools, watching as they pulsed in sync with their movements. Not in words, but in awareness. "Yes," she whispered. "I feel it too."

Another pulse from Aerthis. Encouragement filling the air around it.

They moved carefully, stepping between the scattered pools as the Vale's presence thickened around them. Silence...

Not just an absence of sound, but something deeper. A stillness so absolute it pressed against them, as though the air itself had been swallowed whole.

Then it came.

A wave of emotions, invisible yet undeniable, surged through them, passing from one pool to the next, weaving through their very beings before vanishing into another. First, warmth, hope, courage, friendship, washing over them like sunlight. A sudden shift, failure, fear, loss, seeping into their bones like ice. Sarah staggered. It was too much, too fast. Each sensation struck her like a whispered truth she wasn't ready to hear, each one unraveling a thread of restraint.

Then... A voice. Sharp. Raw. Her own. "Shut up! Leave me alone!"

The words ripped from her throat before she even realized she had spoken. Uncontrolled, spontaneous...triggered, by some invisible force that penetrated her very soul and forced her to react!

The moment the words left her lips, shame crashed into her. Her hands flew to her mouth as if she could take them back, as if they had never existed at all. But they had. The Vale had pulled something from her, something buried, something raw. And now, there was no hiding from it.

Ethan spun around, his heart still pounding from the sharpness of Sarah's outburst. "Whoa, Sarah, what was that? That was... harsh." His voice held both shock and concern.

Sarah's breath caught as shame twisted in throughout her body. She opened her mouth, but her words were stuck. Her gaze dropped to the ground, hands drifted from her mouth to her sides. "I... I didn't mean to say that."

She whispered, barely able to meet Ethan's eyes. The echo of her voice still rang in her ears, raw and unfiltered. Where had that even come from?

Aerthis hovered beside them, its presence steady, unwavering. "What you just experienced, Sarah, was a triggered reaction, an unmanaged part of you that the Vale has revealed."

Sarah forced herself to look up, her eyes wide with unease. "It felt... horrible," she admitted. "Like someone else was inside me, someone I didn't recognize, racing out of me, raw and cruel. Uncaring."

Aerthis pulsed, as if reassuring her. "To discover these parts of yourself is the essence of the Symphony of Stillness," it explained. "You see, Explorers, many struggle to exist in silence. Because in silence, they are no longer distracted. They are left alone with the part of themselves that is wounded, the small child within who feels wronged but does not know how to express that pain with clarity. Instead, it reacts, bypassing every control you've randomly placed before it."

Ethan frowned, his mind racing to process the weight of Aerthis's words. "So, what are we supposed to do? Just... build better controls?"

"No, Explorers," Aerthis answered, its voice steady with knowing. "Control is a cage. And caging emotions does not tame them, it enrages them. When locked away, those feelings grow restless, desperate, willing to break free by any means necessary. And when they do, they will shatter everything in their path just to be heard."

Sarah and Ethan exchanged glances, the confusion in their eyes mingling with contemplation.

"What do we do?" Sarah asked, almost fragile.

Aerthis's glow softened. "You must guide it. Let the emotion rise. Let it breathe. Do not fear it, do not silence it. Feel it fully, its strength, its vulnerability. Only then can you begin to understand it, to negotiate with it, to calm it. If you wish for your emotions to trust you, you must first learn to trust them. But if you imprison them... they will see you as the enemy."

The words settled heavily between them, reverberating in the quiet.

Sarah said with hesitation. "So... the feelings that overtook me, they came from the silence?"

Aerthis drifted closer. "No, Sarah. The silence only created the space. The emotions that surfaced... they were already inside you."

Ethan exhaled, rubbing the back of his neck. "A space? Like a void?"

"Yes," Aerthis confirmed. "The world is filled with distractions, sounds and movement, even the faintest whisper of air passing your ear can distract. These things anchor your awareness outward, giving you something to focus on. But in true silence, when all external noise is stripped away, what remains? You! And what is within. And if what is within is unresolved, unmanaged... it will rise. This challenge is an opportunity to meet those emotions, to see them without fear, and to learn how to respond, not react."

Sarah and Ethan stood in the stillness, their breath the only sound between them. The weight of what lay ahead settled deep within their bones. This challenge was not about mastering silence, it was about facing what lived inside of it. The Whispering Vale held its breath.

The air thickened, charged with something unseen yet undeniably present. The silence was no longer just an absence of sound, it had weight, pressing gently yet firmly against their very being. The pools, once tranquil, now pulsed with an eerie rhythm, mirroring the unspoken turmoil within Sarah and Ethan.

Aerthis hovered between them, its mirrored surface flickering with waves of golden light, as though reading the tension that neither of them had words for.

"The challenge before you is not about silence," Aerthis said, its voice weaving seamlessly through the stillness. "It is about what the silence reveals."

Sarah hugged her arms tightly to herself, as if shielding something fragile beneath her skin. Her jaw was tense, her breath shallow. She was still shaken by the rawness of what had just erupted from her.

"I didn't even know that part of me existed," she murmured. "It just... came out. I wasn't trying to be cruel, but in that moment, I felt like I had no choice."

Ethan studied her carefully, his expression shifting from confusion to understanding. "Yeah. One second everything was fine, and then bam!" He snapped his fingers. "It was like something inside you just... took over."

Aerthis pulsed with steady light. "That, Explorers, is the difference between emotional reaction and emotional responsiveness. Reaction is automatic, raw, and unfiltered. A response, however, is a conscious choice."

Sarah exhaled, frustration flickering across her face. "So how do I stop myself from reacting like that again? Because if I can't control it, what's the point?"

Aerthis shifted, its golden surface capturing the faint reflection of her troubled expression. "The first step is not control, Sarah. It is awareness."

"Reactions do not appear from nowhere. They have roots. Have you noticed what triggered yours?"

Sarah hesitated. "It was… the emotions. They hit me all at once. I wasn't ready. It felt like I had no control over what was coming up."

Ethan tilted his head. "Is that why you lashed out? Because it was too much?"

Sarah's gaze flicked to him for the briefest moment before dropping again. "Maybe. I think… I felt exposed. Like something was being threatened inside me. And before I could even understand it, the words were already out."

Aerthis pulsed, warm and steady. "Good, Sarah. You are beginning to see it. Emotional reactions are often the mind's way of defending itself. But before you can change how you respond, you must first recognize not just the reactions, but the signals that appear before the reactions take hold."

Ethan frowned. "Signals?"

Aerthis drifted closer, its light reflecting off the rippling pools. "Your body always warns you before a reaction takes over. A racing heart, clenched fists, a tightening in your chest and most importantly, the holding of ones breath, these are not just sensations, Ethan. They are alarms. Your body is saying, 'Something feels unsafe. Defend yourself.' The key is to hear these warnings before they turn into actions."

Sarah hesitated, pressing her fingers to her temples as if trying to physically feel what Aerthis described. "Okay… so I notice the reaction coming. What then?"

"You pause," Aerthis said. "Breathe. Give yourself space. Let the feeling exist, but do not let it consume you."

Ethan raised an eyebrow. "Breathing is supposed to stop an explosion?"

Aerthis pulsed with amusement. "Not stop. Slow. When people react, their breath shortens, sometimes even halts for seconds at a time. This sends a message to the body, 'we are in danger', which amplifies the reaction. But a deep inhale, a steady exhale, reminds your nervous system: 'We are safe.' That breath creates the space to choose how to respond."

Sarah chewed on her lip. "So, I breathe, I pause... and then what? Just ignore it?"

"No, Explorer," Aerthis said. "You must shift perspective. Ask yourself, what is this emotion trying to tell me?"

Ethan crossed his arms. "Emotions talk now?"

Aerthis pulsed. "In a way, yes. Emotions are not commands. They are messengers. Fear warns you of danger. Anger signals a boundary being crossed. Frustration reveals an unmet need. But emotions, left unchecked, can distort reality. If you react instantly, you might mistake discomfort for danger, or challenge for threat. But if you pause, if you listen, you may realize the truth is something else."

Sarah's awareness emerged. "So... when I snapped, it wasn't random. My emotions were reacting to something real inside me?"

Aerthis pulsed brighter. "Yes. But instead of allowing pain to lash out unchecked, you can choose to be Self present. Acknowledge the feeling. Let it exist and carefully examine it and when you do that, response begins to emerge, which paves the way for you to express it in a way that aligns with who you truly are."

Ethan exhaled, rubbing the back of his neck. "Okay, so instead of reacting, we pause, reflect, and respond... got it. But what if the emotion is... too strong?"

Aerthis's glow softened. "You give it space. You allow it to be felt. You do not resist it, nor force it down.

Suppressed emotions do not disappear, Ethan. They wait. And when they rise, they do so with the force of everything left unspoken."

Sarah shivered. "So… if I had done that earlier… instead of snapping, I could have just said, 'I feel overwhelmed right now. I need a moment'?"

Aerthis pulsed warmly. "Yes, Sarah. And with time, this awareness will become second nature. You will begin to recognize which emotions require expression and which require patience. But one thing remains crucial, where you place your trust."

Sarah asked with deep contemplation. "Trust?"

Aerthis continued gently. "Your emotions are yours to hold, but trust determines where you share them. Some will see your vulnerability as weakness, and others may try to use it against you. But there will also be those who honor your truth, who listen, understand, and stand beside you. Trust is not about closing yourself off, but about knowing who is worthy of your openness."

Ethan confused. "Honestly, it just seems easier to avoid people altogether. Most don't care, they just judge."

Aerthis pulsed, its light flickering like a quiet sigh. "Ethan, people need connection. Without it, they are left with silence. And as you are about to learn, silence can be far more destructive than rejection."

Sarah tilted her head. "How so?"

Aerthis's glow dimmed, its tone laced with something almost… sorrowful. "Those who isolate… erode. Not just their connection to others, but to themselves. They begin to fade, not in body, but in spirit. Without connection, their sense of purpose weakens.

Their ability to trust, to feel joy, to embrace growth, it all diminishes. And the more they withdraw, the more they convince themselves that they were never meant to belong. Until, in time, they become nothing more than a shadow of who they were truly meant to be."

A chill passed through Sarah. "What erodes them, surly spending time alone doesn't do that?"

"Like all things, Explorers," Aerthis whispered, its voice carrying both warmth and weight. "Balance is everything. Linger too long in solitude, and you may lose yourself in the silence. Stay too long in the presence of others, and you risk forgetting who you are. Social overstimulation drowns out the stillness you need to reflect, while emotional loneliness is not just a feeling, it is a quiet unraveling of the soul."

The Whispering Vale seemed to hum in agreement, the pools rippling softly.

Ethan struggling to understand "So, exactly where do these voices come from, I mean this is a challenge of silence, yet I'm not hearing silence!"

Aerthis pulses with subtle amusement. "The silence is all around you, the voices are from within, it is the absence of distractions, the stillness that calls them to rise."

Ethan and Sarah exchanged a glance, something unspoken passing between them. The challenge before them was no longer just about silence. It was about everything the silence revealed within them. They were just beginning to understand. They needed to transition from reactions to responding to their inner thoughts within the silence.

Sarah took a steadying breath and stepped closer to one of the pools. A discordant hum wrapped around her, whispering memories of past failures.

You didn't do that right… You're not enough…

The familiar weight of inadequacy pressed against her ribs, but instead of recoiling, she closed her eyes and listened deeper.

"This is just sound," she reminded herself. "An amplified reflection, not a truth."

She took a deep breath in and then exhaled, and with that breath, the chaotic hum softened, shifting into something gentler. The pool's surface rippled, the silence gave way to a strange vibration, that of *growth*.

Ethan, watching her, squared his shoulders and moved toward a different pool. The voices were sharper here, biting. *You're weak. You're too sensitive, be a man!* The weight of his brother's taunts, the dinner table silences, the feeling of never quite belonging, slammed into him like a tidal wave. His pulse quickened, anger curling in his chest like a burning coil.

Aerthis drifted closer to Ethan, its presence steady and reassuring. "Distractions can offer relief in difficult moments," it murmured. "Beside the Tone Pools, you'll find the Resonant Stones. Pick one up, feel its weight, its texture. Let it ground you, even for a moment. Shift your thoughts, steady your breath… then return, ready to face what lies ahead."

Ethan turns to see Sarah standing firm, her presence an anchor in the shifting storm of emotions. A pleasant and comforting distraction from both silence and chaos. Ethan shifted his thoughts, if she could do it, so could he. He reached down and picked up one of the small Resonant Stones near the pool's edge. Feeling its smoothness, its soft edges as he rolled it in the palm of his hand. "That is not me," he whispered, steadying his focus. "I am strong, I am connected, I am… me and I choose my responses."

The cold stone beneath his fingers warmed, and the voices quieted.

The dissonance softened, and in its place, a steady hum of resilience resonated through the Vale.

The Orb of Reflection pulsed approvingly. "Yes, Explorers, yes."

Ethan, showing the small Resonant Stone between his fingers, looks at Sarah. "This really works, you need one of these!"

Sarah smiled, reaching down picking up one of the stones that held an intricate pattern.

The Orb glowed approvingly. "The final challenge awaits you at the Vale's center."

A wall of shimmering mist blocked their way, whispering fragmented sentences, some positive, some painful. To pass through, they had to navigate not the silence, but the inner voices the silence triggered within them without being consumed by them.

Together, they walked on. The mist curled around them, testing their resolve. Ethan flinched as his father's disappointment echoed in his ears. Sarah tensed as the echoes of isolation whispered her name. The Resonant Stones rolled through their hands, feeling the structure and the coolness against their fingers. It helped them to focus, to move forward and not be caught in the emotional echoes they heard inside.

The Whispering Vale stretched before them, veiled in thick, shifting mist. A hush settled over the landscape, a silence so deep it pressed against Sarah and Ethan's ears, swallowing even the sound of their own footsteps. The stillness was unnatural, weighty, like a presence lurking just beyond sight.

As they moved forward, the mist curled around them, tightening, thickening. The silence was not just an absence of sound; it was an amplifier of their thoughts, filling the space with restless energy.

The kind of silence that night brings when the world sleeps, but the mind refuses to rest.

Sarah closed her eyes and concentrated, pushing through the barrage of thoughts and images. At first, they swirled chaotically, overwhelming her senses. But she focused inward, picturing the Flame of Focus, distant and faint, barely visible through the noise. She steadied her breath, grounding herself in the moment. Slowly, the flame flickered, uncertain but present. With each deep breath, she fed its glow, bringing it to life, letting its warmth spread through her mind.

Ethan watched her, taking strength from her determination. He reached for his Resonant Stone, rubbing its surface between his fingers, grounding himself in its texture. He let Sarah's focus guide him, syncing his breath with hers, allowing the steadiness of the moment to push back against the mist's influence.

Together, they pressed forward, using the tools they had, Sarah's unwavering focus and Ethan's steady grounding. The mist swirled around them, but they no longer walked alone in their struggle. With each step, the weight of the silence lessened, and the Vale no longer felt like an obstacle, but a journey they would navigate together.

They did not push the mist away; they walked through it, unshaken by its illusions. Applying all they had learned so far. And then, just like that, they emerged on the other side. The air stilled. The chaotic echoes faded into harmony. The Vale had accepted them. As they stood in the quiet expanse, the Orb of Reflection hovered between them, its mirrored light revealing not just their reflections, but something deeper, clarity.

Serenity fell over the Whispering Vale, the weight of the lesson lingering like a final note of a fading melody. The air, once thick with tension, now carried something lighter, something almost reverent.

Sarah and Ethan stood side by side, their minds clearer than when they had first stepped into the Vale's silent expanse.

The air shifted. The pools of liquid light rippled in unison, casting golden waves outward, their glow intensifying. The mist that had once clouded the Vale thinned, swirling into delicate spirals before drawing inward, toward the space before them. The air shimmered, bending and folding in on itself, as if reality were trying to shape something long forgotten.

It slowly emerged. The Harmonize Enigma. It no longer flickered like a half-formed mist when it first appeared, no longer felt distant or uncertain. Now, it stood before them in a defined, yet still ethereal form. Its body was woven from strands of golden light, pulsating like the rhythm of a living heartbeat. The shape was humanoid, though still fluid, as if its very essence was a song still being written. Its presence was warm, resonant, both grounding and celestial at once.

Sarah and Ethan exchanged a glance, their eyes wide in awe. The Enigma's voice, rich and layered like a chorus of harmonies woven into one, echoed through the Vale. "You have done well, Explorers. Once again, you have proven that the Realm is not beyond salvation. That balance can be restored."

The pools shimmered at its words, a soft, melodic hum vibrating through the ground beneath their feet.

Sarah sighed, her voice softer now. "We made it Ethan."

The Enigma's golden form pulsed. "Growth is not easy, only the strong can transform," it regarded them both, its luminous form shifting like a quiet song in motion. "Tell me, Explorers, what have you learned in facing the Symphony of Stillness?"

Sarah exhaled, gathering her thoughts before speaking. "I learned that silence isn't empty. It's revealing. It strips away all distractions, forcing us to hear what we've buried inside.

And if we're not careful... those buried emotions can control us before we even realize they exist."

The Enigma pulsed, as if in approval.

Ethan rubbed the back of his neck. "I learned that emotions aren't enemies. They're not something we have to fight or suppress. They just want to be heard. And if we don't listen, they'll find a way to make us. The hard way."

A long pause followed. The Enigma shimmered in golden light, its form pulsing in perfect rhythm with the Vale itself. The pools glowed in response, the very air humming with something almost... celebratory.

"You have understood the lesson well," the Enigma said. "And with understanding, you have earned your reward."

From the Enigma's shifting form, two radiant objects emerged, floating weightlessly before Sarah and Ethan. The Symphony of Stillness Card and the Symphony of Stillness Pin. The card was edged in soft gold, its surface etched with a flowing script that shimmered as if the words themselves carried sound. The pin, small yet impossibly intricate, took the shape of a delicate spiral, like ripples spreading outward in perfect harmony.

Sarah and Ethan reached out, their fingers grazing the glowing gifts. As soon as they made contact, warmth spread through their palms, seeping into their very being. The Vale seemed to hum in acknowledgment, the pools vibrating with a resonance they could hear.

The Enigma's voice, now softer yet deeper, wove through the stillness. "Hold these close, Explorers, for they are more than just symbols. They are reminders. Of what you have faced. Of what you have overcome. And will assist you in what still lies ahead."

Its golden light pulsed once more, slower now, almost tender. "You are stronger than you know. Wiser than you realize. But most of all… you are capable. Trust that. Trust yourselves."

Sarah's throat tightened, an unexpected wave of emotion rising within her. Ethan swallowed hard, his fingers pressing against the card.

The Enigma's form began to flicker, its edges blurring like a song reaching its final note. "Until we meet again, Explorers." And with that, the Harmonize Enigma faded into light, dissolving into the golden mist of the Vale.

The Whispering Vale exhaled, its energy settling into a peaceful stillness. Sarah and Ethan stood there for a long moment, the weight of their journey settled into their bones. At the exact same time, they both let out a breath, steady, deliberate. This challenge had changed them.

A gentle ripple moved through the Whispering Vale as Aerthis floated forward, its mirrored surface shimmering with golden streaks. It drifted toward Sarah and Ethan, its presence unwavering, yet beneath its glow, there was an urgency. The challenge had been overcome, but the journey was far from over.

"Come, Explorers," Aerthis urged, its voice smooth yet insistent. "The next challenge awaits."

Ethan rolled his shoulders, still feeling the lingering weight of the Symphony of Stillness. "Yeah, no offense, but… what are we walking into next?"

Aerthis hovered closer, the golden glow of its core pulsing. "That would be the Labyrinth of Scented Memory… within the Shifting Labyrinth."

Sarah's brows furrowed. "A labyrinth inside a labyrinth?"

Aerthis pulsed once, a quiet confirmation.

Ethan sighed. "Yeah, that doesn't sound like a difficult challenge at all."

Sarah ignored him, a deeper question pressing at her thoughts. She hesitated for a moment before voicing it aloud. "Aerthis… what happened to the Custodian? The one who was supposed to," she gestured vaguely at the forest, at the shifting realm around them. "You know, take care of this place?"

A sudden stillness fell over Aerthis. Its glow, once steady, faltered, as though the question itself carried a weight too heavy to bear. Then softly, almost mournfully, it answered. "Sadly, Explorers…like so many, they were never taught how to take care of it, instead, the Eternal Guardians of Origins kept control."

Sarah's breath hitched. The finality in those words sent a chill down her spine.

Ethan's face twisted. "What does that even mean?"

Aerthis sadly replied. "It means Ethan, the custodian never evolved into its rightful role, it remained a child, allowing their E.G.O. to rule. We must move forward if we are to succeed."

A hush settled between them, heavy with unspoken thoughts. The sky darkened, as if the very air recoiled from their progress. Without warning, a violent gust of foul wind tore through the trees, sending leaves spiraling into chaos. The ground trembled beneath them. A low, guttural rumble of thunder rolled across the sky, deep and resonant, like a warning growl from something ancient, something watching.

Ethan instinctively reached for a stick laying on the ground as a weapon, only to remember they were in a realm where combat wouldn't save them, it would only draw more danger.

Sarah winced as the wind lashed at her skin, her eyes narrowing. "The Dragons…"

Aerthis pulsed brighter, its energy crackling against the storm. "Yes. The E.G.O., they feel your growth and are reacting to it." A bolt of lightning split the sky in a jagged arc, striking somewhere within the Mystical Forest. The very trees trembled, their crystalline leaves ringing with a sound like distant chimes. The storm was alive, shifting with the chaos of the Realm itself.

Sarah gritted her teeth. "Someone needs to teach them how to respond, instead of react!"

The Orb, shimmers in golden light, knowing well that is exactly why Sarah and Ethan were there!

Ethan stared ahead into the twisting path of the Mystical Forest. The next challenge awaited, and the dragons were fighting back. With a final glance at one another, the three stepped forward, into the unknown.

Chapter 13

The Labyrinth of Scented Memory

The Mystical Forest deepened around them, the towering crystalline trees casting shifting patterns of ethereal light across the moss-covered ground. The air felt thick with energy, pulsating in waves that echoed with the very thoughts in their minds. Sarah and Ethan moved cautiously behind Aerthis, the sentient Orb floating effortlessly through the dense foliage, its golden glow illuminating the path ahead.

As they ventured deeper, an all-too-familiar voice whispered in their minds, clawing its way into their thoughts.

What about the goose in the jar?

Sarah flinched, shaking her head as if to dispel the voice's weight. "Not this again," she muttered.

Ethan sighed, rubbing his temples. "I swear, if I hear that phrase one more time…"

But the voice did not relent. Instead, it coiled around their minds like an insidious vine, demanding attention, demanding resolution. Their frustration grew, and soon, their irritation turned toward each other.

"This is ridiculous," Sarah snapped. "The goose is trapped. We need to find a way to get it out before it drives us insane."

"That's what I've been saying!" Ethan interjected. "We can't just ignore it. If it's in there, it's suffering. We have to do something."

"Don't you think I know that Ethan," Sarah snapped at him. "But how?"

Ethan pulled back, recoiling from the aggression Sarah was feeling.

Aerthis, who had remained a silent observer, drifted between them, its golden light dimming momentarily before pulsing with steady rhythm. "To solve a problem," the Orb stated. "You must first understand the problem. Only then can it be solved."

Sarah and Ethan fell silent, their frustration giving way to contemplation. Aerthis' words rang with undeniable truth.

Sarah took a deep breath. "Alright," she said, forcing herself to calm down. "Let's go through the riddle again. Out loud."

Ethan nodded, scratching his head. "Okay. Hypothetically, there is this silly ancient glass jar, a relic of unparalleled importance. Its base is wide and sturdy, meant to hold the weight of time and the ashes of the ancient ones."

Sarah continued. "Right, and these ashes aren't just any old ashes.

They hold wisdom, enlightenment, generations of knowledge according to the riddle and yet, the jar's neck is extremely narrow, deliberately so, to protect what's inside."

Ethan inhaled. "Agreed, then somehow, a weird little goose egg, containing life, something full of potential, fell inside. Against all odds, it hatched. And now the goose is trapped, growing bigger every day." Sarah twisted her brow. "Yeah, It's alive in there, Ethan. It's in a cage of sorts, trapped!"

"The darn paradox is," Ethan's voice took on a determined edge. "To harm the goose would desecrate a sacred law of life. To let it starve violates compassion. To keep feeding it corrupts the purity of what's inside. And breaking the jar..."

"Would scatter the ashes, severing the link to the Ancient one's wisdom." Sarah finished.

They stood in silence, the problem crystallizing in their minds in a way it hadn't before. The goose, the jar, the ashes, all interconnected, all important in some way. This was no mere riddle. The question that toiled within them was, how could they set the goose free while still preserving the jar and the ashes?

Aerthis pulsed in silence. Sarah and Ethan exchanged a glance, and smiled at each other in agreement, they were determined to find the solution, their previous argument now forgotten.

The trees thinned ahead, revealing the entrance to the Shifting Labyrinth. The glowing crystalline maze pulsed in synchronization with their emotions, its swirling mists curling like sentient fingers reaching out to connect. They both hesitated, sensing the enormity of what lay before them.

As they stood at the entrance, Aerthis hovered between them and spoke in a resonant tone.

"Before you proceed, you must understand the difference between what lies ahead and the trials you have already faced. The Aromatic Illumination Challenge introduced you to the presence of Self. It was a lesson in recognizing the connection between scent and emotion, in observing how memories surface and understanding them without judgment. You encountered emotions both pleasant and painful, yet your task was not to change them, only to accept them. That was your first step into empowering growth."

The mist before them swirled intensely, and Aerthis' light flickered as it continued.

"The Labyrinth of Scented Memory is different. It is not just about recognizing emotions but confronting them. Here, you will relive painful moments. The shifting corridors represent the chaos of your subconscious, twisting and disorienting, just as unhealed wounds do. Where Aromatic Illumination required observation, the Labyrinth demands resolution. You must engage with what you have buried, rewrite your past narratives, and transform your burdens into strength. This is not just about understanding yourselves; it is about integrating what you have learned and choosing how it shapes you moving on."

Sarah swallowed hard, her fingers brushing up against the pins she wore. "So... we're not just facing memories. We're facing how we let these memories impact us?"

Ethan rubbed his hands against the pocket holding the skill cards. "I don't know, that sounds scary!"

Aerthis' glow pulsed. "Fear, Explorers is the refusal to try. To fear what is within you is to remain forever lost, letting fear stop your growth, which leads to erosion. Remember, emotional memories from the past do not define you. They are but simple echoes. True strength, true courage is facing these memories without the fear they have implanted within you.

To truly understand yourself, is to know without any doubt what you are capable of."

"The labyrinth responds to your emotional memories," Aerthis continued. "Remain focused and your path through the labyrinth will be straight, while fear, hesitation, or anger will lead to dead ends and loops, making the challenge to escape the labyrinth impossible. Know that at the heart of each memory lies a lesson, not just pain. Reflect on what it wished to teach you, while also understanding that time and neglect have twisted many memories together. Understanding this, accepting this will reveal the path you seek. Denial, will hide the path forever."

As they stepped forward, the mist thickened, and the walls shimmered with shifting hues. A scent, warm and familiar, drifted toward them, old books. Sarah hesitated as a ghostly image of a school library formed before her. A memory stirred. The challenge had begun.

The labyrinth twisted and shifted, towering walls rose up and moved mystically, each exuding an aroma that triggered twisted memories within them. Exposing both the concealed pain and lost growth. With every step, Sarah and Ethan felt a surge of emotion as their past began pressing in on them, forcing them to confront what they hid from.

The first scent brought Sarah to a library memory, a sudden, overpowering scent filled the air, a familiar mix of lavender and ink. The moment the aroma touched her senses, her vision blurred, and she was no longer in the labyrinth. She was back in her childhood home, sitting on the floor of her bedroom, a torn friendship bracelet in her trembling hands.

The memory was suffocating. She saw herself at twelve years old, standing in front of her best friend, Lila, her face burning with shame and anger. The accusation had come sharp and unexpected:

"You stole money from me, Sarah!" Lila's voice rang through the air, sharp and unrelenting, echoing from all directions.

Sarah's stomach clenched. "I didn't," she whispered.

But the accusation repeated, louder this time, reverberating in the space around her. The walls of the labyrinth contracted, pressing inward. The more she resisted, the heavier the atmosphere became, suffocating her, trapping her inside the moment she had tried so hard to forget.

Lila's face twisted with hurt and betrayal. "I trusted you!"

"I didn't steal anything!" Sarah shouted, her voice raw.

The walls around her shifted, twisting shadows into ghostly figures of classmates, family members, strangers.

"You're a liar."

"I'm going to tell everyone."

"No one will believe you ever again!"

The words pounded against her like waves, eroding the very foundation of her identity. She knew the truth, she hadn't stolen the money, but with every repeated accusation, she felt herself shrinking. Her confidence crumbled, and doubt coiled around her like a serpent. Was she still the person she thought she was? Or was she being forced into being someone else?

Her mind warred against the onslaught, but the lie was relentless. The more she tried to fight it, the more powerless she felt. The walls whispered, wrapping their fingers around her heart, dragging her into despair. Tears welled in her eyes as she collapsed to her knees, her hands trembling. "It wasn't me..." Her voice cracked.

Aerthis pulsed beside her, its golden light cutting through the haze. "Blame is an easy burden to place upon another, Sarah," the Orb said softly. "It allows the accuser to release their anger, to avoid facing the truth.

But their accusation does not define you. The weight of their words belongs to them, not to you."

The walls wavered at the edges of her vision, its grip loosening.

Aerthis pulsed again. "The more anger grows Sarah; the less truth is sought. This anger opens a gateway in those expressing it, that allows every bottled-up emotion to be released inappropriately. They often place an ugly lie upon those that are the recipients of their anger, while using the emptiness of blame, not because it was just, but because it was convenient. Sarah… you know the truth. You know who you are. That is your strength. Remember, anyone can say anything to anyone, about someone else, this does not make it true. What makes truth Sarah, is standing by your authenticity."

Sarah inhaled shakily, lifting her head. She could still feel the sting of the accusation, the wound it had left, but she was beginning to understand, this pain had never been about her. It had been about Lila's anger, her need to direct it somewhere, anywhere. Sarah just happened to be the easiest recipient of that anger.

"The truth is I'm not a thief and I am not a liar," she whispered, her voice steady this time. "I am not the person they think I am! They are blinded by their bottled-up emotions, and I am not responsible for that!"

As soon as she said it, the labyrinth groaned and shifted. The walls shifted back, revealing a clearer path ahead. Sarah wiped her tears, steadied herself, and stepped forward.

Sarah looks at Ethan, his face dripping with empathy.

"Sarah," Ethan bashfully said "You are the most honest person I have ever met! I trust you with my life."

Sarah instantly noticing Ethan's bright red cheeks and smiled.

Ethan stepped forward, and the walls began to shift, this time far more quickly. A sharp, pungent scent filled the air, cooked cabbage. His stomach lurched, his breath hitched. The walls around him shifted even faster, the labyrinth twisting violently, the light dimmed into the confines of a childhood memory.

He was three years old. His brother teased him as Ethan played with his toys, trying hard to ignore him. From out of nowhere, a toy struck him hard, bouncing off his tiny body before smashing into the ceramic swan perched on the shelf. The delicate figure shattered as it hit the ground. Ethan's eyes filled with tears, his small body trembling with fear. He knew how much that swan meant to his mother.

Before he could process what had happened, his older brother yelled out, his voice dripping with feigned innocence.

"Mom! Ethan had another one of his temper tantrums and threw a toy. He broke your swan." Footsteps thundered from the kitchen. His mother appeared, exhaustion lining her face. She barely spared Ethan a glance before grabbing his arm and shoving him into the corner.

"You stay here and think about what you've done," she snapped. "Wait until your father gets home."

Terror gripped him. He knew what that meant.

Hours later, as his mom was making dinner, Ethan, still standing in the corner, could smell the thick aroma of cooked cabbage as it hung in the air. Each minute Ethan stood there brought him closer to his father's wrath, yet he was powerless in doing anything, being three years old.

He heard his father's truck pull into the driveway, fear riffed through Ethans body. The door closed and his father's voice rang out. "I'm home".

Ethan's body trembled in fear. He pushed his tiny head into the corner, wishing he could disappear forever into it. The angry voices of his mother and brother shattered Ethans trust as Ethan's mother and brother retold the lie, painting him as the reckless troublemaker. His father's expression darkened. Without a word, he grabbed Ethan by the arm and dragged him into the bedroom. The belt came off. Each strike burned, each cry ignored. His father's anger fed off Ethan's screams.

"No daddy no!" as if punishing the emotion itself.

Back in the labyrinth, Ethan gasped, his hands clenched. The walls closed in, whispering his brother's lies, his mother's indifference, his father's fury. The cooked cabbage scent suffocated him. He was drowning in the past.

Aerthis pulsed beside him. "Ethan," its voice steady. "These lies do not define who you are either. Their cruelty is an expression of their inner turmoil. Your pain is real, and yet you have a choice, to bare it with understanding, or with resentment. One will open the path forward, the other will keep you trapped in the pain, never letting go."

Ethan choked on a sob, the walls trembling around him.

"They made you believe you were small, weak, wrong," the Orb continued. "But you are none of those things. You were a child. You were innocent. The blame they placed upon you was never yours to carry."

Tears-streaked Ethan's face. For so long, he had believed their lies, had internalized their blame. But now, standing amongst the shifting walls, he began to understand, he had never deserved their hate. He had never deserved their unacceptance. He inhaled deeply, forcing air into his lungs. "I was just a kid," he whispered. "I didn't deserve that!"

The labyrinth shuddered. The walls shifting once again. The scent of cooked cabbage faded.

The path ahead lay open.

Ethan straightened, his body still trembling, but his heart felt lighter than it had in years. The ghosts of his past still lingered, whispering from the shadows, but they no longer had the same grip on him. He had overcome them. And he would continue overcoming them.

Sarah stepped toward him, her expression soft with understanding. She could see the weight of everything he had just faced, the raw vulnerability still etched in his eyes. Without hesitation, she wrapped her arms around him in a firm, grounding embrace. Ethan stiffened for a moment, still unaccustomed to such comfort, but slowly he let himself melt into it.

When she pulled back, she met his gaze and gave him a small, reassuring smile. "Looks like we both could use a little understanding," she said gently. "Just know, I'm here Ethan."

Ethan's lips curled into a faint smile, though the battle inside him wasn't over yet. The memories still flickered at the edges of his mind, but for the first time, they were beginning to lose their power. His voice was quiet. "It's not right."

Sarah frowned. "What's not right, Ethan?"

"People," he said, his voice thick with frustration. "I can see it now. People just... react. They don't take the time to understand. They don't question. They just accept whatever is put in front of them as if it's the truth. And that hurts innocent people. A lot!"

Sarah didn't respond with words. Instead, she reached for his hand, holding it tightly in silent solidarity.

Aerthis pulsed beside them, its light warm and steady. "Young ones," it said, its voice deep and resonant. "You are not always given choices. Instead, you are given lessons. You do not choose your family. You do not choose your culture. But you *do* choose how you face the challenges before you. Much like this labyrinth, life will test you, push you to your limits. But through these trials, you will grow stronger. Not just in body, but in mind and spirit. And when you wield all three, your strength, your intellect, and your heart, you become unstoppable. However…"

The Orb's light flickered, its glow dimming as if to emphasize the gravity of its words. "If you possess none of them, if you choose to avoid the challenges and the lessons they teach, you will remain like this labyrinth... trapped. Trapped in fear. Trapped in uncertainty. Uncertain how to feel, how to think, how to act."

Ethan and Sarah exchanged a look, realization dawning between them. Aerthis was more than just a guide through this strange, mystical world. It was a teacher. A guardian. A voice of wisdom showing them not just the way forward, but the way through life itself.

Sarah and Ethan turned toward the now open path ahead, their hearts still steadying from the emotional trials they had endured. Before them, bathed in a soft, otherworldly glow, stood a magnificent archway, an exit from the Labyrinth of Scented Memories. Relief mingled with quiet anticipation as they took their first steps toward it.

But just as they neared the arch, the air around them thickened again. Wisps of silver mist began to swirl, condensing into a form, a figure emerging from the ethereal fog. The mist shimmered, shifting, refining itself with more definition than before.

The Learnspring Enigma stood before them once again, no longer just a wisp of curiosity, but a presence more whole, more knowing. It was as if Sarah and Ethan's growing bond had given it strength, pulling it further into existence.

For a few long moments, it observed them. Its translucent form flickered like a flame caught between worlds, its deep-set eyes filled with an ancient curiosity. What potential did they hold? Could they truly shape the future of the realm?

The Learnspring Enigma spoke. "You have done what few before you have accomplished. You have faced the Labyrinth of Scented Memories and emerged not just unbroken but transformed."

Sarah and Ethan exchanged glances, the weight of what they had endured still lingering in their bones.

"Tell me," The Enigma continued. "What have you learned?"

Ethan spoke up. "I learned that pain doesn't just disappear. It lingers in the spaces we try to avoid, waiting for a trigger that twists its influence on our emotions. But more than that, I learned that blame is a weapon, and when wielded carelessly, it can shatter a person from the inside out. I carried guilt that was never mine to bear... and I let it define me. But not anymore." His voice, raw but resolute, carried through the mist. The Enigma listened, motionless, absorbing every word.

Sarah's voice came next, quieter but equally powerful. "I learned that silence can be just as painful as accusation. That standing still in the face of a lie is the same as letting it become the truth. I let fear stop me from fighting for myself. But I see now... I don't have to live in the shadow of someone else's judgment."

As she spoke, the air between them hummed with something unspoken, something sacred.

The Learnspring Enigma was no longer just evaluating them, it was recognizing them. A slow, approving nod. "You have seen the labyrinth for what it is, not just a test, but a potential passageway through thought. And because you have faced your truths without turning away, you have earned these."

The Enigma extended its mist-like hands, and from the shifting vapor materialized two objects:

The Labyrinth of Scented Memories Skill Card, a small card, glowing with fragments of light, swirling with hues of lavender and gold. The Labyrinth of Scented Memories Pin, a delicate silver emblem, its intricate design resembling the twisted walls, frozen in time.

"These will serve as reminders," the Enigma said, its voice layered with meaning. "When darkness falls and the air is thick with illusion, when scent becomes a trap meant to ensnare you, remember what you have learned here. Use these, and you will not be lost."

Sarah and Ethan reached out, taking their rewards with quiet reverence. The moment their fingers closed around them, a warm energy pulsed through their bodies, washing away the residual ache of their memories. A sense of pride filled them, replacing the pain with something deeper, a knowing that they had been trapped in a horrific past and now had escaped it.

The Learnspring Enigma rose, its form beginning to blur at the edges. Before it faded, it paused once more. "You have shown bravery. Courage. Devotion. You have given hope where there was once only fear." As its final words echoed through the clearing, the mist began to dissipate. "We see the truth now. Do you?" And then it was gone.

A silence settled between Sarah and Ethan, heavy yet peaceful. They stood there.

Aerthis pulsed beside them. "There is little time to linger," the Orb of Reflection said. "Two more challenges await within the Mystical Forest."

Sarah exhaled and glanced at Ethan before asking. "And then what?"

The Orb hovered for a moment before dimming. "Then, Explorers, we will reach the edge of the forest... and the end of its protection."

Ethan frowned. "What's beyond the forest?"

A pause. And in a voice laced with sorrow, the Orb said. "The Barren Lands... and Dysquinox."

Chapter 14

The Flavor of Resilience

The air twisted with a menace as Sarah and Ethan stepped beyond the archway of the Labyrinth. Overhead, the sky growled, dark clouds swirling like a cauldron stirred by unseen hands. A crack of lightning split the heavens, its jagged fingers illuminating the twisted landscape ahead. The wind carried a foul scent, something acrid and decayed, curling around them like the breath of an unseen predator.

Sarah wrinkled her nose. "That smell... it's getting worse."

Aerthis hesitated. "It's the Dragons... They're getting angrier. Every challenge you pass, their grip weakens and no doubt it is upsetting them."

Sarah met Ethan's gaze. Unspoken understanding passed between them. Dysquinox had already taken so much from the Realm, and with each trial they overcame, the Guardians, once protectors, now corrupted, seemed to lash out harder, their presence manifesting in ways neither of them fully understood.

Ethan sighed "Losing control over something you are tasked to protect, that's got to create some kind of emotion!"

The Orb slowed and floated between them "They have become accustomed to living in pain, they know no different now, to them, pain is comfort. They use fear and trickery to keep control, blinding them from what they truly are protecting."

Sarah asks "What is that? What are they protecting?"

"Their fear, pain and vulnerability," the Orb replies. "You see, pain does not cling to them, they cling to it, you have often heard the saying, let it go, and yet, no one teaches you how to do just that. To let go of something, you must first become aware you are holding onto it. Some believe their very existence is based on that pain, without it, they would not know who they are. They have lived with it most their lives, it has guided them, even protected them."

"How can pain protect anyone." Sarah asks.

"Pain is a reminder of experience; it stops people from repeating the same experience again and again." the Orb replied.

"Yeah but, doesn't it stop us from...I don't know, experiencing other things?" Ethan asks.

"Indeed, it does Ethan, pain, held onto inappropriately, is like poison to a plant, stopping its growth which then leads to it eroding."

"You mean dying..."

"Not exactly young ones, erosion doesn't mean dying, it means living in a self-imposed prison, where fear is the gate keeper.

Life is a wonderful experience, for those who learn how to navigate it effectively. Yet for those trapped in fear, all they see is a world full of negativity, hurt and discord. To them, they either hide away, removing themselves from life or they lash out in retaliation, believing all those who approach are a threat."

"That sounds horrible!" Sarah exclaimed.

"To them Sarah, its comfort, their pain is the only comfort they know"

"Can't they just try something different?" Ethan wondered.

"The unknown is what they fear the most Ethan, to step out of the pain they have grown comfortable in, is to step into the unknown. Their fear kicks in and convinces them that anything unknown is dangerous, so they remain trapped in their Dysquinox states."

"Brutal," Ethan proclaims. "I sure hope I never turn into that kind of person!"

The Orb cuts in again, changing the subject. "The Resonant Tasting Hall should be just past that ridge."

They set off, their boots pressing into the damp, uneven terrain. The wind howled through the jagged trees lining their path, their twisted trunks swaying as if trying to escape the storm.

After a moment, Sarah broke the silence. "I've been thinking about the Enigmas. About their place in all of this."

Ethan nodded, his expression thoughtful.

Aerthis replies. "They are more than just guides Explorers. Each one embodies something essential, something people need to face and understand the world and themselves fully."

Sarah tilted her head. "Like the Endurancevale Enigma. What exactly does she embody?"

Ethan, looking puzzled, gave her a curious look. "You mean he, right?"

Sarah blinked. "Wait, what?" Thinking Ethan is just overwhelmed by the last challenge. "Never mind!"

The Orb floats around them. "The Endurancevale Enigmas teach resilience through discernment, revealing that every experience, sweet or bitter, shapes the soul. As Guardians of Taste, they challenge seekers to endure discomfort, savor wisdom, and reject what weakens the spirit, for only those who choose wisely may unlock true endurance."

Ethan hesitated, looking at Sarah confused. "Yeah, the Enigmas, like the Mindwright, the Insightborne, even the Endurancevale. They remind me of a teacher I had once; he kind of understood me, guiding me in a way."

Sarah's looking confused. "To me, they seem like my grandmother, nurturing, caring and understanding. It's like her voice speaking to me."

"You mean your grandfather, right?"

"No, I never knew him, he passed away before I was born."

A strange shiver passed through them, though the air was warm. Neither spoke for a few breaths, it was if they weren't seeing the same Enigma's at all? The thought curled at the edges of Sarah's mind, stirring an unease. But before she could follow the thread further, the wind shifted, and a voice slipped into their thoughts, soft as silk and sharp as glass.

What about the goose in the jar?

Ethan stopped dead. "Not that again!"

Sarah rolled her eyes, her pulse quickening. "For the love of... ugh!"

The voice, so foreign yet familiar, echoed in the recesses of their minds, carrying with it an inexplicable weight. The question hung in the air as if it contained an answer they weren't yet ready to grasp.

Ethan swallowed hard. "What the heck is with this riddle, why does it keep haunting us!"

Sarah's breath caught. Ethan turned sharply, scanning the shadows. The voice rippled through their thoughts, pressing against their awareness like a hand against glass. It belonged to no one, and yet, it demanded to be answered. Before they could react, Aerthis slowed and positioned itself between them again. Its surface rippled, casting fragmented reflections of their faces, eyes alight with unspoken truths.

"The riddle will continue to seek an answer," the Orb said knowingly. "It will press upon your mind, whisper through your dreams, curl around your every thought... until you give it one."

Sarah and Ethan stood frozen as the Orb's light pulsed, its presence wrapping around them like a lingering touch.

"But be warned," Aerthis continued. "To give the wrong answer is to be bound by the question. The voice will linger forever, never accepting another answer, even if it is correct. You will know no silence, no peace, only its echo, repeating without end."

Ethan swallowed harder. "That's horrible, I mean even now it's a royal pain!"

"Only the correct answer on your first attempt will free you, not just from the riddle, but from so much more," the Orb confirmed. "You will either be set free by understanding its true power or be forever trapped within it."

A chilling pause followed, the storm above rolling like a beast unsettled.

Sarah turned to Ethan. "We need to be careful."

Ethan nodded, but his mind was already spiraling. "The goose in the jar... it could be..."

"Wait," Sarah interrupted. "We need to think about this logically. I don't want to be stuck with this voice in my head!"

Ethan bristled. "And you think I do?"

"I didn't say that," she countered, frustration creeping into her voice. "I just mean that sometimes you rush into things without..."

"Oh, so now I'm reckless?" Ethan snapped, crossing his arms.

"I didn't say that either!" Sarah shot back, the tension between them sparking like flint and steel.

"You implied it."

"Maybe if you actually *listened!*"

"I *am* listening!"

The air trembled around them, heavy with the weight of their unspoken emotions. Overhead, the storm rumbled, echoing the tension between them, as though the sky itself could feel the struggle in their hearts. The Orb pulsed... once, then again, its glow a steady heartbeat in the turmoil.

"Explorers," it spoke at last, its voice cutting through their fraying argument like light piercing fog. "The conflict you feel is not the enemy, it is the call to understanding. Look at the problem not as a battle, but as a reflection. Is the struggle within you, or is it merely a shadow cast from something else?"

Ethan turned to Sarah, his expression softening as regret flickered across his face. He let out a breath he didn't realize he was holding. "I'm sorry," he murmured, the weight of his frustration giving way to something gentler. "I didn't mean to take it out on you."

Sarah held his gaze for a moment before offering a small, knowing smile. "Me too," she admitted. "You're not the problem, and neither am I. The problem is the riddle. It has no feelings, no pride to wound. But we do. Let's stop fighting each other and start working on the answer. Together."

Ethan's lips curved into a tired but genuine smile. "Together," he agreed, reaching out his hand. And in that moment, the storm overhead grew louder as they kept moving forward. As the three of them made their way through the Mystical Forest, Sarah and Ethan each presented different ideas on how to solve the riddle, yet each answer they seem to test had some flaw that would break one of the riddles rules.

Before they knew it, the Orb announces. "We have reached the Resonant Tasting Hall."

At once, the oppressive weight of the moment shifted. The wind stilled. The storm, though still present, seemed to recede, as if the dragons themselves held their breath, hoping to see them fail. Sarah and Ethan turned to find themselves standing at the threshold of a magnificent structure, perched on the edge of a towering mountain. Its walls, translucent crystal, shimmered with shifting colors, refracting light into dazzling patterns that moved like living things. The very air hummed with energy, vibrating in response to their presence. Aerthis hovered between them, its mirrored surface reflecting the glowing runes etched into the floor.

"This challenge is unlike the ones before it," the Orb explained. "It is not about perception or fusion, but resilience. Emotional endurance, sensory insight, and balance. You must face the harmony and discord within yourselves, integrating opposing forces to find strength through discomfort."

Sarah exhaled, her hands turning sweaty. "And I'm guessing taste is at the center of it."

"Indeed," Aerthis confirmed. "Taste is not merely a sensation, it is an experience of emotion, memory, and reaction. Here, you can learn to transform bitterness into wisdom, sweetness into patience, and the overwhelm into the refined. You must take what repels you and weave it into something whole."

Ethan's jaw tightened. "That sounds complicated!"

The Orb's light dimmed. "Explorers, look what you have accomplished thus far, hold true to your growth, resilience is not found in avoidance, but in embracing what challenges you."

A beat of silence passed between them. Sarah and Ethan exchanged a look, both hesitant, both determined.

"Inside," Aerthis continued. "You will find the Alchemy Plates. Each holds a challenge, each flavor a trial of endurance and self-awareness. The path forward is not in resistance, but in acceptance."

Ethan let out a slow breath. "So… we taste our emotions?"

Sarah met his gaze. "I think it means the tastes make us more aware of our emotions."

"Funny," Ethan fessed. "All my life I have been taught to ignore my emotions and here I am, now supposed to learn as much as I can about them?"

Aerthis hovered before him, its mirrored surface shifting, its voice neither harsh nor gentle, but firm, unwavering. "Ethan," it began. "Do you understand the weight of what you have been carrying?"

Ethan replied puzzled. "Actually, they're not that heavy." He muttered, tapping his hand against the pocket of his shirt, referencing the Skill cards.

Aerthis pulsed with quiet knowing and a chuckle. "Not those Ethan, the weight of un-expressed emotions?"

Ethan's puzzled look grew.

"Ethan, men have been told a lie," Aerthis continued. "A lie that has been passed down through generations, whispered into their ears before they could even speak. 'Men are not permitted to feel. Men are not allowed cry. Men must be strong and emotionless. Emotions are a weakness in men.' And so, they swallow their pain, bury their emotions, locking them away, thinking that by doing so, they are proving their worth."

Ethan's throat tightened. He knew this lesson too well. His father's voice echoed in his head: *Stop being so sensitive, Ethan. You have to be tough if you want to make it in this world.*

And Jason's taunts: *Crybaby.*

Aerthis floated closer. "Tell me, Ethan, what happens when something is caged for too long?"

He didn't answer. He didn't have to. He had seen it in his father, in the way his eyes carried exhaustion like a shadow, in the way his silence filled the house like an unspoken warning. His fathers very breath was full of tension.

"You have been told that locking your emotions away keeps you safe," Aerthis said. "But it does not. It poisons you. It poisons everything around you."

Ethan swallowed hard, his pulse quickening.

"Look at the world around you. How many fathers can teach their sons emotional strength when they were never taught it themselves? How many men hold back their pain because they were told it made them weak? They are not without feeling, Ethan, they are simply lost within themselves, unable to give what they do not understand. All trapped in that lie!"

Aerthis pulsed again, its light reflecting Ethan's face, his doubt, his resistance, his fear. "You have spent your whole life being told that pain must be endured in silence, by men who endure pain in silence.

That to break is to fail. But you are not a machine, Ethan. You are not steel. You are flesh, blood, and spirit. And when you deny your emotions, you deny yourself."

Ethan's breath came shallow. His heart pounded against his ribs like it was fighting to escape the weight he had buried it under.

"Tell me," Aerthis pressed. "What happens to something bottled up for too long and you keep adding to it, building pressure?"

Ethan exhaled shakily. "It explodes."

"Yes," the Orb's glow deepened. "Emotional tension is not harmless, Ethan. It is the root of worry and stress. And stress, unchecked, unchallenged, becomes physical illness."

Ethan's stomach twisted as he thought his father having so many medical problems. Ethan believed the medical problems was the cause of his father's stress, but was it? Could it be that his fathers stress was the cause of his medical problems?

"You remember the poison given to the plant," Aerthis continued, its voice dipping lower, heavier. "How it seeped into the roots, how it spread until even the strongest parts began to wither. It begins to rot from the inside out. That is what happens when you deny what you feel. You think you are containing it, but in reality, it spreads. Your body begins to ache under the weight of it. Your mind turns against you. The sickness grows, slow, silent, until one day, you wonder why everything feels wrong, why nothing feels right."

Ethan's hands trembled, his body rigid as though resisting the truth. He had felt it, the exhaustion that never left, the weight in his chest, the quiet voice in the back of his mind that whispered that something was broken inside him.

Aerthis' light dimmed, as if sharing in his pain.

"When you were younger Ethan, you were not given the tools to understand this. Yet now, you hold the responsibility to take care of yourself. You must learn how, not from those who themselves have not learned, for no one can heal what they refuse to face."

Ethan swallowed past the lump in his throat. "So… what? I'm just supposed to let it all out? To… feel everything?"

Aerthis pulsed. "Firstly, accept that to feel is to be human. To understand what you feel is to be whole."

The words cracked something inside him, something he had long held together with clenched fists and forced silence.

"Strength is not found in suppressing pain," the Orb said. "It is found in embracing it, understanding it, and choosing to rise despite it. Do not let the world's lies dictate who you are. You are not weak for feeling. You are strong because you do."

Ethans chest tightened with something that felt dangerously close to relief. His whole life, he had been taught to hide. Maybe, just maybe, it was time to unlearn.

With that, the great doors of the Resonant Tasting Hall groaned open, revealing the mysteries within. And the next challenge began. Sarah and Ethan stepped cautiously through the threshold of the Resonant Tasting Hall, their breath catching in their throats at the mesmerizing sight before them.

The vast, crystalline walls rippled with living light, refracting hues of indigo, molten gold, and iridescent violet that shimmered and shifted as if the very air pulsed with awareness. A soft, resonant hum vibrated through their bones, neither sound nor silence, but something in between, a soft whisper of energy that responded to their presence. Beneath their feet, the intricate mosaic floor pulsed with a faint glow, the delicate runes shifting subtly in sync with their emotions.

It felt as though the hall too was watching. Waiting.

At the center of the chamber, a raised circular platform floated just inches above the ground. Suspended in the air above it, plates of glowing ingredients hovered weightlessly, each pulsing with an otherworldly aura. The air itself carried a heady mixture of scents, some rich and alluring, others sharp and acrid, each one stirring something within them, an instinctual pull that neither of them fully understood.

Ethan's stomach tightened with an unfamiliar hunger. "I don't know about you, Sarah, but this place is making me crave something, and I don't even know what it is!"

Sarah stepped forward, her fingertips brushing the air, feeling the strange current of energy that crackled around them. "Look at the colors," she murmured, eyes scanning the luminous plates. "Everything seems... so edible, so delicious!"

As if responding to her thoughts, Aerthis, the Orb of Reflection, pulsed between them, its mirrored surface rippling like liquid mercury. Its voice was smooth yet edged with caution. "What you feel, Explorers, is desire, and desire can be deceptive. The Resonant Tasting Hall tempts you with cravings you do not yet understand. But beware, desire is a double-edged blade. Left unchecked, it traps you in illusions, binding you to limiting beliefs that can shatter your emotional world. Many chase what is sweet and easy, avoiding what is difficult yet necessary for growth. But in doing so, they distort not only their taste, but their perception of reality."

Sarah straightened her shoulders. "You said this challenge is different from the Essence of Fusion. How so?"

Aerthis shimmered, its mirrored surface distorting before steadying. "The Essence of Fusion presented to you the presence of SELF.

It showed you the importance of emotions, how they, like flavors, combine to create something either harmonious or discordant. But the Flavor of Resilience is far more demanding."

Its glow intensified, its voice both firm and knowing. "This challenge does not only ask you to understand emotions. It requires you to endure them."

Ethan stiffened. "Endure them?"

Aerthis pulsed once, deliberately. "Resilience is not the absence of pain, nor is it the blind charge through discomfort. It is the ability to experience every sensation, bitter and sweet, harsh and smooth, without turning away. It is the transformation of hardship into strength, of contrast into balance."

Sarah frowned. "And that's done through... taste?"

"Taste," Aerthis confirmed. "Is not merely a physical sensation. It is an emotional experience, tied to memory, tolerance, and endurance. What you are about to face is not just about food, it is about what you hold within yourself," the Orb hovered closer, its voice dropping into something almost reverent, as if speaking a truth rarely uttered aloud. "If you judge too quickly, rejecting what is unfamiliar, unpleasant, or challenging, you will struggle to find truth. Many mask their true natures beneath protective layers, just as fruit and root grow tough skins to shield what is delicate within. What may seem unpalatable at first, may in fact be something beautiful, something nourishing, but only if you have the patience to taste beyond its surface."

Ethan swallowed. "So... you're saying people are like that too?"

Aerthis pulsed. "Yes. Many who have been wounded by the very world meant to protect them grow what you, Ethan, call thick skin. These barriers are not just shields, they are warnings, bitter to the taste, sharp to the touch.

But if you look beyond them, if you have the courage to peel away the layers, you may find a heart far different than the exterior it wears."

Sarah's breath hitched, something in her tightening at the truth of those words. How often had she hidden herself behind intellect, behind sharp remarks and cool distance, all because she was afraid to show how much she felt?

Aerthis continued, its voice unwavering. "Every ingredient here holds more than a flavor, it carries a truth about yourself. You must face them, taste them, and learn to find harmony in both what comforts and what repels you. You must expose who you truly are, and in doing so, learn to accept others, even when their outer layers seem unpalatable. If you can do this, if you can blend your true essence with theirs, you may not only create something wondrous...," the Orb's glow pulsed, brighter, deeper. "...But you may also set them free."

Sarah and Ethan stood motionless, the weight of the challenge settling over them. This wasn't just about taste. This was about truth. Ethan's mouth salivated. He wasn't sure he liked where this was going, yet his desire to consume was overpowering him greatly.

Sarah hesitated, her fingers hovering just above the first floating plate, her pulse quickening. A single violet fruit rested atop it, its surface glistening like liquid dusk. It looked harmless, inviting, yet something inside her warned against the unknown sensation that awaited. With a steadying breath, she plucked the fruit from its delicate perch and placed it in her mouth. The moment the taste hit her tongue, a wave of sensation crashed into her, sharp, unrelenting, as if regret itself had taken form. Tartness sliced through her senses like a raw wound, and suddenly, she was no longer in the Resonant Tasting Hall.

She was ten years old again. Her father sat across from her at the dining table, disappointment heavy in his gaze. "You're better than this, Sarah. You need to find better self-discipline." She had stayed up too late studying, again, desperate to be the best, to be enough, only to fall asleep in class the next day. Shame had burned through her, coiling deep in her chest like a slow-moving poison. She had pushed herself harder ever since, convinced that anything less than perfect made her unworthy.

Her breath hitched, and she stumbled back, gripping the edge of the platform to steady herself against the weight of the memory. "I... this isn't just taste." She choked out, voice trembling.

Ethan was at her side in an instant, his grip firm but gentle on her arm. Concern shadowed his eyes. "Sarah? What happened?"

Her hands curled into fists, her nails digging into her palms as she forced herself to swallow the lingering bitterness. It wasn't just on her tongue, it was in her soul. "I felt it," she whispered. "I felt everything."

Aerthis pulsed knowingly. "Each flavor holds an emotion, tied to a piece of yourself you may have ignored, denied, or buried. To move forward, you must not only face them but integrate them."

Ethan swallowed hard, his mouth dry. But his desire to consume, forced him closer. His gaze flickered over the hovering plates before settling on a small, dark root. He reached out, hesitating a second, and bit down. Acrid. Overpowering. Bitter in a way that sank into his bones. And then...His father's voice.

"You need to toughen up, Ethan. Stop being so sensitive."

The sting of his older brother's laughter rang in his ears, the sound curling around him like a vice.

"You always take things so personally. Just get over it."

The words had followed him for years, carving deep into the way he saw himself. He had tried to fight it, tried to ignore it, but no matter how much time passed, the bitterness had remained, festering, waiting for moments like this to remind him of his inadequacy.

Ethan staggered backward, sucking in a sharp breath. He coughed as if the bitterness had lodged itself in his throat. "This is really bitter!"

Aerthis floated closer, its glow unwavering. "Do not resist it. Do not try to suppress or reject what you feel. Resilience is not found in avoidance, but in acceptance."

Sarah wiped at her eyes, her body trembling from the lingering impact of the fruit. "But this, this feels horrible. It tastes horrible!" She turned back to the floating plates, her voice shaking but determined. "This is important, isn't it? We have to go through this, don't we?"

The Orb dimmed, its glow taking on a solemn hue. "Yes, if you wish to succeed. True resilience comes from facing what challenges us, not avoiding it. Life is meant to be experienced in all its complexity, for it holds a sweetness, it also holds bitterness, sharpness, as well as intense spiciness. It is the blending of these contrasts that makes life rich and meaningful. But if we reject the bitter, shy away from the sour, and fear the spice, we risk creating a world that is dull, flavorless, and void of true depth."

Sarah let out an exasperated groan. "Well, that sounds incredibly boring."

The Orb pulsed, its glow flickering like a distant ember. "Indeed," Aerthis replied, its tone layered with something deeper, a quiet sorrow. "And yet, there are those who desperately seek the comfort of a 'boring' life."

Ethan frowned. "Why? Who would want that?"

The Orb's glow dimmed further, the air between them thickening with a silence that felt heavier than words. When Aerthis spoke, its voice carried the weight of countless unspoken truths. "Because, Ethan, they have not learned the skills needed to face life. Instead, they retreat, hiding from all that is, all that could be, believing that if they avoid hardship, they will remain safe."

Sarah crossed her arms, a crease forming between her brows. "And are they?" she asked. "Safer?"

Aerthis hovered between them, its mirrored surface swirling with shifting reflections. "If you consider a mind trapped within its own walls, bound by fear and limiting beliefs, to be safe... then yes," its glow pulsed once, then dimmed again. "But the truth is, they are so consumed by the fear of being hurt by the world around them, that they fail to see how their own world within them is crumbling."

Ethan swallowed, his throat dry.

Aerthis continued, its voice now a whisper that vibrated through the space around them. "The more they reject the contrasting flavors of life, the bitter, the sour, even the spice, the more they confine themselves to an existence without depth. And the deeper they retreat, the tighter their prison becomes, until the walls they built for protection become the very thing that suffocates them."

With hesitation curling in their movements, Ethan and Sarah pressed forward. Each new ingredient pulled forth a memory, an emotion, a wound. Some were sharp and painful, the bitterness of disappointment, the saltiness of tears unshed. Others were unexpectedly soothing, the sweetness of joy, the depth of quiet strength. But the real challenge came when they had to balance them.

Ethan found himself drawn to grounding flavors, flavors that resonated with his need for control, realism, and certainty. Bitterness felt familiar to him, even when it hurt.

Sarah, however, reached for sweeter, more uplifting elements, flavors that offered relief, that softened the edges of pain. Their differences soon clashed.

"Not everything has to be bitter, Ethan," Sarah snapped, frustration bubbling beneath her exhaustion. "Resilience isn't just about enduring pain."

"And not everything should be sugar-coated, Sarah!" Ethan shot back, his voice taut. "Sometimes, you have to face things as they are!"

The room responded. The crystal walls darkened, their iridescent glow dimming as tension swelled between them. The air vibrated with discord, the plates quivering where they floated, flickering between states.

Aerthis interjected, its voice cutting through the building storm. "Resilience is not a battle against each other. It is the understanding of contrast, opposites working together. Different tastes are not enemies. They are partners in balance."

Sarah took a breath, applying the skills she had learned so far. This allowed her to pause and think. She turned to Ethan, seeing him differently this time, the tightness in his shoulders, the quiet pain in his eyes.

"You're right," she said, her voice softer now. "Resilience isn't just about forcing things to be sweeter, yet it's also not about being consumed by the bitter parts. Maybe... maybe it's about knowing when to endure acceptance a little more and when to understand when to decline that which is unacceptable. Each time we push through to accept, we build a little more resilience."

Ethan swallowed, his jaw unclenching. "Yeah. And each time we cave into rejection, we lower our resilience and become more unaccepting."

Together, they began to adjust. They experimented, gently and incrementally combining flavors that seemed incompatible. A pinch of bitterness for strength. A touch of sweetness for hope. A trace of sourness for clarity. A hint of salt for perseverance.

They learned that sugar-coating life created false spikes of depth, blinding them from seeing things clearly. That bitterness, left unchecked, hardened the soul, turning resilience into cynicism. That too much sourness made life unbearable, warping perception into distrust. But when blended together, in the right measure, at the right time, life was whole, full of flavor that excited the inner most emotions.

As they placed the final dish on the altar, the Resonant Tasting Hall erupted in a symphony of light. The shifting colors aligned, forming a breathtaking spectrum of harmony. The air hummed with resonance, vibrating in time with their newfound understanding.

Sarah and Ethan exchanged a look, their eyes reflecting the transformation they had just undergone.

This challenge had been about more than taste. It had been about life itself.

As the final echoes of their trial settled into the shimmering walls of the Resonant Tasting Hall, Sarah and Ethan stood side by side, their hearts still pounding from the intensity of the challenge. The air hummed with a quiet expectancy, the floating plates now still, their mystical ingredients depleted.

The hall itself, once shifting with their emotions, had settled into a golden, tranquil glow, a reflection of the balance they had fought to create within themselves.

From the center of the chamber, the Endurancevale Enigma emerged. Its towering form of swirling, translucent crystal refracted the golden light around it, its opalescent eyes radiating warmth. A soft pulse rippled through its being, like a heartbeat woven from pure energy. As it moved, the floor beneath them bloomed with crystalline flowers, each petal shifting in color, amber for resilience, silver-blue for clarity, rich violet for growth.

The Enigma regarded them with quiet reverence before speaking, its voice a symphony of resonant tones.

"You have tasted the many faces of life, the bitter, the sweet, the sharp, the grounding. You have endured. You have blended these flavors not in rejection, but in acceptance. Tell me, Explorers, what have you learned?"

Sarah and Ethan exchanged a glance. A silent understanding passed between them, each of them carrying the weight of revelation.

Sarah spoke up first. "I learned that resilience isn't just about enduring hardship. It's about embracing all of life's experiences, the joys and the sorrows, the victories and the failures, without rejecting any part of them. I've spent so much of my life trying to perfect everything, to avoid the bitter moments, to drown them in sweetness. But now I understand that by rejecting the difficult parts of life, I was robbing myself of its depth."

Her voice softened as she continued. "We don't grow by only experiencing what's easy. We grow by learning to balance it all, by understanding that the bitterness of failure teaches us strength, that the sharp sting of regret pushes us to do better, and that the sweetness of joy is only meaningful because we've known loss.

I see now that life isn't meant to be one flavor. It's a symphony, and every flavor plays its part."

The Enigma's form pulsed with light, its gaze steady as it turned to Ethan. "And you?"

Ethan hesitated, his hands trying to find their place. His voice was quieter, raw. "I learned that I've been carrying too much bitterness," he let out a shaky breath. "I thought if I could just keep moving forward, keep pushing past all the stuff that hurt me, I'd be strong. That I'd prove them wrong, the people who told me I was weak, too sensitive. But... that's not strength. Strength isn't about rejecting pain. It's about feeling it, understanding it, and then choosing how to move forward."

He looked down at his hands, as if seeing himself for the first time. "I get it now. If I hold onto bitterness, I become bitter. If I drown in what's sour, I turn sour. And if I pretend everything is fine and force sweetness where it doesn't belong, I lose sight of reality. But if I learn to balance it all, to accept it, rather than fight it, to learn from it and grow from it, I can move forward with real strength. Not just the kind that endures, but the kind that transforms."

The Enigma pulsed with a golden radiance, its energy wrapping around them like a gentle embrace.

"You have both discovered a truth that many never grasp. Resilience is not weathering the storm under a false blanket of safety; it is learning to dance in the rain. It is knowing when to fight, when to accept, and when to weave the lessons of hardship into the strength of your being. You have done well, Explorers."

It raised its shimmering hand, and two brilliant objects materialized before them.

The first was a glowing Skill Card, Flavors of Resilience, etched across its surface in shimmering script.

"This Skill Card will remind you of the strength you have gained today. It will guide you when desires overcome you, when bitterness threatens to consume you or when sweetness tempts you into illusion. With it, you will remember how to balance yourself."

The second was a small, elegant pin, a swirling symbol of interwoven colors, representing the many flavors they had endured. "This is the Flavors of Resilience Pin. A mark of your achievement. A reminder that you have faced the depths of yourself and emerged stronger."

Sarah and Ethan each took their rewards, feeling a warmth seep into their palms as the objects settled into their hands.

The Enigma's form began to shimmer, its radiance growing until it glowed with golden light. Its voice softened, but its words carried quiet power. "You have come far. One final challenge remains here, within the protection of the Mystical Forest."

Ethan straightened, his grip tightening around the Skill Card. "Yes, just one more! What kind of challenge is this last one?"

Sarah nodded curiously, a new edge of determination in her voice. "What can we expect?"

The Enigma's eyes gleamed, unreadable. It took a single step backward, its form beginning to dissolve into light. "You will see." And then, in a dazzling burst of golden energy, it was gone.

As silence settled over the Resonant Tasting Hall, Aerthis floated forward, its mirrored surface reflecting their expressions. "Come, Explorers," the Orb murmured. "Your final Mystical Forest trial awaits."

With one final glance at the now-still tasting hall, Sarah and Ethan followed Aerthis back into the Mystical Forest. But something was different. The moment they stepped into the woods, they noticed the air had changed.

The once-lush, vibrant forest now felt eerily still, as if it were holding its breath. The wind, once warm and alive, had vanished, leaving a suffocating stillness. Then... A blast of thunder cracked the sky, shaking the ground beneath them.

A sudden, foul stench curled around them, sharp and pungent, making Sarah gag.

She covered her nose. "There's that smell again!"

Aerthis dimmed, its glow flickering uneasily. "Indeed, Explorers, the scent of decay."

A chill ran through Sarah's spine. She turned to Ethan, the unspoken realization settling between them like a weight. "The Dragons." she whispered.

Ethan's hand covered his nose. "The Eternal Guardians of Origin… in Dysquinox," his hand now waved in front of his face, coughing. "Man, they stink!"

Before they could say another word, the wind howled through the trees, carrying with it the foul scent of something rotting. And from a distance, beyond the thickening fog, a guttural growl rumbled through the storm. Sarah and Ethan looked at each other, realizing their journey was far from over.

Chapter 15

The Harmony of the Beasts

The Orb of Reflection shimmered ahead of them, its soft glow cutting through the gloom of the Mystical Forest. Sarah and Ethan trudged forward, their every step muffled by the thickening decay beneath them. Once-vibrant leaves curled in on themselves, dark veins slithering through their emerald skin before crumbling into dust. Flowers, once blooming with iridescent light, wilted into shriveled husks. The air thickened with the stench of something rotting, pungent and suffocating, twisting Sarah's stomach into knots.

Ethan pressed a sleeve to his nose, gagging. "That smell is so intense!"

Aerthis, the Orb, pulsed. "Dysquinox has begun to take root here," its voice carried a weight they hadn't heard before, somber and edged with urgency. "It's erosion of the Realm of the Mind is advancing with rotting beliefs, decaying thoughts left unchallenged. The poison in this air is the stench of stagnation, of ideas left to fester instead of grow."

Sarah's eyes burned as she pushed forward. "It's like being in a house that has never been cleaned." she murmured.

Aerthis spun in agreement. "Precisely. Those consumed by Dysquinox have grown accustomed to its stench, unable to sense the decay, much like spoiled food left too long in a refrigerator. Left unchecked, these beliefs taint everything."

Ethan's eyes began to water. "This is horrible; we need to keep moving. How far do we have to go?"

The Orb replied. "Not far."

Their pace quickened despite the oppressive weight of the air around them. The deeper they ventured, the more the world withered, and the more the foul stench intensified. The towering trees that had once sung with life now loomed skeletal, their hollow trunks whispering eerie echoes. The further they walked, the quieter the world became, until it was silent. A thick, unnatural stillness that made the hairs on Sarah's arms rise.

Then, the voice. Low and raspy, creeping from the shadows like fingers dragging across damp stone.

What about the goose in the jar?

The words sent a chill down Ethan's spine this time. His breath hitched as he scanned the darkness, but the forest around them remained unmoving, as if it, too, was waiting for an answer.

Sarah's fingers twitched as she reached to touch the pins that decorated her shirt. "We need to solve this riddle, Ethan!"

Ethan let out a sigh. "Yeah, somehow Sarah, if we don't find the answer to that darn riddle, this is going to haunt us our whole lives!"

Sarah leaned forward, eyes glimmering with thought. "What if the goose becomes part of the ashes? Like, it sheds its physical form and integrates into the wisdom of the jar."

Ethan tilted his head, considering. "So, you're saying the goose transforms into something spiritual, merging with the ashes while leaving the jar intact?"

Sarah nodded. "Yes. The jar stays whole, the ashes remain undisturbed, and the goose's life becomes part of the legacy of the Ancient Ones."

Ethan frowned. "But isn't that just another way of destroying the goose? Even if it's a spiritual transformation, it still means losing its life as it is. Besides, that also means keeping it trapped in the jar until, what, it decides to transform? The riddle says we can't harm it. I think that means physically and emotionally."

Sarah sighed. "You're right, transformation sounds beautiful, but it still means an end to the goose as we know it. And that goes against the sanctity of life."

Ethan laughed, shaking his head. "Here's an idea. What if we find a magical potion in this forest that shrinks the goose? We just need a few drops, and we can give the potion to the goose through a straw, never touching the ashes."

Sarah's eyes widened. "What makes you think there is a magical potion like that here in this forest, Ethan?"

Ethan grinned. "I mean, look around you. This isn't any ordinary forest, this is the Mystical Forest. Surely there must be a mystical shrinking potion hidden somewhere?"

Sarah frowned, thoughtful. "It's an interesting idea, but somehow, I don't feel that's the right answer. We can offer that to the Orb if you feel it's the right answer?"

Ethan sighed. "No, not yet. We only get one answer. We need to make sure it's the right one."

Sarah hesitated. "How will we know, though?"

"When we find that magic potion." Ethan laughed.

Aerthis glowed brightly now. "Magic will not solve this problem for you, Explorers. Wisdom will."

They pressed on until the trees gave way to an opening. Before them appeared the Velvet Cavern, its entrance partially lined crystal formations pulsing with a faint, rhythmic glow, partly dull and lifeless. As they stepped inside, the cavern reacted instantly.

The moss beneath their feet shimmered, the walls vibrating like a quiet heartbeat. Bioluminescent veins webbed the ceiling, shifting in color from soft blues and greens to sharp flickers of red and orange. The ground trembled as if a new source of energy had found its way to it.

Sarah and Ethan stood just inside, carefully examining every inch of the cavern before moving in deeper. The Velvet Cavern pulsated with life, as the bioluminescent reached up into the velvet walls shifting in color as Sarah and Ethan stepped inside. The floor beneath them rippled like liquid light, soft moss glowing electric blue beneath their hesitant steps. The cavern was reacting to their presence, mirroring their emotions, cautiousness filled the air.

The Orb of Reflection floated ahead, its mirrored surface catching and amplifying the cavern's glow. Its voice was calm and resonant. "Welcome to the Velvet Cavern, where your emotions become your environment.

To proceed, you must bring balance to this sacred space by calming the chaos of the three Harmony Beasts. Your success depends not on control, but on alignment, of yourselves and each other and with them."

Sarah ran her fingers lightly along the crystalline walls, watching them pulse in response to her heartbeat. "This place feels... scared, nervous, as if it fears me."

Ethan took a cautious step forward, feeling the moss beneath his foot harden into rough stone. A shiver ran down his spine. "It's not just afraid, it's rejecting us."

He turned to the Orb, a thoughtful frown creasing his forehead. "How is this different from the Emotional Reflection challenge? That one also forced us to confront our emotions."

Aerthis pulsed, as if pleased by the question. "The Emotional Reflection challenge was an inward journey, a test of your ability to recognize and embrace your emotions. But the Harmony of the Beasts requires mastery of alignment. Not only must you understand your emotional state, but you must express the balance you hold within, showing the beasts that you are not a threat, while at the same time, teaching them to accept you. Your emotions influence this cavern and the creatures within it. To succeed, you must harmonize your internal world with your external surroundings."

The air in the Velvet Cavern had thickened, pressing against Sarah and Ethan like unseen hands tightening around their throats. The walls pulsed with eerie luminescence, casting long, writhing shadows that seemed to move of their own will. Then, the beasts emerged.

Sarah gasped and stumbled back, her pulse pounding so hard she could hear it in her ears.

This was nothing like the Emotional Reflection challenge, there were no small, timid creatures waiting for gentle reassurance. These were predators.

The Sabletooth prowled first, its sleek, panther-like form gliding towards them with liquid grace. Its rippling black fur gleamed like the endless void between stars, violet eyes glowing with cold, calculating intelligence. It didn't charge, it didn't need to. Each step was deliberate, a test, a promise of violence if provoked. It *felt* Sarah's fear, tasted it in the air like the scent of prey before the kill.

From above, the Hollowcry descended. Its skeletal wings barely made a sound as it landed, its translucent feathers pulsing like dying embers. Empty, hollow sockets locked onto Ethan, and with one slow beat of its wings, it shed glowing motes of sorrow. The motes drifted down like dead memories, fragments of pain, regret, and all the wounds that never fully heal. Ethan's breath hitched, his stomach twisting as waves of sadness coiled around him.

Then Shadowfang emerged into view, but it had no single form. It flickered, its shape warping between wolf, mist, and something darker, something shapeless and terrible. It *was* fear, raw and untamed. When Sarah and Ethan hesitated, it grew wilder, its shifting body moving faster, feeding on the chaos inside them.

The cavern itself twisted in response to the beasts. Jagged ridges erupted from the walls like teeth. The floor turned deathly cold, stealing the warmth from their skin. The once-harmonious hum of the cavern became a grating, dissonant screech. The creatures were not waiting. They were hunting.

The Orb of Reflection hovered between them, its light flickering under the cavern's growing storm.

"Harmony is achieved not through control," Aerthis spoke, its voice unyielding. "But by aligning with the rhythm of chaos. Let the beasts feel your calm, and they will mirror your serenity."

Sarah's breath hitched as the Sabletooth circled her, its glowing eyes locked onto hers. It moved in a stealth-like manner, slow and deliberate, savoring the tension in her muscles. Every instinct screamed at her to run, to *do* something, but no matter what she did, the beast seemed to sense it. Her fear was fuel, feeding its aggression. Her fingers trembled. She tried to breathe, but it was shallow, ragged.

The Sabletooth slinked closer, and its rumbling growl vibrated through her bones. *It knows.*

Sarah was frozen. Even her breath seemed to stop. "Uh... guys," she choked out. "I'm really scared."

As if responding to her panic, the cavern continued to roar to life. The ridges in the walls sharpened even as the jagged spikes grew, and the air turned heavy with suffocating pressure. The Sabletooth bared its fangs. It was no longer testing her. It was about to strike.

Sarah's body moved before her mind did. She turned and ran. The scream tore from her throat as she bolted for the cavern's entrance, her heart hammering like a drumbeat of pure terror. Behind her, the Sabletooth's claws scraped against the ground, its breath seemingly hot on her heels.

Ethan barely registered her fleeing. Consumed by his own thoughts. Hollowcry's mournful screech sliced into him, peeling back every layer of defense he had ever built. He saw flashes, memories of things he had done, things he had failed to do. Regrets like burning scars. Words he never said. Apologies he had swallowed. Faces of those he had let down.

The cavern began to close in, walls pressing tighter, the light dimming into suffocating blackness. Ethan's hands clenched into fists. He couldn't breathe. A hot gust of breath skimmed the side of his face.

His blood ran cold. Slowly, as if time had slowed to a crawl, he turned his head.

The Shadowfang was right there.

Its shifting, flickering form loomed beside him, its warped spectral face inches from his. Its breath smelled of something ancient, something wrong. It exhaled slowly, as if savoring his fear, waiting for him to break.

Ethan's body locked. His legs refused to move, his arms felt numb. His entire being screamed to run, but he couldn't. His mind was trapped in Hollowcry's sorrow, while his body was frozen in Shadowfang's grasp.

His throat tightened. His heart slammed against his ribs. In an instant, Ethan found himself, uncontrollably fleeing from the cavern. Seeing Sarah, peeking out from behind a dying tree, he joined her hoping she had found a place of safety.

Aerthis moved. The Orb of Reflection swept forward, its glow intensifying, and with it came its voice, calm and unwavering. "Fear is one of the greatest forces of the mind," it said, its voice cutting through the storm of chaos held by both Sarah and Ethan. "It is felt by many, yet it is often mistaken for threat. But fear holds three powers."

The words slowed Sarah's frantic heartbeat. They reached Ethan's spiraling thoughts.

Aerthis pulsed. "The first is the power to escape, known as flight," its light flickered toward Sarah, who was still visibly trembling. "The second is the power to freeze, to create the false illusion of not being seen."

The light turned to Ethan, as if still caught in Shadowfang's snare.

"The third power, the one most fall prey to, is fight," Aerthis hovered between them, glowing brighter now. "In rare moments, these powers hold meaning. They can save you. But far more often, they create mistrust, uncertainty, and unpredictability."

Sarah's breathing slowed, while Ethan's fingers uncurled.

"These beasts are not your threat," Aerthis whispered. "You are. If you feed them fear, they will respond with fear. But if you offer them kindness, compassion, and trust, they will eventually return those to you."

"Before or after they eat us?" Ethan announced.

Aerthis pulsed one last time. "Courage is not the absence of fear. Courage is accepting fear, while trusting the skills you have worked so hard to achieve in calming it."

"Did you see that thing?" Sarah shouted, her voice trembling. "It's a friggin' *panther*, with really sharp *teeth*, and it looks really *hungry*! I am *not* about to risk that!"

Ethan, standing beside her, threw his hands up, frustration mixing with his fear. "Seriously! There's a bird, or, or a thing that's half-cooked and still alive! It's shedding sparks! And let's not forget that ghost wolf, or whatever that thing is! If we stay in there, we're dead."

Aerthis remained still, its mirrored surface capturing the frantic expressions of both of them. It pulsed once, a slow, measured glow that seemed to contrast their spiraling panic. When it spoke, its voice was calm, almost sorrowful. "What you are seeing," it said evenly. "Is nothing more than a manifestation of your own fears."

Sarah and Ethan froze.

Aerthis continued, its tone unwavering.

"Fear is controlling your sight, your hearing, your sense of smell and taste, and most importantly, your actions. Everything you perceive is being amplified and distorted. This is what fear does."

Sarah swallowed, her hands trembling. "And what's that supposed to mean?" she demanded.

Aerthis tilted, as if studying her. "Fear is an ancient emotion, one of the first to evolve. It is the guardian of survival, designed to keep those who possess it safe. Like all emotions, it can become reactionary. In fact, fear is one of the most reactionary emotions of them all."

Ethan shook his head. "So what? We're just supposed to pretend that those things aren't real? Because I'm pretty sure that if that panther gets close enough, I'm going to find out real fast if it's real or not."

Aerthis pulsed again, softer this time, as though offering understanding. "I am not telling you to pretend. Instead, I am suggesting you try to see fear for what it truly is."

Sarah hesitated. "...And what is it?"

Aerthis's glow deepened, as if it were about to reveal something hidden in plain sight.

"Fear is like a child," it said. "A child that has not yet learned the difference between what is truly dangerous and what appears to be. It cries out at shadows, flinches at the unknown, and clings to what is comfortably familiar. Sadly, this child called fear is taught. Taught that anything unknown, is dangerous."

Sarah's contemplated, her mind racing.

Aerthis continued, its voice unwavering. "Because of this, hypervigilance grows. Fear spreads like a wildfire, encouraged by a world that constantly tells you to be safe, as though everything must be feared. But the truth is, few things are true threats.

Most are just perceptions, illusions formed in your mind by the influences of the external world, a world that thrives on fear, for it, like the dragons, use fear to control and to manipulate those who easily fall victim to its power, as the two of you just did."

Ethan, still breathing hard. "So, what, you're saying the panther, the bird, the wolf-thing… aren't real?"

Aerthis paused for a long moment, then spoke. "They are real Ethan. Yet the fear you hold does not come from them, it comes from you!"

Sarah stiffened. "What?"

"The beasts are reacting to you," Aerthis said. "They sense your fear. They feel your doubt. They do not see themselves as threats, you make them threats. Because you see them as dangerous, they mirror your expectations. If you feed them fear, they will respond with fear. If you feed them hostility, they will become hostile. But if you offer them kindness, compassion, and trust, they will eventually return it."

Ethan scoffed. "You're telling me to walk up to a nightmare and pet it?"

Aerthis pulsed. "No, what I am suggesting is to try and change how you see it."

Sarah bit her lip, glancing back at the cavern's entrance. Her mind racing with the though that the beasts still linger within, pacing in the darkness, their glowing eyes watching.

Aerthis's voice grew softer, more deliberate. "To change fear, begin by recognizing it. Why are you afraid? What are you afraid of? Identifying the cause often lessens its power."

Ethan inhaled shakily. "I'm afraid of being torn apart."

Sarah hesitated before whispering. "I'm afraid of being powerless."

Aerthis tilted toward them. "Good. Acknowledge it. Accept that fear exists, without shame or judgment. The more you can approach fear, the more others sense you as approachable. Fear isolates, it creates walls. But courage is accepting fear," Aerthis said. "While trusting your skills. The skills you have worked so hard to achieve so far."

The words struck something deep within them both.

Aerthis continued, its voice gentle but firm. "Challenge your thoughts. Fear thrives on worst-case scenarios. Ask yourselves, is the danger real? Is the outcome you imagine certain, or is it fear distorting your mind?"

Ethan stared at the cavern. "So… what, we just walk in there and hope they don't eat us?"

Aerthis pulsed. "If you are certain, it will eat you, it will. Because you will act as prey, and the beast will respond accordingly. Ask yourselves instead, are you reacting to the fear created by the beast, or is the beast reflecting your fear? Is it truly a monster, or is it merely sensing you as the threat, seeing you as the monster?"

Sarah and Ethan stood in silence, the weight of Aerthis's words sinking in. Sarah looked back at the caverns entrance. Taking a breath, she closed her eyes, her hand touching the first pin she earned, as she did, small flame appeared within her mind. Calmness began to settle in as all her focus was brought to the flame.

Ethan sat down, pulling out the skills cards he began to read each one again, The Flame of Focus, Resonant Listening, Aromatic Illumination, Essence of Fusion, Emotional Reflection, Eye of Insight, Symphony of Stillness, the Labyrinth of Scented Memory and the last one, the Flavor of Resilience.

Ethan paused as he closed the last skill card, His heart pounded as he turned to Sarah, who stood beside him, arms crossed tightly, her face pale with fear. The cavern entrance loomed before them, dark and waiting. The beasts still stirred within.

"We can't just go back in there and expect things to be different," Ethan said, voice raw. "We have to change something. We have to change."

Sarah let out a shaky laugh, though there was no humor in it. "Oh yeah? And how do we change the fact that there's a panther in there that looks like it wants to eat me?" Her hands shook as she gestured toward the entrance. "Or the fact that you've got a half-dead burning bird haunting you? And let's not forget that nightmare of a wolf that can't decide if it's real or a ghost."

Ethan exhaled, trying to steady himself. "That's just it, Sarah. We're seeing them wrong."

Sarah scoffed. "Oh, so I'm just imagining the fangs and claws?"

Ethan turned to her, his eyes intense. "Think about what we've learned, what we've actually learned. We've been through so many challenges, and every single one of them was about seeing past what we think is happening and understanding what's really going on."

Sarah hesitated. "You think the beasts aren't real?"

Ethan shook his head. "No, I think they're real enough. But I also think they're responding to us. Just like the Resonant Listening challenge taught us, we're not just hearing with our ears, we're perceiving with our emotions. What if we're projecting our fear onto them, and they're just reflecting it back?"

Sarah bit her lip, considering. "So... you think they're not actually trying to kill us, they just seem that way because we're afraid?"

"Yes," Ethan took a deep breath. "The Eye of Insight taught us that what we see isn't always the truth. Fear twists perception. What if those things aren't monsters, but something else? And what if they want harmony, but they can't find it because we're the ones radiating chaos?"

Sarah looked down at her hands, her palms cold and sweaty from fear. "...Then that means it's not about fighting them, is it?"

Ethan shook his head. "No. It's about understanding them. Calming them. But before we do that, we have to calm ourselves first."

Sarah swallowed hard. "Okay... how?"

Ethan let out a breath and started counting on his fingers. "Flame of Focus. We learned that if we don't control our focus, the outside world will control it for us. Right now, fear is controlling us. We need to take back control."

Sarah nodded. "So... we need to stop letting panic make our decisions."

"Exactly," Ethan met her eyes. "And then there's Aromatic Illumination. That one taught us to trust our instincts. Right now, our instincts are screaming at us to run, but what if that's just conditioning? What if our instincts are based on past fears rather than the truth?"

Sarah exhaled shakily. "Like how The Labyrinth of Scented Memory taught us that our past experiences can shape how we react in the present. If we let old fears decide how we handle this, we'll never see what's actually in front of us."

"Yes!" Ethan's voice lifted with hope. "And what about Essence of Fusion? That challenge was all about balance. We learned that harmony doesn't mean forcing things to be the same, it means letting things coexist. If we go in there and try to control them, force them to be something they're not, it's going to fail. We have to work with their nature, not against it."

Sarah frowned. "But how do we even begin to do that?"

His expression softened. "Symphony of Stillness."

Ethan continued, voice steadier now. "Stillness isn't just about not moving. It's about being present. When we panic, we react, fight, flight, freeze. But when we choose stillness, we give ourselves space to actually see what's happening.

That's what Aerthis was telling us. The beasts aren't our enemies. They're mirroring us."

Sarah let that sink in. The idea both terrified and reassured her. If the beasts were mirroring them, the real battle wasn't with them, it was within themselves.

Ethan took a breath. "That brings us to The Flavor of Resilience. That one taught us that struggle isn't something to be avoided, it's something to learn from. We've spent this entire journey preparing for this moment. Every lesson, every challenge, it's led us here. And now we have to trust what we've learned."

Sarah stared at him for a long moment. "So, this is not about winning them over, is it?"

Ethan shook his head. "No. We're supposed to understand them. Accept them. And show them that they don't have to fear us either."

Sarah looked back at the cavern. Wondering if the beasts were still waiting. Still watching. But something felt… different.

She turned back to Ethan, her fear still there, but something stronger had settled beside it. Resolve.

"Alright," she whispered. "Let's go try this again."

Ethan stood up, reaching for Sarah's hand. As she took Ethan's the Orb pulsed excitedly. Sarah and Ethan slowly re-entered the cavern. As the made their way in, Ethan led Sarah to a smooth rock and they both sat down.

Sarah closed her eyes, as did Ethan and together they took in several breaths. Then calmly opened their eyes.

From a dark corner, the Sabletooth appeared. It no longer seemed aggressive, its pacing had slowed, its ears twitching, watching, waiting, almost confused.

The Hollowcry flew from the darkness and landed on a jagged rock, keeping its distance from Sarah and Ethan, its mournful glow was dimmer now, its ethereal wings shifting with uncertainly.

The Shadowfang then appeared, it flickered in and out of form, but it no longer felt like it was stalking them. It was watching.

Sarah took a slow breath as her eyes drifted from one beast to the other, not with fear, but with curiosity. Seeing their beauty for the first time, yet she also felt the need to respect them.

Ethan exhaled, his mind slowing down. As he gazed into each of the beasts eyes, he saw sadness, not aggressiveness. Ethan began to think, these beasts, this cavern, the forest, the realm all were in danger, all were being threatened. Ethan though back to his life and how he felt when his world was threatened, how he wanted to hide, how he felt lost and alone as if nobody cared. If someone would just...care a little, maybe, maybe his world wouldn't be so...lost!

Aerthis pulsed. "You have a choice," it said. "You can keep running. You can keep freezing. Or… you can face the fear. Not as something to conquer, but as something to understand."

Sarah met Ethan's gaze. He nodded. And together, they turned back toward the beasts.

"We want to help," Ethan said to the beasts. "We know this is hard for you."

Sarah speaks up. "We do care, and we promise, we will do whatever we can to save your world, but right now we could use your help."

The Sabletooth, slowly took a step forward, as if in some kind of gesture to tell them more.

"We came here, to learn how to transform the dragons." Ethan stated.

The beasts all lurch with a sudden fear, reacting to the mention of the Dragons.

"Yes, we understand, the dragons are a problem, I mean, they need our help too. We are here to find and align with the five Mystical Enigmas," Ethan said. "With their help, we believe we can bring the realm back to harmony."

The beasts, upon hearing Ethan mentioning the five Enigmas, perked up, as if the Enigmas were their friends.

"We are not asking you to be our friends, we are letting you know, we are not your enemy." Said Sarah.

The air stood still, the beasts carefully watched in silence as Sarah and Ethan sat looking at them. The Shadowfang's form solidified into a giant wolf, it stepped towards him, cautiously. Each step getting closer to Ethan. It piercing eyes locked into his. As it drew closer, so too did the Sabletooth and the Hollowcry.

Ethan reached out with gentle touch, brushed the Shadowfang's head. It's fur ruff and course to the touch. A shock wave struck Ethan as his finger connected with the Shadowfang. It was if Ethan could feel the Shadowfang's every emotion, it was scared, lost and angry.

The Sabletooth approached Sarah, its deep black coat glistening in the cavern's luminescence. The panther looking beast, walked up to Sarah, gently bowing its head. She, feeling the invitation to touch it, reached up and scratched the beast between its ears. As she did, Sarah was bombarded with a surge of frustration, isolation and remorse.

Then the Hollowcry, let out a giant screech, it raised is flaming wings and shook its body, as it did, it transformed into a beautiful bird, part peacock and part Phoenix, a mystical firebird. The cavern filled with the sense of hope restored, and the three beasts, turned and faded into the cavern's darkness.

The cavern hummed, not with discord, but with harmony. The walls smoothed, the moss beneath their feet grew warm, and a blue glow spread across the cavern like dawn breaking.

The glow overtook the cavern, and a calm stillness settled in. A soft, shimmering light coalesced before Sarah and Ethan. The very air around them tingled with warmth as the light took shape, more solid than before, yet still fluid, like soft silk weaving itself into form.

With a burst of excited energy, the Mindwright Enigma emerged.

It was radiant, its translucent body pulsing with golden hues, its form flickering between tangibility and energy. But unlike before, when it was a mere whisper of an existence, it now felt present, alive. And most notably, it was beaming with joy.

"Quite frankly," it said, its voice bursting with excitement. "I never thought anyone could do that. Impressive!"

Sarah and Ethan exchanged a look of sheer astonishment. The Mindwright Enigma, one of the Five Mystical Enigmas, had doubted them?

Sarah blinked. "Wait... you didn't think we could, do it?"

The Enigma shimmered, bouncing in the air. "Oh, not at all! I mean, most people just, fail, when fear takes over. But you two? You harmonized the beasts! That's unheard of!"

Ethan exhaled a short laugh. "Well... good to know we broke a record."

The Enigma twirled midair before settling into a composed stance. "Now tell me," Its golden eyes glinting with curiosity. "What did you learn?"

After standing there for a moment to reflect. Ethan spoke first.

"We realized that fear isn't just something that happens to us, it's something we create," he said. "It's a primal reaction, meant to protect us, but if left unchecked, it distorts reality. The beasts weren't attacking us; they were reacting to us, mirroring the fear we projected. When we let fear take control, they became threats. But when we learned to manage it, to respond with awareness instead of panic, they changed. Because it was never them, we were truly fighting. It was our own perception."

Sarah nodded, her voice quieter but just as certain. "And it wasn't about overpowering them or forcing them into submission," she said. "It was about understanding them, just as we must understand fear itself. Fear isn't just an outside force; it's often an illusion shaped by our own thoughts, often born from past wounds. Each time we let it control us, it grows stronger, feeding on itself, distorting reality. But when we stop running, when we face it, question it, and see it for what it truly is, we take away its power. Fear isn't always the enemy, it's a signal. And more often than not, what we really need isn't fear. It's understanding."

The Mindwright Enigma shimmered with golden light, then without warning, it bounced into the air in excitement.

"YES!" it cheered, twirling, darting, spinning across the cavern in sheer joy. "Yes, yes, YES! You get it! You truly get it!"

Sarah and Ethan watched, stunned, as the Enigma twirled in exuberance, ricocheting off the cavern walls, streaking trails of gold wherever it moved.

Finally, it came to a slow, graceful stop, hovering before them, still vibrating with delight.

"Well then," it said, its voice practically humming with pride. "I think you two earned these."

A soft golden light swirled before them, and in its radiance, two objects materialized, the final Mystical Forest challenge card and its accompanying pin.

Ethan reached out first, his fingers brushing against the Harmony of Beasts card. The moment he touched it, a warm pulse ran through him, as though the very essence of the lesson had embedded itself within him. Sarah followed, accepting the Harmony of Beasts Pin, feeling the weight of its meaning settle against her palm.

The Enigma twirled in the air again, vibrating with joy. "Oh, this is so exciting! You're going to be amazing in what comes next!"

Sarah tilted her head, eyeing the Enigma suspiciously. "What comes next?"

The Enigma grew still, its golden glow deepening with quiet intensity. "Find the Village of Witherhollow," it said, its voice calm yet resolute. "There, our journey together will continue."

"Witherhollow?" Ethan repeated.

The Enigma's glow began to flicker. "Hurry," it added, its voice quieter now. "The storm is approaching." Then, just like that, it began to fade.

Sarah stepped forward instinctively. "Wait, what storm? What's happening?"

But the Enigma was already gone, its last golden spark dissipating into the cavern air. Silence fell.

Sarah and Ethan turned to find the Orb of Reflection waiting for them at the cavern's entrance. There was something different about its glow, something prouder, warmer.

A familiar voice cut through it. "Well done," Aerthis said, its mirrored light reflecting the cavern's golden hues. "Remember, fear is not your enemy, it is a guide.

It stands for *Face Every Adversity Realistically*. There will be times when fear serves a purpose, warning you of real danger. But not all fear is truth. Learning when to trust it and when to let it go is the key to true wisdom. You have grown much," it continued, floating toward them. "Your success here was not just in understanding the beasts, but in understanding yourselves."

Sarah exhaled. "That was… a lot."

"A lot doesn't even cover it." Ethan sighed.

Aerthis pulsed. "Come," it said. "There is something you need to see."

Without further question, Sarah and Ethan followed Aerthis out of the cavern, stepping into the dying Mystical Forest. There was deliberate change in the air, something darker, empty even. As they walked, both in celebration and concern, Sarah and Ethan couldn't help but wonder: Where were they headed now?

Chapter 16

A Glimpse of Chaos
and
Into the Shadows

The remnants of the Mystical Forest stretched around them, its once-vibrant glow reduced to nothing more than faint flickers of dying embers. Each step forward deepened the realization that the forest was not just withering, it was being robbed of life, as negativity drains all vibrant life, leaving behind lifelessness. Leaves, once crystalline and shimmering with energy, now lay cracked and brittle beneath their boots. The towering trees, the majestic giants that not only bring life to the realm but protect the mystical and magical, the creativity and the imagination of the realm, stood hollow, their bark peeling in strips like pages from a forgotten book. Without the Mystical Forest, creativity and imagination die.

The air was heavy, not just with silence, but with something unseen, something sorrowful. Every step they took stirred brittle, crumbling leaves, the remnants of a once-vibrant sanctuary now stripped of its vitality. Twisted branches stretched overhead like skeletal hands, reaching for something long lost, their energy drained into an eerie stillness.

Ethan halted abruptly, his brows knitting together as he kicked at the lifeless foliage beneath his feet. A cloud of dust rose, clinging to the air like a memory unwilling to let go. "Why does it feel so... empty?"

His voice was hushed, almost reverent, as if anything louder might fracture the delicate remains of this place. He turned to Aerthis, seeking an answer to a question he wasn't sure he wanted to understand.

The Orb of Reflection hovered before them, its once-brilliant glow dimmed to a soft, pulsing shimmer.

"This forest," Aerthis said, its voice a whisper laced with sorrow. "Is surrendering. It reflects a truth that many refuse to acknowledge."

Sarah's emerald eyes flickered with curiosity and unease. "What truth?"

Aerthis' light faded, then returned. "There was a time when the wisdom keepers, those who had endured hardships, gathered knowledge, and guided others, were revered. They did not want the youth to suffer as they had. Instead, they pushed forward, creating, improving and encouraging the youth to rise beyond the struggles of the past, to build something better. And so, the youth listened. They learned. They advanced."

The Orb's glow flickered, like a memory being relived. "Over the centuries, life became easier, more efficient. The struggles that once defined entire generations centuries before faded, replaced by new challenges of a different kind.

The very technology that the wisdom keepers once dreamed of became a reality. But with progress came an unexpected consequence. No longer the sole keepers of knowledge, the elders found themselves outpaced by the very future they had helped shape. Their wisdom, once a guiding light, began to dim, gave way to technology they struggled to understand. The youth, no longer looked to them for answers, for they had none to offer."

Sarah frowned. "But wasn't that the goal? To move forward? To make things better?"

Aerthis' light softened, heavy with understanding. "Yes. And yet, as the world evolved, the wisdom keepers watched the life they had known slip through their fingers. Their stories, once vital, became relics. Their guidance, once sought after, became dismissed. And slowly, their wisdom twisted into something else, remorse. Not just for the hardships they had endured, but for the fading of a world they once understood."

Ethan let out a dry chuckle, though his eyes betrayed a flicker of sadness. "Sounds like my grandparents," he muttered. "Always telling me how easy we have it. How much harder their lives were." He shook his head. "Like we don't have our own battles to fight."

Sarah scoffed. "I hear it too. Like we're the ones who ruined everything. Like we're responsible for fixing a mess we didn't make."

Aerthis pulsed once more. "And yet, you are."

Both Sarah and Ethan recoiled. "That's not fair," they blurted in unison. "Why do we have to clean up their mess?"

Aerthis paused, its mirrored surface rippling with contemplation. Then, it turned to them, its voice softer, but unwavering. "You don't."

Ethan and Sarah exchanged confused glances.

"But you just said…"

"Responsibility is not something forced upon you," Aerthis interrupted. "It is something you choose to accept. Each generation carries the weight of shaping the world for those who follow. Taking the world, left to them by those of the past, and reshaping it with the hopes of it being better. The wisdom keepers once embraced this role in the best way they knew how. Yes, mistakes were made, but learning is best achieved by understanding the failures of others. Over time, they forgot. They abandoned the duty of teaching and, instead, clung to what they knew, afraid of that, that was new. Their focus was no longer on guidance, it shifted to criticism and judgment instead. The youth, in turn, feeling rejected, were left to seek wisdom elsewhere, not because they wanted to, but because they had to."

Sarah's expression softened. "So… what happened?"

Aerthis pulsed, its glow flickering like a heartbeat. "As technology advanced the elders forgot something vital."

"What?" Sarah asked.

"They forgot how to tell stories."

A solemn stillness settled between them. Aerthis continued, its voice carrying the weight of countless lost tales. "Once, their stories were vessels of meaning, woven with lessons, filled with purpose. But as their relevance faded, so too did their ability to share them. They became desperate, clinging to fragments of the past, not as a way to teach, but as a way to hold on to a time when they mattered."

Ethan frowned. "But isn't it good to hear about their lives? Their experiences?"

Aerthis pulsed. "It can be, when stories are told to inspire, to stretch the imagination, to illuminate the right paths. But when they are told out of fear, out of longing for what was, they cease to be bridges. They become walls."

The weight of this revelation settled into Sarah's chest. "So… they lost their ability to tell meaningful stories. And because of that, we've lost the desire to listen?"

Aerthis pulsed again. "Not entirely. You see, it is difficult to stretch an imagination when it has been stretched farther than one can grasp."

Ethan's eyes darkened with understanding. "Technology," he murmured. "It's taken over everything. Even imagination."

Aerthis nodded. "The very game you play, the one that brought you here, it is filled with vibrant images, intricate worlds, adventures at your fingertips. But they are not born from within you. They are given to you. The stories you once would have imagined on your own are now crafted for you, pixel by pixel. The elders… they do not know how to compete with that. They cannot."

Sarah's throat tightened. "So, people stopped listening. And they stopped telling."

Aerthis dimmed. "More than that young ones, everyone stopped caring. And so, the connections began to fray. The bridges collapsed. The wisdom keepers became relics, and the youth, overwhelmed by noise, by distractions, lost interest in the very stories that once wove the fabric of community, of family, of understanding, they felt lost, alone and isolated."

Ethan looked around at the dying forest, seeing it now for what it was, a reflection of that loss. Of stories left untold. Of wisdom left unheard.

Sarah exhaled. "So… what can we do?"

Aerthis pulsed with quiet certainty. "You remember them. You listen to them. You tell new stories to them, not just ones given to you, but ones born from within. And when you do, you rebuild what was lost."

Sarah shivered, rubbing her arms as she took in the scene around them. "So, what happens now? If the youth are avoiding the elderly, and the elderly are stuck in fear and negativity, doesn't that mean no one's growing?"

Aerthis dimmed for a moment, as if contemplating. "That is why this divide must be mended. The elderly must embrace change and share wisdom without fear, without demand. The youth must seek knowledge and guidance, not from resentment, but with patience. Only then can both face the storms of influence and grow together and help their realms thrive once more."

The wind whispered through the brittle leaves, as if the forest itself was listening.

Sarah broke the silence. "Aerthis... earlier, you mentioned the Storms of Influence. What are they?"

Aerthis shimmered, as if taking a breath before speaking. "The Storms of Influence are the greatest challenges you will face, for they are not born from you, but they will shape you."

Ethan raised an eyebrow. "That... doesn't sound good."

Aerthis turned toward him, its glow shifting like ripples across a pond. "They are neither good nor bad. They simply exist. But when left unchecked, they can become forces of destruction. These storms are external pressures, formed from the collective thoughts, fears, and emotions of others largely based on the impacts of Dysquinox in other realms. They seep into the Realms of others, warping perception, distorting truth, and reshaping how individuals see themselves and the world around them."

Sarah folded her arms. "So... these storms just appear out of nowhere? How do they start?"

Aerthis pulsed in thought. "They form from patterns, cycles repeated across generations. From the expectations placed upon you, the fears instilled in you, the unchecked anger that spreads like wildfire. Imagine the weight of a thousand minds, all carrying the same resentment, the same fear, the same doubt. That energy does not disappear, it gathers, festers, and eventually, it erupts into a storm."

Ethan kicked at a dried leaf, watching as it crumbled beneath his foot. "And when that happens... what does it do to us?"

Aerthis' glow dimmed, its voice deep with sorrow. "It changes how you think. How you feel. How you see the world. Each storm carries its own essence."

The air around them shifted, a vision unfolded before their eyes. The sky darkened, and the forest around them flickered with different hues, each color pulsing with the energy of an unseen storm.

Aerthis' voice resonated through the air. "For example, The Storm of Anger twists perception. It fuels resentment, turning kindness into mockery, turning friends into foes. It does not allow peace, only an endless cycle of fury."

The trees flickered red, their bark cracking as if set aflame. Sarah clutched her arms, feeling an unfamiliar heat pressing against her skin.

"The Storm of Doubt," Aerthis continued, as the colors shifted to a sickly gray. "Makes you question everything. Your worth. Your choices. Your dreams. It whispers until you believe its lies, until you stop moving."

Ethan's breath hitched as the weight of the storm pressed against his chest, making every step feel heavier.

"The Storm of Conformity," Aerthis spoke, its voice reverberating through the shifting air. Around them, colors twisted and dulled, bleeding into lifeless shades of gray.

"It does not bind with ropes or walls, but with something far stronger, your own doubt. It whispers that you must follow, that you must blend in, that your voice is too much, too different, too unwelcome. It makes you fear standing apart until, piece by piece, you forget who you are."

Sarah's heartbeat pounded in her chest. The images Aerthis conjured weren't just visions, they were her. Every unspoken thought, every moment she had shrunk herself to fit in, every time she had swallowed her truth just to belong. She watched, horrified, as the essence of her thoughts faded into the shadows, slipping from her grasp like something that had never truly been hers to hold.

Aerthis' voice grew solemn. "Then there is the Storm of Distraction. The most subtle of all. It does not rage, it does not burn. It pulls your attention away from what matters, from what needs to be done. It lulls you into comfort, until one day, you look back and realize you have lost time… lost purpose…lost true connection with those who cared."

The vision faded, and the forest returned to its hollowed-out silence. Sarah and Ethan shaken by the storm's lingering presence.

Sarah removing her hands from her mouth after trying to silence her shock. "These storms… they're in our world too, aren't they? We just don't see them like this."

Aerthis pulsed. "Yes. They are in your world, shaping your choices, molding your beliefs. But you can stand against them, if you are willing."

Ethan looked down at the decaying world at his feet. "But how? How do we fight something that isn't even real?"

Aerthis turned toward him, its glow unwavering. "They are real.

You feel their weight every day. You fight them by recognizing them. By questioning what is being forced upon you. By deciding who you are, beyond the storms that seek to shape you."

Sarah nodded, a fire igniting in her eyes. "So, if we understand them, if we see them for what they are... we can break free?"

Aerthis pulsed brighter. "Yes. The storms thrive on unawareness. The moment you see them for what they are, and use the skills you have acquired, they lose their hold. But be warned, there are those who have lived in the storms for so long that they no longer see them as a threat, they see them as places of comfort. They will resist change. They will try to pull you back into the chaos."

Ethan's jaw tightened. "Then we push forward anyway."

Aerthis glowed, warmth returning to its light. "Yes. And in doing so, you will not only save the Realm...you change yourselves, isn't that what you desired? Real change?"

Sarah and Ethan exchanged a glance. The Mystical Forest still stood in decay, the weight of lost stories and forgotten wisdom pressing upon it. But now, they understood. The storms were not just something to endure, they were something to challenge.

They moved on, the last remnants of the Mystical Forest stretched behind them, the impact of Dysquinox very apparent. Ahead, the world was broken. The Barren Lands stretched into what seemed like infinity, an expanse of fractured earth and twisted remains of trees that clawed at the sky like skeletal fingers. The once-vibrant Plains of Rejuvenation had become a wasteland of ruin, swallowed by the storms of Influence.

Ethan stepped forward, the soft hum of the forest vanishing behind him, replaced by an eerie silence.

He crouched, brushing his fingers against the cracked ground. It was dry, lifeless, like all the warmth had been bled from it.

"This…" his voice barely carried over the stillness. "This was supposed to be a place of healing.

How could it have become… this?"

Beside him, Sarah stood rigid, her emerald eyes scanning the devastation. "It's like the land itself just… gave up," she murmured.

A shimmer of light flickered in front of them as Aerthis floated into view. Its glow was dimmed, as if even it had absorbed the despair of this place. "Once, this was a sanctuary of creativity and peace," Aerthis spoke, its voice softer than usual. "But it has been consumed by the storms of Influence, tainted by the imbalance of the Dysquinox Dragons."

Sarah's stomach twisted at the name. The Dysquinox Dragons, the creatures that had torn this realm apart. The ones they would have to face.

Aerthis continued. "Beyond this wasteland lies the Core of the Realm, where the storms rage and the dragons reside. To restore balance, you must endure the storms of Influence and complete your alignment with the Five Mystical Enigmas."

At those words, five luminous figures emerged around them, familiar, yet more vivid than before. The Five Enigmas had come to offer their wisdom for the trials ahead.

The Insightborne Enigma spoke first. "The storms will try and blind you, distorting your vision of the path and of yourselves. See beyond the illusions."

"The winds will howl with voices of fear and doubt. Hear the truth beneath the chaos." Proclaims the Harmonize Enigma.

The Endurancevale Enigma approaches Sarah and Ethan next "Hunger, fatigue, and despair will gnaw at you. Savor every moment of strength, for it will guide you towards the right path."

"The air will carry scents of comfort and deception. Let curiosity guide you to what is real." The Learnspring Enigma states.

The Mindwright Enigma floated closer, giggling as if it knew something they didn't. "Oh, the chaos will come," it said, its glow pulsing playfully. "It'll be messy, relentless, and about as gentle as a stampede of startled goats."

It spun once in the air before adding. "But don't stress too much. Your strength isn't about dodging the storm, it's about holding on to each other and figuring it out as you go. Together, you'll manage. Probably."

The four Enigmas exchanged long, knowing glances before turning to the Mindwright, shaking their heads in perfect synchronization. The Insightborne sighed dramatically. The Harmonize crossed its arms like a disappointed teacher.

The Learnspring covered its face as if reconsidering all its life choices while saying. "Wisdom comes in many forms… unfortunately, so does nonsense."

Then Endurancevale simply muttered. "Mindwright, you really need to get out more!"

The guardians of sight, hearing, smell, and taste gracefully faded away, except for the guardian of feeling, who had to be dragged along like a reluctant toddler refusing to leave the playground.

Sarah and Ethan chuckled, their laughter light but fleeting as the weight of what lay ahead settled over them.

Ethan placed both hands on his forehead, pushing his hair back as if to see even more. "This… this feels bigger than anything we've done. It's like we're standing at the edge of the world."

Sarah turned to him. "We are. But look at what we've already faced. We've confronted some of our fears, turned weakness into vulnerabilities that can be overcome… and we're still here. Stronger. More resilient."

Ethan looked at her, the uncertainty in his eyes giving way to something steadier. "Yeah… and the dragons don't know it yet, but we're coming to help them."

Sarah smirked, nodding. "Together."

The forest behind them flickered one last time as they stood overlooking the Barren Lands. Ahead, the storms churned, restless and waiting. Before they could take another step, A voice cut through their minds like a sharp knife, questioning.

What about the goose in the jar?

Sarah placing her hands over her ears, to no avail. "Enough already!"

Ethan, clearly turning to frustration. "This is getting really annoying"

"Let's just give an answer Ethan," Sarah blurted out. "I want this to stop!"

"Sarah, if we give the wrong answer, it will be stuck in our heads forever, do you want that?"

She paused, removing her hands from her ears. "No, that would be horrible."

Sarah's brow furrowed, looking at Ethan. "Let's just break the darn jar to free the goose?"

"No Sarah, we can't do that."

Sarah hesitated. "Yeah... you're right. What if we transferred the ashes into another jar first?"

He rubbed his chin. "That might work. But if we tipped the jar over to move the ashes, wouldn't some of them fall onto the goose?"

Sarah groaned, exasperated. "This riddle is the hardest one I've ever faced. There has to be a solution."

But Aerthis did not answer. It simply floated there, reflecting their faces back at them.

Sarah stared at it for a long moment before realization dawned. "...It's not about the answer, is it?" she murmured. "It's about how we think."

Aerthis pulsed, and for the first time in a long while, Sarah and Ethan caught a hint.

A sudden gust of wind howled across the wasteland, carrying a low, bone-chilling roar. The sky churned, black and crimson clouds twisting violently above them. The earth trembled as jagged arcs of lightning split the horizon. And then... A shadow moved within the storm. For a fraction of a second, its form became clear. A Dysquinox Dragon.

Its jagged scales glistened like obsidian, each edge catching the fleeting light like a blade poised to strike. Its burning red eyes cut through the darkness, unblinking, all-consuming, filled with an intelligence far beyond their own. With a single movement, its massive wings unfurled, sending shockwaves through the storm, bending the howling winds to its will. And then, just as suddenly as it had emerged, it was gone, devoured once more by the swirling chaos, as if the storm itself had reclaimed its own.

Ethan's breath hitched, his pulse hammering in his ears. "Did you see that?!"

Sarah exhaled shakily, her voice barely more than a whisper. "I saw… something," her eyes searched the storm's depths, a cold dread settling in her bones. "It's like the storm is alive."

Another flash of lightning split the sky. Beyond the veil of rain and shadow, colossal figures shifted, their presence undeniable, their forms stretching against the chaos. The dragons were waiting.

Aerthis rose higher, its voice echoing with finality. "The storms are but the beginning. To reach the Core of the Realm, you must confront their chaos, and yourselves. The path forward lies not in certainty, but in resilience."

"We've faced every challenge so far. We'll face this too." Ethan said with determination.

Sarah stepped forward, her resolve solidified. "Whatever's out there, we're ready to face it… Together."

"Together." Ethan proudly proclaimed.

They took their first step into the Barren Lands, the threshold where the Shadows of the Realm began.

The dragons were waiting.

Watching.

Mystical SELF
Book 2

Shadows of the Realm Teaser

The Barren Lands stretch endlessly before them, a wasteland of shattered dreams and stolen light. Once known as the Plains of Rejuvenation, this land pulsed with creativity, joy, and imagination, until the Storms of Influence came. They did not simply destroy; they twisted, eroded, and silenced, leaving behind hollow villages and the haunting remnants of what once was.

Now, Sarah, Ethan, and Aerthis, the Orb of Reflection, must journey through these broken lands, knowing that every step forward could unravel reality itself. Somewhere beyond the swirling fog lies Witherhollow Village, a once-vibrant haven of self-expression, now drowned in illusion and shadow.

The fog is alive. It coils through the ruins, warping perception, twisting memory, feeding doubt. Whispers echo through the mist, their voices rising and falling, pleading, accusing, deceiving. Lanterns flicker between golden warmth and eerie blue, shifting unpredictably between guidance and deception. The ground beneath them shifts like something restless beneath the surface, making every step a test of trust and instinct.

In Witherhollow, the storm does more than obscure the way, it infiltrates the mind. Figures move just beyond sight, their forms flickering like dying embers. Footsteps echo from nowhere. The voices of the past refuse to stay buried. Every hesitation feeds the storm, thickening the fog, warping the truth until even the past feels uncertain.

But hidden within these ruins are truths that refuse to die. Each village in the Barren Lands holds a fragment of what was lost, waiting to be uncovered. Yet the Storms of Influence are relentless. They don't just deceive, they erode confidence, twist perception, and turn certainty into shadows.

And in the distance, the Dysquinox Dragons wait. Watching. Hunting weakness.

To survive, Sarah and Ethan must battle more than the storm around them, they must conquer the storm within. Every moment demands trust, resilience, and the courage to separate illusion from truth. If they fail, they will be lost, not just to the storm, but to themselves.

If they succeed, they will do more than reclaim what was stolen. They will prove that even in a world consumed by doubt, truth, imagination, and the power of self can never be erased.

But first, they must step into the storm.

And hope it doesn't swallow them whole.

Basic Glossary
of the
Mystical SELF

This glossary is designed to help readers better understand the terms and characters within the *Mystical SELF* universe. To deepen this experience, we've created exquisite collector cards, just like the ones Ethan carries, offering insight into both the *Mystical SELF* world and its real-life reflections, helping readers explore themselves along the way.

Go to www.thelivingadventurers.com to learn more.

Aerthis, Orb of Reflection – A sentient, luminous sphere that acts as a guide within the Realm of the Mind, revealing hidden truths and aiding those on their Mystical Quest toward self-awareness.

Benevolent Dysquinox – A deceptive state where kindness is used manipulatively, masking deeper imbalance. Though it appears well-intended, it subtly distorts true harmony.

Chamber of Secrets – A hidden chamber of knowledge within the Mystical Forest, where the Orb of Reflection hides the Book of Wisdom from Dysquinox influence. Only those who demonstrate true authenticity may access its truths.

Custodian (of Balance) – The guardian of the Realm of the Mind who ensures the equilibrium between Quinox and Dysquinox, preventing chaos from overwhelming the land. The Custodian is also known as SELF.

Dragons – Representation of human behaviour. In their Quinox state, their behaviour is that of harmony, yet in any one of the Dysquinox states, their behaviour is distorted, often causing chaos and disruption.

Dysquinox – A state of imbalance that severs one's connection to the Ethereal Nexus, SELF and the Enigmas. It manifests in different forms, Benevolent, Malevolent and Shifting, creating internal or external chaos and deep emotional challenges.

Endurancevale – The Guardian of Taste. This Enigma represents the human sense of taste, resilience and discernment and how it can influence our lives.

Eternal Guardians of Origin – The E.G.O. is the part of the mind that shapes your identity, self-perception, and decision-making. In psychology, it mediates between instincts and morals, helping you navigate reality. Spiritually, the ego is often seen as the false self, creating attachment and suffering. A healthy ego builds confidence and boundaries, while an overactive ego leads to defensiveness and insecurity.

Ethereal Nexus – Known by many names, Nirvana, Valhalla, Jannah, Swarga, Tír na nÓg, Elysium, Aaru, Sekhet-Aaru and Heaven.

Explorers – Those who move beyond seeking for answers to questions to bravely venturing into the unknown to learn new questions and to discover their answers.

Insightborne – The Guardian of sight. This Enigma represents the human sense of vison, perception, and self-awareness and how it can influence our lives.

Harmonize – The Guardian of hearing. This Enigma represents the human sense of sound, emotional clarity, and resonance and how it can influence our lives.

Learnspring – The Guardian of smell. This Enigma represents the human sense of scents, memory, and intuitive insight and how it can influence our lives.

Malevolent Dysquinox – A destructive form of Dysquinox where imbalance manifests as dominance, aggression, or uncontrolled chaos, leading to harm for both oneself and others.

Mindwright – The Guardian of touch and feeling. This Enigma represents the human sense of connection, both physically and emotionally and how these can influence our lives.

Mystical Enigmas – Guardians of the senses. Sensory guides that help travelers unlock deeper self-awareness. They ensure that wisdom is earned through knowledge and experience.

Mystical Forest – A vast, ever-changing woodland filled with echoes of past memories and future possibilities. Each path taken reveals different insights about one's journey. It represents the learning aspect of the human mind.

Mystical Quest – A transformative journey of self-discovery undertaken within the Realm of the Mind. Travelers must face internal and external trials to achieve true growth.

Mystical Skill Cards – Artifacts containing wisdom, lessons, or abilities earned through overcoming trials. These cards are given by the Mystical Enigmas when successfully having endured a challenge.

Quinox – A state of harmonious balance and self-actualization, allowing full access to the Ethereal Nexus. It represents harmony between thought, emotion, and purpose.

Sacred Book of Wisdom – A legendary tome said to contain the essence of all true wisdom. It is written in shifting symbols, revealing only what the reader is ready to understand.

Seekers – Those who have awakened to the call of self-discovery and have begun to embark on their own Mystical journey.

SELF – The representation of the conscious mind known as the Custodian. It's the guiding philosophy of the *Mystical SELF* journey, representing Strength, Evolution, Love, and Fulfillment. It serves as both a compass and a path to true self-discovery.

Shifting Dysquinox – A dynamic and unpredictable state of imbalance, where behaviours swing between false kindness and aggression, causing confusion and instability.

Storms of Influence – Powerful, swirling tempests that infect the Realm of the Mind, representing external influences such as fears, or doubts. These storms test one's ability to stay true to their path.

Epilogue

The Birth of

The Mystical SELF

Every great journey begins with a question, one that lingers in the heart and mind, demanding to be answered. For Annet van Duinen and Randy Grasser, that question was simple yet profound: *How do we help people truly understand themselves?*

As Highly Sensitive, High Sensation Seekers, Annet and Randy had spent their lives navigating the paradox of their nature, deeply feeling the world's intensity while also seeking adventure and challenge. They understood firsthand the complexities of emotions, self-awareness, and resilience.

Through years of personal exploration and professional expertise, they recognized a crucial gap in mental health education.

Too often, books and programs approached mental well-being with only scientific facts and structured methodologies, making them informative but lacking emotional connection. There was no bridge between understanding mental health and truly experiencing how it influences everyday life. They envisioned something different, something that would take readers beyond the clinical and into the mystical.

Thus, *The Mystical SELF Universe was born.*

A Journey, Not Just a Lesson

Annet and Randy believed that storytelling is one of the most powerful tools for transformation. They knew that people, especially young adults, learn best when they connect deeply with a journey, when they can see themselves reflected in characters facing challenges similar to their own.

From this vision, *The Mystical SELF Saga* emerged. The series follows Sarah and Ethan, two young adventurers who uncover the Realm of the Mind, a hidden world shaped by thoughts, emotions, and self-perception. Through their struggles and triumphs, readers are guided to see their own minds in a new light, gaining insights into their mental and emotional landscapes.

More than just a story, *The Mystical SELF* is an interactive exploration of self-awareness, blending fiction with research-backed psychology. It provides young adults, parents, and educators with a way to approach mental health as an adventure, rather than just a subject to be studied.

Beyond the Pages: The High Responsive Training Program

While *The Mystical SELF* is designed to inspire young minds, Annet and Randy knew that the journey of self-discovery and emotional intelligence doesn't end with adolescence.

In parallel with the book series, they developed the High Responsive Training Program, a program that mirrors the lessons of *The Mystical SELF*, translating its wisdom into real-world strategies. This program is designed for individuals of all ages who seek to better understand their emotions, sensitivities, and unique strengths. By embracing their high responsiveness, participants learn to thrive rather than struggle in a world that often misunderstands emotional depth and intensity.

A Mission for the Future

At its core, *The Mystical SELF* is more than a book series, more than a program, it is a movement toward deeper understanding and greater fulfillment. Annet and Randy firmly believe that helping young people successfully navigate the transition from childhood to adulthood is vital to the well-being of future generations. They also recognize that self-awareness, emotional intelligence, and resilience are skills that benefit everyone, no matter their age.

Through this journey, they invite readers to explore their own minds, embrace their strengths, and find empowerment in who they truly are. Because the greatest adventure is not found in distant lands or imagined worlds, it is the journey within.

Your Story Begins Here

As you close this book, remember: your journey does not end here, it is only beginning. Like Sarah and Ethan, you have the power to explore, understand, and shape your own mind. The path to self-discovery and growth is always open, waiting for you to take the next step.

So, will you answer the call? Your *Mystical SELF* awaits.

Additional information about the Authors and the HRT Program can be found at - **www.thelivingadventurers.com**

As authors of this book, we genuinely value your thoughts, ideas, and questions. Your insights mean so much to us, and we love hearing how the book resonates with you. Please feel free to share, your voice is an important part of this journey!

Email us: info@thelivingadventurers.com

The Realm Keepers Reflections

As you reach the end of this part of the journey, the Orb of Reflection offers you these questions designed to guide you deeper into your own mind, much like Sarah and Ethan's path through the Mystical Forest. Each question is a key, unlocking hidden truths and unseen strengths within you, while helping you discover even more about the Mystical SELF story. Take your time, answer with honesty, and let the wisdom you hold unfold.

Did you see yourself in any part of Sarah and Ethan's journey as they faced their personal struggles and past experiences?

How did Sarah and Ethan's sensitivity, initially seen as a weakness, become their strength? Have you ever had a similar realization about yourself?

What lessons did Sarah and Ethan learn about embracing their authentic selves? And how can you apply these lessons to your own life?

What does courage mean to you after reading this book? Has your definition changed?

Sarah and Ethan faced multiple challenges that required patience, resilience, and adaptability. Can you recall a moment in your life when you had to develop these traits?

What role did fear play in the challenges they faced? How do you typically respond to fear in your own life?

The idea of persistence is a key theme in the book. What is one challenge you have faced that required you to keep going, even when it felt impossible?

Sarah and Ethan had moments of self-doubt but pushed forward despite their uncertainties. How do you handle self-doubt in your own life?

Throughout the book, Sarah and Ethan learned to trust themselves and their instincts. How can you strengthen your own self-trust?

The bond between Sarah and Ethan grew through their shared experiences. How has connection with others helped you through difficult times?

How did their journey help them understand the importance of empathy? How can you practice more empathy in your daily life?

The characters initially felt alone in their struggles, but they found strength in each other. Have you ever experienced a moment where connection with someone changed your perspective?

What qualities do Sarah and Ethan demonstrate that make them good friends to one another? How can you cultivate these qualities in your own relationships?

The book highlights the idea that everyone is on their own journey of self-discovery. How does recognizing this help you interact more compassionately with others?

The Realm of the Mind is shaped by thoughts, emotions and behaviours. How do your own thoughts and beliefs shape your reality?

The five Enigmas represent different aspects of perception. Which one do you think you naturally align with the most, and why?

What is one key lesson from The Emergence that you want to carry with you moving forward?

There are several subtle hints within the story that were purposely placed, one example is when Sarah and Ethan are confused with the Enigmas being seen as male or female. What might this mean?

If the Enigmas represent our senses, what do the dragons represent?

And finally, "What about the goose in the jar?"

To learn more about your own Enigma's, take the Enigma Assessments created by The Living Adventurers. You can find them at: www.thelivingadventurers.com/mystical-self-book/